TANNER'S *Angel*

DOREEN ORSINI

Ellora's Cave
Romantica Publishing

An Ellora's Cave Romantica Publication

www.ellorascave.com

Tanner's Angel

ISBN 9781419962134
ALL RIGHTS RESERVED.
Tanner's Angel Copyright © 2010 Doreen Orsini
Edited by Briana St. James.
Cover Art by Syneca.

Electronic book publication February 2010
Trade paperback publication 2010

With the exception of quotes used in reviews, this book may not be reproduced or used in whole or in part by any means existing without written permission from the publisher, Ellora's Cave Publishing, Inc.® 1056 Home Avenue, Akron OH 44310-3502.

Warning: The unauthorized reproduction or distribution of this copyrighted work is illegal. Criminal copyright infringement, including infringement without monetary gain, is investigated by the FBI and is punishable by up to 5 years in federal prison and a fine of $250,000. (http://www.fbi.gov/ipr/)

This book is a work of fiction and any resemblance to persons, living or dead, or places, events or locales is purely coincidental. The characters are productions of the author's imagination and used fictitiously.

TANNER'S ANGEL
ಙ

Dedication

ഇ

I dedicate this book to my mom, the woman most likely to blush while reading this book.

Trademarks Acknowledgement

ഇ

The author acknowledges the trademarked status and trademark owners of the following wordmarks mentioned in this work of fiction:

Chrysler: Chrysler Corporation
Dumpster: Dempster Brothers, Inc.
Girl Scouts: Girl Scouts of the United States of America
Hershey's: Hershey Foods Corporation
Jack Daniel's: Jack Daniel's Properties, Inc.
Jack Rabbit: California Exotic Novelties LLC
Jeep: Daimler Chrysler Corporation
Marlboro: Philip Morris Inc.
Palm Pilot: Pirani, Amin
Saks Fifth Ave: Saks & Company
Stetson: John B. Stetson Company

Chapter One
൭

Tanner tilted his head back and peered up at the Chrysler Building. Sunlight glinted off the glass. An elbow jabbed into his spleen.

"Watch it," he yelled over his shoulder. The heat of the sun warmed his face and drew his attention back up to the little slice of blue peeking out between the buildings.

"Better go home, cowboy, before you get trampled," another passerby said in a sultry voice that reached into his jeans and squeezed.

Tanner spun around. He scanned the pedestrians rushing past. No one glanced his way or even acknowledged his presence.

"New York City...home of cowards," he muttered. Watching them file by, with their eyes focused on the back of the person in front of them the way cows just followed the ass of the cow in front of them, he shook his head. "Or cows."

Crossing his arms over his chest, he gave the sky one last look. He didn't give a damn that his stance broadcasted to those rushing past him on the sidewalk that a tourist stood in their midst. Hell, if they couldn't tell by his Durangos, worn-out Stetson and football t-shirt that he lived far from this fine city, he doubted staring up at one of their skyscrapers would give it away.

Lowering his head, he merged into the crowd.

His stomach growled but the smell of hot dogs from a vendor's cart mingling with the fumes of the taxis, buses and cars cramming the street left him more homesick than hungry. Horns blared and curses flew when he bolted from the herd and weaved between the cars to the other side of the street.

Leaning against the glass window of some sex shop, he caught the faint scent of urine.

God, he missed Texas. The mountains towering in the distance, the smell of dirt and horses and homemade pies. And the silence. How he missed being able to hear the rustle of a gentle breeze flowing through the trees or a lizard scurrying through the grass.

Gritting his teeth, he swept back into the moving mass of people. Something soft, smelling of jasmine, cinnamon and fresh-baked bread slammed into his chest.

Before she could run off, he wrapped his arms around her and held tight. She let out a breathy gasp and tensed. Grinning down at the mass of black curls below his chin he drew in a deep breath. "Damn, you smell like home."

The brim of his hat sank into those dark curls a second before she tilted her head back. Doe eyes burned with enough malice to singe and her lips compressed thinner than a blade of grass. But her cheeks flushed and her expression softened after only a few moments.

"Do they manhandle women back home?"

"Sweetheart, any cowboy worth his weight in horseshit knows that when something that smells sweet and feels soft bumps into you, you wrap your arms around it and hold on tight," he said in what the ladies back home called his bedroom voice.

When she opened her mouth to answer, the sight of those lips forming a slight "O" entranced him for all of two seconds before his cock woke up and took notice. Her eyes widened and he knew she felt his sleeping giant wake up and burrow into her soft stomach. She stiffened but instead of turning tail and running, she shifted her hips ever so slightly as if she were trying to determine if it was really as long as it felt. That sweet mouth opened and closed about ten times, bathing his face with little puffs of her breath. The gentleman his mother had worked so hard to produce, the gentleman who usually knew how to treat a lady keeled over and dropped dead.

"Damn," he muttered. Closing the distance between their mouths, he tightened his hold on her and took possession of her lips. She wriggled some, just enough to tell him she didn't normally kiss strangers. He smiled against her lips when she moaned, leaned in and let him have his moment in the sun.

Pain shot out from his groin in every direction. Stars flashed before his eyes. Air whooshed out of his lungs into her mouth. Releasing her, he doubled over, grabbed his thighs to stop himself from squealing like a girl and blinked away the tears blurring his vision. A package near her feet caught his attention.

Tanner squeezed his eyes shut then glanced at the package again. A vibrator lay beside a black paper bag. The damn thing was nearly as long and fat as *his* Long John and had a mess of pearls filling its bulging base. According to the package, they'd named the pink hummer Jack Rabbit. He figured that came from the long-eared bunny poking its head up from the bottom.

Slender fingers blocked his view as she scooped the vibrator back into the bag.

"No offense, miss, but you're too pretty to need an electric boyfriend," he said on a wheeze. Gritting his teeth against the pain, he straightened and raised one brow. "Especially not one with a bunny riding shotgun."

He watched her doe eyes widen then narrow.

His throbbing balls shrank up tight as he steeled for another blow. Before he knew what hit him, she dazzled him with a mischievous smile and said in a deep, sultry voice that sounded way too familiar, "When I find a man who can make me scream louder than Jack and who doesn't burn out if I want to go all night, I'll stop buying batteries."

A whole other pain hit him and judging from the way her eyes kept straying down, the lady responsible knew damn well she just gave him a wicked hard-on. Tanner chuckled.

"Well, now, maybe I oughta know a little about the competition before I enter this rodeo, Miss...?"

"Rose—" Her eyes widened again. Her jaw dropped when he crossed his arms over his chest and scowled down at the bag. "You can't be serious?"

"Oh, I'm serious, all right."

Her curls whipped her face as she shot a glance over each shoulder as if she were searching for an escape route.

"Calm down, I'm not just looking for a good time. I'm looking for a wife to take back home." He tipped his Stetson and flashed his best smile. "Back home to Texas."

"I told you to go back home, cowboy." She drew up her shoulders and crossed her arms, jutting out two apple-sized breasts. Her brow furrowed but her eyes shone with amusement. Lips he suddenly wanted to feel against his again quirked up in a smile. "You following me?"

She acted indignant, all right, but he hadn't made it to the ripe old age of thirty without learning a thing or two about a woman's body. This little lady's body told him all he needed to know. Yup, something about him turned her on. Those doe eyes were getting darker by the minute and her halter dress did little to hide the imprint of her pebbled nipples. Tanner's mind took off at a gallop just imagining how well her breasts would feel in his hands with those little buttons pressing into his palms.

"Now that's the thing. I considered following you and meeting the gal with the sultry voice, but you disappeared into the herd."

"Herd?"

His cheeks burned.

Her eyes narrowed. "I see. You just happened to bump into me."

"No offense, but you bumped into me."

"Because you were following me." Her eyes flashed with

challenge.

"A while back, I asked God to send me an angel. Way before that, I prayed for a rodeo I could win...after losing my first. I've won every one since. Maybe this is his way of answering me." He nodded down at the bag clutched in her hand.

"Yeah, right. God led you to me so you could screw with my head, among other things. Go home, cowboy." She moved to walk around him.

Tanner sidestepped, blocking her way. "Let's start over." He held out his hand. "Name's Tanner. Tanner McQuade. Pleased to meet you, Rose."

She glanced down at his hand. He wished he didn't have so many calluses. Then again, the ladies at home seemed to like the feel of them over their skin. His hand hovered between them for what felt like an eternity.

"I'm really not a bad guy once you get to know me."

He'd just about given up on her when she slowly slipped her slender hand into his. He wrapped his long fingers around it, had to stop himself from whistling from the shot of molten lead rushing straight to his cock.

"M-my name's not Rose. It's Angel. Angel Roselli." She tugged her hand free and smiled up at him.

"Can I buy you some lunch, Angel?"

"Oh, I don't think..."

Bright white teeth snagged her lower lip for a second before letting it slide free. The sight sent more lead down south in the most painful way. He cleared his throat, took off his hat and held it to his chest. "Please."

"Just lunch, right?"

"For now." He winked then, placing his hand at the small of her back, started toward the pub across the street before she could change her mind. "Angel. Now that's a pretty name."

She followed, shifting away from his hand. "Actually, it's

Angelina. My dad always called me his angel and the name just stuck." A smirk played across her mouth. "Of course, if he knew I was having lunch with a cowboy who just offered to ride me in a rodeo, he might rethink calling me Angel."

Chuckling, Tanner held open the door to the pub. As she passed him, he leaned over and brought his lips to her ear. "I've won every rodeo I've entered since that prayer, Angel. There's not a filly that can unseat me once I've settled in." When Angel stilled but didn't turn or reply, he added, "But they sure do buck and scream a lot."

* * * * *

Sitting in the booth across the table from Tanner, Angel wondered what subway she'd left her brains on this morning. She couldn't believe she was actually considering letting this tall, sinfully handsome cowboy try to prove he could outdo her rabbit. As if any man could.

But one look in those sapphire blue eyes, one feel of those large rough hands and her ever-needy pussy started purring with anticipation. She made matters worse when she felt then snuck a peek at the impressive bulge in his jeans. And when he'd taken off his hat and raked his fingers through that mane of sun-bleached hair when a wayward lock tumbled back down over his brow, she silently moaned.

Walk away from this cowboy? The idea had never entered her mind.

Still, she hadn't even considered taking him up on anything more than lunch until he'd whispered in her ear at the door. Now all she could see was him holding on while she bucked and screamed under him. Yup, her brains were definitely on the E train heading all the way downtown. "So what brings you to New York?" she yelled over the music.

"What?" Tanner leaned his elbows on the table.

Candlelight highlighted his rugged features. Blond stubble graced his cheeks and chin. She could almost feel it scratching her inner thighs. She always left Tilley's Toys aroused, but this was ridiculous. Blinking away the image of those blond locks peeking out from between her legs, she told her body to get a grip then shoved the candle to the edge of the table. Needing something to hold on to, she picked up a packet of sugar and twirled it between her fingers.

She glanced up.

He winked.

Her stomach tumbled.

Licking her lips, she tried again to steer their conversation to a more mundane topic. "What brings you…?"

Angel's words lodged in her throat when he slid out of the booth, unfolding what had to be over six feet of muscle. He hiked up his jeans, drawing her attention again to a bulge that would take a whole drawer full of socks to build, then joined her on her side of the table. He leaned close.

The side of his body, from shoulder to knee, melded to hers.

Growing up in New York City, Angel had erected a barbed-wire electrical fence around her personal space years ago. Unless they were crammed into a subway or elevator or vying for the same shoes during a Black Thursday sale, no one, man or woman, made it past that fence. "Back off, cowboy," she said, pointing the sugar packet at him to emphasize each word.

Tanner leaned back, moving his upper body a fraction of an inch away. "Sorry, but I can barely hear you over the music."

His musky scent and the heat of his thigh still pressing against hers set off alarms that one peek at the bulge in his pants silenced. She could almost hear the last dying buzz of her security fence. She realized this cowboy had bumped into her at the worst time. Leaving Tilley's Toys with yet another attempt to fill the void in her life, starved for the feel of a real flesh-and-blood man between her legs, she wondered if she'd be here even if he didn't have the equipment to rival her biggest dildo. Damn, this was New York. Men propositioned her on the street every day. She'd never given them a second look, much less followed them into a dark pub. Glancing up at his face just as his tongue darted out to moisten his lower lip, she crossed her legs and squeezed.

"I said," she repeated, trying to smile as if his nearness had no effect, "what brings you to New York?"

Tanner chucked her under the chin. "I told you. I'm looking for a wife."

The sugar packet ripped. Other than forcing that amazing kiss on her, Tanner had acted and looked quite sane. A little too sure of himself. But sane.

Until now.

Wiping the pile of sugar to the side, Angel cleared her throat and searched the bar for the waiter, for any able-bodied male who might help her out of this mess. "You came here for a wife?"

When he nodded with a wink, she wondered if she'd missed some major flaw outside while checking out his face and family jewels. She slid closer to the wall of the booth and examined her cowboy.

Growing up a Roselli had its advantages. As a child, she'd helped out in Roselli's Bakery more than she'd played with other kids. As the years passed, she grew to admire how her father knew just how to handle each customer in a way that suited their personality. The only heir apparent to his hundred-year-old family business, she'd studied her father and constantly questioned him about his uncanny perception. As a bonus, she now could peg a nutcase the minute one entered the shop.

Until now. "Why couldn't you find one at home?"

"Oh, there are plenty to choose from. Plenty who would have accepted my proposal, but I wanted someone...well..." he hesitated then glanced at the black paper bag on the table.

"Someone who wouldn't accept a man unless he could outdo her favorite toy."

Angel couldn't help but laugh at the way he shrugged. "So you came all the way to New York to find her. The City of Sin is Las Vegas, cowboy. You came to the wrong town."

"No. I'm not looking for a sinning kind of woman. I'm looking for an angel who doesn't mind sins of the flesh."

He brushed her lips with his thumb. Angel's lungs seized. Trapped in his gaze, she wondered if she could drown just by looking into eyes as blue as a Bermuda sea. Or lose herself, vanish like a boat sucked into the Bermuda Triangle. Realizing that she had somehow leaned closer, she lowered her gaze. Found his lips moving.

"...I want a woman whose eyes flash with fire when she's angry and burn with passion when she's not."

Angel tried to drag some air into her lungs then lost it all when he leaned over and brought those hot, satin lips to her ear again. Someone must have turned off the jukebox and told everyone seated in the booths surrounding theirs to shut up. She heard nothing but her pounding heart and Tanner's husky drawl.

"Your eyes, Angel mine, were spitting fire at me outside when I kissed you. And judging by the way they're looking at me right now, I know you'll crash and burn beneath me...if you let me in the saddle."

Tanner's scorching breath seared a path over her cheek. She tilted her face up for just one kiss, just one taste. Just one—

She shoved him away. "Calm down, cowboy. Number one, you picked the wrong girl if you're looking to bring a wife back to Texas—which, by the way, is the lamest line I've heard yet. Number two, you haven't seen the competition." She lowered her voice. "You have no idea what you're up against."

"So show me this great wonder of the single woman's bedroom." He reached for the bag.

Snatching it off the table, Angel shook her head. "No

way."

"Why not? It's dark, loud and the waiter won't be back with our food for a while." Tanner picked his Stetson up from the table. "We could hide it between us and use my hat to cover it if he comes back."

"Forget it." Sweat trickled down between her breasts.

"Please," he lowered his voice, "just one look."

He pouted. She couldn't believe it, but he actually pouted.

That damn lock of hair fell over his forehead. And fool that she now knew she was, she reached up and brushed it back. The silken strands slid through her fingers. The purring of her needy pussy got so loud, she couldn't hear, much less think straight enough to get up and leave. Years with nothing but her toys to keep her happy had damaged her ability to just say no.

Grateful they at least had their beers, Angel chugged down half her bottle then opened the bag. Pulling out the vibrator, she held it between them for a few seconds before shoving it back in the bag.

"Whoa, sweetheart. That's not fair. I need to see how it works before I can tell if I'm capable of besting it." He snatched the package out of her hands and cracked open the plastic. "You do have batteries in there, don't you?"

Angel's cheeks burned. Every sane part of her brain told her to slip under the table and bolt out of the pub.

The insane, physical part of her brain and body refused to let her go.

She slid the package of batteries out of the bag and placed them in his calloused palm. Just as they had on the sidewalk, the feel of those calluses made her nipples harden. God, she loved a man with rough hands. "I-I don't think this is a good idea. I mean, I have no intention of letting you...uh...prove anything with me."

"You date much, Angel?" Tanner asked as he loaded the batteries into the remote.

"Enough," she said, inching closer to the wall until her hip hurt from the pressure, "Not that it's any of your business."

"Well, I'll tell you something. I'm a nice guy. Real nice." He snapped the cover over the batteries and looked up at her with an earnest expression. "I don't usually handle a woman's toys on a first date, but my ranch is in the hands of a somewhat capable foreman who tends to go on drinking binges. I figure one's due by the end of the month."

Angel nodded, wondering what an alcoholic had to do with her and her vibrator.

"Now I wasn't kidding when I said I was looking for a wife. I like you. Quite a lot, considering we just met. You've blushed at least ten times in the last hour but handed over this rabbit gadget. That tells me you're not one to hit the sack with just anyone, but you're also pretty open about dealing with matters some women prefer to act like they know nothing about. You're here and that tells me you're also open to trying something new, and you don't let conventions rule you."

Knuckles nearly as rough as the palms of his hands brushed down her heated cheeks. She opened her mouth to speak, to ask him what the hell he was talking about, just as his tongue swept out to moisten his lips again.

"Did you want to say something?"

All she could do was shake her head.

His finger hooked her chin. She closed her eyes, waited for him to lean down and give her what she so desperately wanted.

A gentle nudge from his finger and her gaping mouth snapped shut. Opening her eyes, she met eyes twinkling with amusement. Another wave of heat seared her cheeks. His finger glanced down her neck before breaking contact with her skin.

"I'm not...I don't..." Groaning, she clenched her hands in her lap before they reached out and dragged his head down to hers.

Tanner cleared his throat. "I like that you're an angel." Smiling, he winked. "I like that you're not."

"But I know nothing about you," she choked out through her throat.

"Sure you do. You know what I like in a woman. You know you're her. I may have every intention of bringing you to heaven and back by the end of the day, but I haven't been crude about it, have I?"

Angel shook her head. She could barely breathe, how could she reply?

"Well, that tells you I'm somewhat respectful. That waiter brought me the wrong beer then insisted I asked for lite when I pointed out his mistake." He shrugged his shoulders. "Sure, it annoyed me, but I let it go. I did that because I'm very picky about what I fight about and I don't let the small things bother me. I read that book. Every damn page." He beamed.

The knot twisting in Angel's gut loosened a bit. "Look...I—"

He rested the pad of his finger over her lips, cinching that knot tight again. "I'll let you in on a secret, Angel. I'm dying a little every minute because looking at you and not touching is more painful than getting trampled by a bronco. I've kept my hands to myself...for now. That tells you I'm a patient man and have some class." He looked down and slid the two buttons on either side of the remote all the way up.

Angel cringed and let out a nervous giggle when the penis rotated, the pearl sac expanded and contracted and the rabbit ears quivered. Her old Rabbit had broken a week ago and her body reacted like Pavlov's dogs. She had to admit, he'd been right about the music drowning out the sound, but she knew Tanner felt the vibrations when he ran his thumb up to the rabbit's nose.

"I'll be damned." He rubbed the back of his neck. "And revealing the humble part of my wonderful personality, I'm willing to admit that, after seeing all the functions on this Jack Rabbit, I may not win this rodeo."

His shocked expression sent a peal of laughter rippling up her throat. He must have noticed the waiter approaching, because he shut the vibrator off and shoved his hat over it a moment before the man arrived at their table.

They ate their hamburgers with the vibrator silent but not forgotten between them. She knew he hadn't forgotten by his furtive glances to his hat and the way he kept saying "damn" and shaking his head. But their conversation remained off the subject of sex and centered more on their respective lives.

"So you're a baker. That explains the smell." He popped a fry into his mouth.

"Smell?" Angel fought the urge to tilt her head down and sniff.

"Cinnamon. Reminded me of my mom's apple pies." Gazing wistfully into the dark pub, he took a deep breath then let it out on a long sigh.

"Your mom...is she waiting for you back in Texas?" Angel watched him nod. For the first time since they'd entered the pub, tense silence brought their conversation to an abrupt halt. Wiping her mouth with the napkin, Angel coughed. She picked up a fry and swirled it around in the pile of ketchup on her plate.

"He died, the bastard."

Her head snapped up so sharply her neck cracked. "Who?"

"My father." A frown furrowed his brow. A hard glint entered his eyes.

Losing her appetite quite suddenly, Angel dropped the fry in her dish. "You weren't close, I gather."

Without answering, he turned and stared at her then once again drew in a deep breath that left on a long weary sigh. "A month ago, I would have sworn we were as close as a father and son could get."

"But now?"

Tanner downed the rest of his beer. "Let's just say he must have thought otherwise."

Memories of the yelling and screaming during the hours before her mother's death made her eyes burn. Before she realized what she was doing, Angel brushed his hair off his brow then rested her hand on his arm. "You fought before he died."

"No." Tanner shook his head and chuckled, but Angel heard no mirth in his laughter.

She dropped her hand.

"So, do your parents run the bakery when you're out buying toys?"

"No. My father and Antonio."

"Antonio?"

"A baker."

Tanner's calloused hand covered hers. "Your mother?"

Slipping her hand free, she reached for her beer. She had no desire to discuss her mother, no desire to reveal the guilt that still ate away at her to a man she grew more and more convinced would replace her rabbit. At least for tonight. "Tell me about Texas."

She couldn't believe how comfortable she felt with him. By the time they were done, she'd consumed two beers and enough knowledge about Tanner to feel like she'd known him longer than a couple of hours. By the time they were done, she wanted him to touch her with those abrasive hands in the worst way.

Tanner must have seen her gaze stray to his hands. He cupped her cheek in his palm and said, "Hope my hands aren't too rough. Your skin is so soft and I've been known to scratch just by rubbing my hand down a lady's thigh."

He slid his palm down her cheek. She imagined that palm smoothing over her thighs and breasts. Liquid heat drenched the slender crotch of her thong.

"Now back to my competition," he said in a husky voice that lulled her into submission.

He retrieved the vibrator from under his hat. After meeting her gaze for just a moment, he slid the button that made the penis gyrate and rested the rabbit's head on the top of her thigh just where the hem of her dress met her skin. The motion of the penis lifted her dress. Staring at it, unable to move, she watched the head burrow under the material.

His voice, deeper, raspier, broke through the haze holding her captive. "I sure can't make you feel this just by touching you."

The bunny started to vibrate.

When her mouth opened on a shocked gasp, he captured her lips in a tender yet firm kiss that took her breath away. Satin lips skimmed over hers, captured her lower lip, her upper lip, again and again. Teeth grazed from one corner of her mouth to the other while the tip of his tongue delved in. She struggled to keep this kiss from going any further, gave up when she felt his deep, rumbling groan beneath hands that had somehow found their way from her lap to his chest. Parting her lips, she almost cried out when his tongue swept in and caressed every inch of her mouth. Lost in the kiss, she barely felt the vibrator slip deeper under her dress.

Stop him, her mind screamed.

But her hands gripped onto his shirt as all her senses concentrated on his mouth and the vibrations working their way up her inner thigh.

He nibbled on her lips, sucked them into his hot mouth and plunged his tongue in again. All the while, he kept inching that vibrator closer and closer to her dripping-wet thong. By the time she felt his fingers push the cloth aside and nudge the fat head of the penis between her throbbing lips, she could only spread her legs wider in response.

The raspy voice of Sister Mary Ellen emerged from her

past, warning that someday the devil would come and try to lure her into hell, that even an angel would find herself powerless if she fell under his spell. Angel felt her muscles coil and wondered how on earth that frail nun knew this day would come.

"And I definitely can't do this," he murmured against her lips then turned the vibrator's functions to the max.

The shaft gyrated, bumping her G-spot while the beaded sac expanded, stretching her. Then, as if he knew exactly what to do, he tilted the vibrator until the rabbit ears clasped her clit and sent a bevy of vibrations to her core.

"Stop," she whispered between pants when she worked up enough willpower to pull slightly away from his kiss.

His calloused hand, the one not holding the vibrator, slid under her dress and up her hip. Every nerve his palm skimmed over tingled long after it left.

"Do you really want me to stop, Angel? I will if you do."

His mouth recaptured hers. Muscles coiled tightly and clenched the rotating penis. Shudders racked her body as she fought the approaching climax.

"Please," she whispered, not sure if she was begging him to stop or continue.

He deepened the kiss and turned off the vibrator. His hand slid down her hip. When she felt him start to slip the vibrator out, selfish need overpowered any morals she possessed. She clamped her thighs on his hand, tore her mouth away and, gazing up into eyes that burned her with their desire, said in a ragged voice, "Don't you dare stop."

"Promise you'll let me enter the rodeo?" Tanner slid one rough hand all the way up to her waist and nudged the vibrator deeper with the other.

"Wha...no."

He pulled the vibrator out, inch by inch. A slight shift brought the head against her G-spot.

"Wait, yes, dammit. Yes."

"As soon as we leave and go to your place?"

She hesitated.

He bumped her G-spot again. "Time's running out, Angel. That waiter will be back with the bill soon."

"God help me, yes."

The vibrator sprang to life. His hand made its way up and over her breast and those wonderful calluses scraped her nipple. Angel shattered and screamed into his mouth from an orgasm stronger than her Rabbit had ever produced before.

Still dazed ten minutes later, she watched him hand his license over to the waiter and listened while he told the man to write down all the information as proof for the "lady" that he was safe enough to walk her home.

Before she knew it, they were in her apartment and Tanner was slipping her dress over her head.

She vaguely wondered if they'd bothered to close her door, vaguely wondered how she couldn't care less if they hadn't. All that mattered were his hands burning a path down her back and his mouth branding her like the cattle that roamed his ranch. Her cat, Raven, let out a long, high-pitched mewl, apparently insulted that she'd forgotten to give him his usual greeting. A siren shrieked past. Tanner growled like an animal gone wild.

She felt wild, untamed, unleashed.

When he nibbled his way down her neck, she arched her back, greedy for the feel of his tongue on her breasts. Her heart pounded in her ears.

His hot, moist mouth captured her nipple. The pounding grew louder. Her heart would surely burst if it beat any faster.

"Angel. You home?"

The sound of her father's voice sent ice through Angel's veins and a yelp to her lips. Slipping out of Tanner's hot embrace, she darted a glance at her door. Luckily, someone had shut it when they'd first come in. A series of dull bangs resounded from the door. The sound of a key sliding into the lock propelled her into action. Ignoring Tanner's bemused expression, she took her dress from his hands and yanked it over her head. The arch of his brow as he stared at her body drew her gaze down. Realizing she'd put the dress on backward and had no time to set it right, she did what any smart woman would do. She fled to the bathroom and locked herself in. Leaning against the door, she listened to the muffled voices coming from her living room.

* * * * *

Tanner met Mr. Roselli's suspicious glare with one of his warmest smiles. The man's bushy black eyebrows pointed south and nearly met over a prominent nose that appeared to have been broken a few times.

Shoving his hands deeper into his pants pockets, Tanner swayed back on his heels. "Angel should be out any minute. She just wanted to freshen up before we, uh, left for lunch."

"Lunch?"

Tanner watched Mr. Roselli's gaze dart from corner to corner as if he expected to unearth some Indian artifact amongst the clothes, books and papers littering the small room.

The man folded his arms across his chest and leaned against the door. "Guess she forgot *we* had a lunch date."

Feeling as if he stood in the crosshairs of a bull stamping his feet before a charge, Tanner felt the familiar stirrings of excitement. Damn, he loved a challenge and this man, all five foot six of him, promised an exciting ride.

"Well," Tanner said in a tone that held a note of uncertainty he just didn't feel, "this isn't our first date, but I..."

"Fine." Mr. Roselli grinned. He bent down and patted the head of a sleek black cat. "Then it's settled. You can take her another day."

Tanner almost laughed. The old coot had hogtied him. "Maybe we should ask Angel."

Waving his hand as if the idea held no more power than a pesky *'squita*, he smirked, "My girl never says no to her daddy."

The bathroom door opened. Tanner turned and sucked in a hissing breath. Sunlight from a small window behind Angel shone through her dress, shadowed her legs and left little to his imagination. She smiled brightly at her father.

"Dad."

The scent of her arousal swirled around Tanner as she whisked past him into her father's open arms. Angel and her father embraced each other with their bodies and eyes. Watching the two, Tanner felt the first stirrings of guilt. He'd have to be recovering from a long ride into the setting sun not to see how much they loved each other. Damn, he hadn't taken into account the notion that he'd be taking a woman thousands of miles from her daddy. It just didn't seem right.

Especially considering his reason for needing a wife.

Thanks to his father, he had to find a wife before the end of the summer or lose the ranch, and time was running out faster than a prairie dog running from a coyote. No one had to tell him that his father's will had set him up for a marriage of convenience. No one had to tell him that his wife would only fill his home and his bed.

He had no intention of wedding one of the proper girls back home, even if he could get past their drooling at the prospect of marrying the owner of one of the largest ranches in Texas. Eventually, word might leak out about his father's will. The ladies back home would take that as a green light to lock the bedroom door and visit the nearest stud farm. Then they'd divorce him and take him for every penny.

In a loveless marriage, only a naughty religious girl would serve his needs. Someone who'd believe him when he said he loved her, who'd satisfy his every need and never stray from their holy vows.

Even if he did.

He'd come here hoping New York City had the sassy, sexy fillies his brother, Ryan, raved about after his last trip. He already knew it held the largest, most important cathedral in the United States. Sassy, sexy and devout. Perfect.

Mr. Roselli's eyes shone with love as he smiled down at his daughter. Guilt washed over Tanner. Left him cold and oddly bereft.

Five minutes in a lawyer's office had killed Tanner's notion that his father had truly loved him. Five minutes and years of memories had soured. He cursed his father and wondered again why on earth he'd written up such a sick stipulation to his keeping the ranch. He knew Tanner loved that ranch. Knew that he'd go to any lengths to keep it. Dammit, the man had even built Tanner his own house, wraparound porch and all. The night his father had died, he'd sat on that porch. The sight of the sun setting had soothed him as he'd gazed out over the expanse of land he'd assumed was now his and his brother's responsibility. The fear of failing and losing the ranch ate away at him and had him cursing his father again. Angel's voice broke into his moment of self-pity.

"What a surprise, Dad."

"Surprise?" Angel's father chucked her on the jaw. "This *is* Saturday, isn't it?"

Tucking a curl behind her ear, Angel frowned. "Yeah, but—"

"You forgot." Shoulders slumping, Mr. Roselli glanced at Tanner. "I have only one child and she's too busy to remember her dad."

Tanner had to hand it to the man. He sure knew how to lead a mare to water. Angel's face fell. Those delicate hands that only minutes ago had held Tanner's face captive and shoved it toward her breasts now cupped her father's cheeks.

"Of course I didn't forget you, Dad. I...I..."

"Forget? Right before you arrived," Tanner stepped up and touched Angel's arm, "Angel explained she always kept Saturdays free for her Dad. I, ah, figured I'd just tag—"

"You figured you'd tag along with me and my girl?" Beaming, Mr. Roselli stepped back and puffed out his chest.

Basking in the warmth of Angel's grateful smile, Tanner mutely nodded. After a few moments of silence he glanced back at Angel's father.

Mr. Roselli's smile had faded. "Normally, I'd have no problem." Rubbing the back of his neck, he glanced at the door as if he could see through it into the hall. "But I brought Antonio."

"No!" Angel shifted closer to Tanner. "Dad, I told you—"

"I know, Angel, but the guy came all the way from Italy for you." He winked at Tanner then shrugged.

"He came from Italy for the bakery. Not me."

Tanner looked down at the woman he'd known for only a few hours. "Antonio? The baker?"

"Best baker ever to set foot in New York. And Italian royalty."

"Royalty," Angel muttered, still scowling at her father. "I've never heard of his family."

Mr. Roselli reached for the doorknob. "Well, we don't want to keep him waiting outside too long. Last time I took him out, the women nearly trampled me to get his attention. You'd think I had Antonio Banderas by my side." Peering intently at Tanner, Mr. Roselli held out his hand. "Ready, Angel?"

Angel slid her hand into Tanner's and squeezed. *"We'll* be out in a few minutes. I have to feed Raven. That should give you enough time to explain to Antonio that I'm bringing Tanner."

27

Chapter Two

Tanner watched Angel lock the door then thump her forehead on the wooden surface. "That man! He just doesn't give up."

He grabbed her shoulders and turned her around. Instead of coming into his arms like he'd expected, she leaned back against the door and closed her eyes. Sliding his finger between two of the buttons on her dress, he skimmed over the warm swell of her breast until the tip of his finger bumped over a nipple. Her teeth snagged her lower lip.

He knew he should just leave. Knew he had no right to upset her life for a marriage that would be nothing more than a piece of paper. Knew she belonged here with her daddy and...

Jealousy took hold of him. "You catch Antonio while he was visiting New York too? Or did he find you wandering through some Tuscan vineyard?"

Angel's eyes flew open.

"No, don't answer that. Where you met doesn't matter since the Italian stud obviously failed in the bedroom."

Angel gasped. "Excuse me?"

Scraping his nail over the hard nub until her lids lowered, Tanner told himself to shut up. He had no right saying what he did, no right even feeling jealous. What she did with her Italian Stallion was her business. "What do you do, my sweet Angel? Take out your electric boyfriend after your limp noodle leaves?"

Eyes burning with indignation met his as her hands pushed against his chest. "You bastard! How dare you just assume that I...I..." Her cheeks pinked. "Look, I know what we, uh, did might make you think...but I never...not with..." She licked her lips and lowered her eyes.

"Not with Antonio?"

"Not with anyone." Angel's cheeks turned bright red. "Just Jack."

Tanner froze. The implications of those two little words stunned him, left him speechless for all of two seconds. Laughter bubbled up his throat. He swallowed it and scowled down at her.

"Just Jack? As in Rabbit?" His finger hooked her nipple and tugged until she yelped and stumbled forward. "You expecting me to believe you gave your virginity to a toy?"

She swatted at his hand. "You try having a social life when you're in a bakery with your father six, sometimes seven, days a week, thirteen hours a day. You try catching some guy's eye when you have so much flour in your hair you look sixty."

"Why does the image of you covered in flour turn me on? Not buying it, Angel. Some guy had to walk into that bakery and see what I saw the minute I laid eyes on you." Her blush spread down her neck and now covered the wide expanse of chest above her neckline. He wanted to rip that dress off and see if her breasts were blushing too. "So, Antonio never made it through the gates. Did he get to play with Jack and you like I did?"

A high-pitched squeal met his ears. "You...you...you have no right to question me, cowboy. We just met. Remember? Who and what I play with is none of your business."

"Take it off." His voice sounded too harsh to his ears, but her nipples poked at the thin cloth of her dress with every deep breath. He had to see those breasts. He'd never spoken to a woman like this. Never had to. But logic had left the minute he realized he just might be his angel's first. Well, first man.

If Mr. Roselli had told the truth, he'd brought a man all the way from Italy to wed and bed the woman who had just spread her legs in a restaurant for Tanner and a buzzing bunny. The woman whose pussy had never felt the hot thrust of a real cock. Although Tanner would have laughed at such a notion ten minutes ago, he'd somehow managed to snag a virgin in New York City. Shit. Not your standard saving herself for marriage or God kind of virgin. He had found kinky virgin. Talk about stepping in shit. But if her father had his way, the Italian Stallion would be Angel's first. A hungry pain shot through Tanner's cock. His balls drew up as tight as fists gearing up for a brawl. Tanner clenched his hands at his sides. "Take that fucking dress off, Angel. Now."

Fear glanced across her face. "Or?"

That fear sliced through his need, shredding it. Gritting his teeth, he closed his eyes. "Or I'll die right here on your floor from wanting you," he whispered, resting his forehead on hers.

Her sigh sent her warm breath over his lips. From beneath his lashes, he watched her trembling fingers fumble with her buttons. When they were all free, he spread the sides apart until he bared her breasts to his greedy eyes.

"There's no time." Her breathless voice dissolved into a moan when he ran his calloused palms over those rose-tinged swells.

"Oh, I won't take you now. A woman always remembers her first time, doesn't she?" Rubbing the roughest part of his palm over the buds stabbing his flesh, he waited for her to nod then captured her mouth with a tender kiss that soon grew into a hungry feeding frenzy. When the pain in his cock grew unbearable, he forced himself to pull away.

"No, much as I'd like nothing better than to strip you down and slam into you, I won't have your first time being a quickie against the door. Just promise me you won't let that limp noodle outside sneak in before me."

Huge round eyes gazed up. "Tanner, I...you've already gone farther than anyone else."

"You mean no one else has done this?" Holding her gaze, he lowered his lips to her breast and proceeded to make his way to the rosy peak that beckoned to him. Clamping it between his teeth, he nibbled until she cried out and her knees buckled. Still holding her nipple hostage, he slid his thigh between her legs. Another bite and her legs gave out completely. He grinned against her breast as her crotch landed on his thigh. A few more nips and he felt her warm juice seep through his jeans. Grabbing her hips, he slid her up his leg. Her fingers dug into his shoulders. "Now, Angel, I find it hard to believe no man ever taught you why women do *not* ride sidesaddle."

"I've never been on a horse. I'm terrified of the—ah!"

Her words fractured when he started to move his leg, all the while holding her firmly in place. Suckling on her like she was the last watering hole before a vast desert, he ground her weeping flesh up and down his leg until her back arched and her body started to shudder. The need to take her hit him so hard that he had to release her breast and grit his teeth just to keep from freeing his cock. Crushing her mouth with his, he slid his fingers beneath her dripping panties, between her slick folds. Muscles stronger then he would have figured possible gripped his fingers and drew them in deeper. He searched until he touched the spot that made her still, made her nails bite into his skin through his shirt, then he stoked the flames until she screamed into his mouth and slammed down on his leg so hard she nearly broke his fingers.

Tanner gathered Angel in his arms. Still savoring the taste of her mouth and the feel of her soft moans gliding down his throat, he carried her to the couch and sat her on his lap. Something salty slid between their lips. Although he could have kissed her until grass covered the desert floor, he raised his head. Tears streamed down Angel's cheeks.

"Damn. Did I hurt you?"

Smiling as she palmed away her tears, Angel cleared her throat and murmured, "I don't know why I'm crying." She glanced up then quickly lowered her gaze to her lap. "I'm a little overwhelmed right now. And confused."

"Confused?"

Angel hopped off his lap and gazed at him as if he'd performed some impossible magic trick. "From the moment you bumped into me, I've been acting like," she flung out her arms and let out a short, nervous giggle then shook her head, "well, not like myself, that's for sure."

When he frowned and held out his hand to bring her back to his lap where she belonged, she jerked away.

"Stop it! Don't you get it? I'm a twenty-five-year-old virgin. In New York City, for crissakes! I rarely date. I never go to bars. And believe me, when I knee some jerk on the street, I usually leave before he catches his breath. And never, never would I go with him anywhere or allow him to do half the things you've done on a first date, much less within the first few hours of meeting him."

Tanner listened as intently as he could, considering that her open dress revealed that her breasts bore the marks of his attention. "Well, I don't normally make a move on a woman I've just met, but I did and I'm not going to apologize. I wouldn't change a damn thing about the last few hours. Not a damn thing." When her eyes welled, he stood up and brushed a damp curl from her cheek. "It's not your fault. It's the boots."

Angel hiccupped. "The boots?"

"That's why no woman can deny a cowboy. We don't normally reveal our secret, but seeing as you're all worked up about it, I figure you deserve to know what turned you into putty in my hands. You women see a man in cowboy boots and you lose all your inhibitions." Tanner worked to keep his face serious while he watched her eyes narrow.

"You're telling me I shouldn't beat myself over the head because your boots worked some kind of Western magic on me?" Her voice rose with every word.

"Yup. Works every time."

"So it has nothing to do with you or me." The corner of her mouth quirked up.

"Nope. It's not because you're the prettiest thing here or in Texas and it's not that I'm the best-damn-looking cowboy you'll ever meet. It's not even because there's a God up in heaven letting out a sigh of relief that two people he created for each other finally met. It's the boots." When she opened her mouth to reply, he brought his lips close to hers. "Don't even ask. They stay on."

Angel giggled. "Even when you sleep?"

"If it means you'll be lying next to me, then even when I sleep. Now let's get downstairs before your father sends Antonio up to rescue you."

Angel's eyes widened. She spun around and started for the door. Laughing, he snagged her waist and brought her back up against his chest. "Whoa."

"What?"

"I don't think it's a good idea to go out with your dress undone."

As she buttoned up, he decided not to tell her that her lips had that swollen, kissed senseless look or that her flushed face, half-mast lids and beard-rouged chest and neck would tell her father and the great Italian Stallion just what had delayed their arrival.

Outside, when Mr. Roselli's eyes narrowed as he took in his daughter's appearance, and Antonio's mouth set in a grim line, Tanner just flashed his pearly whites and draped his arm possessively over Angel's shoulders.

Halfway down the block, his smile faltered.

Angel's father hadn't exaggerated. Women of all ages seemed taken with Antonio. Tanner watched them wink, smile, giggle and stop in their tracks as they caught sight of the tall, dark-haired, perfectly chiseled Italian. He'd wink with those dark brown eyes and smile, baring perfect white teeth and a set of deep dimples. Dimples!

Tanner drew Angel closer. Wished he could see her face, her reaction.

As they crossed the street, a cool breeze swirled around them, seemed to latch on to his upper thigh. Glancing down, he realized that his jeans still bore the mark of Angel's release. Turning to Antonio, catching the way the man's eyes darted between Angel and the dark, wet smudge, Tanner couldn't help but whistle a happy, nameless tune.

* * * * *

"Will someone either sit down or move so I can?" Angel stood behind the three men in Munsey's Cafe. As soon as they'd entered the café, all three of them had rushed to the booth then tried to leave a small gap for Angel. But every time Angel tried to enter that gap, the man on the other side would shove his shoulder into the other's and close the gap as he attempted to get her to enter the booth closer to him. Five long, embarrassing minutes passed with Angel shuffling from side to side. Now the three men totally blocked the booth and stared each other down.

"Hello? I'd like to sit down."

When no one moved, she pushed her way between her father and Tanner then dropped down onto the wooden bench.

Antonio, Tanner and her father converged to her side of the booth. When her father landed beside her, Tanner and Antonio shoved and pushed to get in the bench on the other side of the table first, obviously vying now for the spot directly across from her.

"Grow up," she muttered, snagging Antonio's attention just long enough for Tanner to cut in front.

The minute he sat down, she felt his boot nudge her feet.

The air-conditioning in the restaurant had already chilled her wet thong. Pushing his boot away, she crossed her legs and picked up a menu. But as she searched for the least-filling dish, the hard toe of his boot shot up her leg and bumped into her crotch. Shimmying back on the bench, she glared into his innocent-looking face. "Stop it."

"Excuse me?" her father asked, lowering his menu.

"G-glaring at each other. Just stop it."

Tanner grinned. "I'm only looking at you, Angel."

"I too only have the eyes for you, *bella*." Antonio reached across the table.

Snatching her hand away before Antonio could touch it, she wondered for the tenth time what had ever possessed her father to bring the man back with him. She did not believe his claim that he'd brought Antonio all the way from Italy so they could have someone else around to watch the bakery.

She glanced up. If she, her father and Antonio were here... "Who's watching the bakery?"

Her father raised the menu and muttered, "I closed the shop for a couple of hours. The tenderloin tips sound good."

"You closed it? So Antonio could have lunch with us?"

"Sure, why not?"

A lump rose in her throat. Every concert, sport event and school play her father had failed to show up at replayed in her mind. Every prom, sweet sixteen and beach party she'd missed because he'd refused to close the sacred bakery or even keep it open without her help. During a wicked argument when she'd turned eighteen, she'd threatened to quit and move out unless she had Saturdays off. He'd refused until he came home the next day and found her packing.

Glancing up, she caught Tanner staring at her, concern etched across his face. She lifted the menu, hoping he didn't see the shimmer of tears she could feel burning her eyes.

The scrape of his boot inching over the edge of the bench

sounded deafening to her ears, but when she peeked around the menu and met her father's and Antonio's gazes, she saw no sign that they'd heard. Tanner on the other hand leaned back and smirked then winked.

Planning on reminding him of her impeccable aim and the painful ramifications of angering her, she uncrossed her legs and pressed one foot into his crotch.

His eyes widened. His smirk turned into a dopey grin.

A rough hand wrapped around her ankle and tugged.

Before she could respond, she slid to the edge of the bench. She felt the bottom of her dress slip back. Her bare butt touched the cool wood. Her tender, still recovering pussy slammed into his boot. A second passed as she met his gaze, absorbed the feel of the toe of his boot teasing her clit with the subtlest movement. Too sensitive, too soon, she felt the stirrings of another orgasm and wondered if the man before her was truly Sister Mary Ellen's devil.

"I don't know about Texas," she hissed through clenched teeth, "but the streets of New York are not that clean."

"I'm well aware of that," Tanner said, shrugging. "I wouldn't worry. Last I saw, you were wearing—"

"Shoes." Angel scowled and tried to back away.

"What are you talking about, Angel?" Her father peered around the side of his menu.

"Shoes, Daddy. We're talking about dirty shoes." She wriggled her leg. "And where they do not belong."

"I do not understand." Antonio lowered his menu. "My English, it is not good."

"It's not you, Antonio." Her father shook his head and turned back to the menu. "Angel's talking nonsense."

Tanner's grip on her ankle tightened, pulled her even harder against his boot. She tried again, nearly moaned from the pleasure spiraling up her stomach.

Deciding to give Tanner a little of his own treatment, she

moved her foot from side to side then realized too late that she'd only heightened her own desires. Her sandal's scant sole did little to hide the feel of the thick, hard ridge beneath her foot. Meeting Tanner's heated gaze with one of her own, she wriggled to break free and lift her foot from the evidence of just how much he wanted her.

Again, a major mistake. He tugged and ground her foot even harder into his crotch.

"Stop fidgeting, Angel," her father said from behind his menu.

"Yes, Angel," Tanner said. "Stop fidgeting."

"What is this? Fidgeting? I do not think I know this word." Antonio closed his menu. "Angelina, do you feel well? You have, what you say, sweat? And you are shakering."

Tanner burst out laughing. "Shakering?"

Antonio's hands balled. "Are you making the fun of my English?"

"Calm down, Tony—"

"*An-tonio.* I say you are making the fun."

"Making the fun of your English? No, would never do that to royalty." Tanner's other calloused hand scraped up and down her calf.

"So you agree. She is shakering?"

Angel fought for control. The more Tanner laughed, the more his boot jerked and twitched, the more she wobbled at the edge of coming. She stared at him with what she hoped were pleading eyes.

"She is shaking." Her father pressed his cool palm to her forehead. "You're hot."

"I tell you, she is all wet," Antonio leaned over and ran his finger down her cheek. "See?"

"You know, Tony, I have to agree with you." Tanner stared into her eyes and grinned. "She's definitely wet."

"We should leave." Her father closed his menu.

Angel watched in horror as her father grabbed her hand. "I'm fine!"

Tanner released her ankle.

Her father yanked her hand as he moved to slide out of the booth.

The edge of Tanner's boot scraped her clit as he finally lowered his foot.

The waiter appeared. "Ready to order?"

"We're leaving," her father explained, staring at her with a concerned expression.

"I'm fine, D-daddy."

He squeezed her hand. "You sure, Angel?"

"Yes, it's just hot in here."

"You're too thin. Did you eat breakfast?"

"Breakfast? No." She didn't want to talk. Or eat. She just wanted to crawl under the table and punch Tanner in his oversized balls.

* * * * *

Angel closed the door of her apartment and let out a relieved sigh. Throughout lunch, the three men in her life, the only men in her life, had either vied for her attention, sparred with each other or clammed up entirely. The fact that she'd already eaten less than an hour earlier and had to force her salad down her throat made the afternoon unbearable. Her stomach, fuller than she ever recalled, roiled with every forkful.

She'd nearly tossed both lunches when her father scowled and asked if the rash on her face and neck had anything to do with why she and Tanner took so long to leave the apartment.

She'd nearly punched Tanner when he'd brushed his knuckles over her inflamed cheeks and stated that he was not the type of man to kiss and tell.

Then, as they'd strolled home, Tanner had held her hand and talked as if they'd been dating for months. By the time they'd reached her apartment, he'd all but admitted that they were considering marriage.

Marriage!

Sliding down the door until her butt thumped painfully on her oak floor, she closed her eyes and prayed she hadn't let some lunatic into her life. Trapped in her father's bakery all these years, she had little experience dating, much less choosing a man. Sweat trickled down her spine. Wouldn't it be her dumb luck to pick some nut and end up spending the rest of her life eluding a crazed stalker?

Antonio's eyes had practically burned with rage every time Tanner had touched her or leaned all the way over the table to whisper in her ear. Come to think of it, she might make the news with two stalkers. After all, the man had come all the way from Italy, leaving his family and job, after her father had shown him her picture. If that wasn't crazy, Angel didn't know what was.

Yup, she'd definitely hooked two nuts. She saw herself coming apart on Tanner's lap and groaned. She'd seen the dark spot on his jeans.

Had her father? Antonio?

Every pedestrian they'd passed on their way to the restaurant?

A soft tap on the door sent her scurrying on her hands and knees across the room. Crouched near the coffee table, she stared at the door and willed whoever stood on the other side to leave.

Another tap.

"Who—ah," she croaked then cleared her throat, "who is it?"

"Who do you think it is?"

Hearing her father's voice, Angel scrambled to her feet and ran to the door. Relief sent a bright smile to her face.

When she opened the door, her father's scowl made her stomach lurch. She covered her mouth and ran to the bathroom.

After she'd flushed both lunches down the toilet and brushed her teeth and hair, she returned to the living room and her father.

"Well, Dad, I didn't expect to see you back so soon."

"Don't give me that innocent look. Who's this Tucker—?"

"Tanner."

"That's what I said. Who's this Tanner guy?" Mr. Roselli strode over to the sideboard. "And what the hell is this?"

Angel's eyes felt as if they'd pop out of their sockets as she watched her father turn around, her vibrator clutched in his hand.

"That?" Avoiding his eyes, she snatched the vibrator and bag from his hands. Giggling, she explained, "This is just a gag gift for...ah...a neighbor's bridal shower."

"Really?" He followed her into the kitchen. "Funny, I would think you'd keep it sealed in the packing. You know, just in case she wants to return it."

Recognizing the voice he'd used countless times when she would lie as a child, she drew up her shoulders and turned. Piercing him with a scathing glare, she lifted a bridal shower card and gift bag from the island. "See? It's opened because the...the idea is that she...she takes it out of the bag like this!"

Angel shoved the vibrator into the gift bag bearing three lacy thongs, her neighbor's real gift, then pulled it back out with her hand wrapped around the pink shaft. "Funny, right?"

The coiled wire attaching the vibrator to its remote snagged the edge of the gift bag and tipped it over the side of the counter. Fumbling to catch the bag, remote and delicate lingerie as they fell to the floor, Angel dropped the vibrator. She felt the ridges of the remote button glance over her fingers.

Heard the motor buzz to life.

Out of the corner of her eye, she saw her father lurch forward to help, saw his fingers grasp the remote then lose contact after they'd slid both buttons all the way up the side of the slender white casing.

"Jesus Christ!" Her father's booming voice did little to drown out the loud buzzing from below, a buzzing amplified by the plastic base hitting her tile floor.

Jack Rabbit, in all its vibrating pearls, fluttering ears and twirling shaft glory, danced across the kitchen floor directly toward her father's feet. She froze just long enough for the vision of Tanner sliding his competition between her legs in the pub to flash before her eyes, then reached for the vibrator.

"Angelina Maria Roselli, don't you dare touch that thing."

She shifted direction and went for the remote. Jack Rabbit hit the toe of her father's shoe. He kicked it away, sending the shaft skidding across the kitchen floor toward her cat, Raven. The attached remote followed, shooting out from under Angel's clawing fingers.

"Dad," she whined, then couldn't help but laugh when Raven screeched and, sliding across the tile, tried to gain enough friction with the floor to make a hasty retreat. The wire caught one of Raven's flailing legs, wrapped around it and held tight. Raven, the remote and vibrator sped out of the kitchen.

Angel watched in horror as her father followed. Her heart leapt into her throat when he snagged the remote and yanked the wire out.

Silence. Suffocating silence.

Burning with humiliation yet grief-stricken by the destruction of her brand-new toy, Angel mutely watched her father toss the deceased Rabbit into the garbage.

A flush spread over her father's cheeks. "That's what goes on at those parties?" Shaking his head, he opened a cabinet with trembling hands and took out a bottle of merlot. "Thank

God your mother wasn't alive to see this."

Later, sipping her second glass of wine and finally calming down, Angel watched her father pour his third. "Don't you think you've had enough, Dad?"

Downing half the glass, he muttered, "One of the benefits of living in the city. I don't have to worry about driving."

"I'm talking about your sugar. You have to stop this."

"Don't you think it's about time you told me who that cowboy is?"

"Just some guy I met."

"When?"

"When?" She tipped her glass and emptied the contents. "Well, a while ago. I really don't recall exactly when." Rising, Angel strolled over to the window. "I don't see why you had to be so cold to him during lunch. You contradicted everything he said."

"Angel, Angel, Angel," her father muttered, rising from the barstool, "Roselli's Bakery has been in our family for nearly a century. You are my only heir. Whoever you marry has to help you run the bakery. You know that. What's his last name?"

Leaning against the windowsill, she glanced down at the people strolling past her stoop. "McQuade. Why?"

"Doesn't sound Italian. Unless, of course, his people were one of the fools who changed their names as they passed through Ellis Island."

The top of a Stetson caught her eye.

Her father continued, his voice a distant hum amidst the sudden roaring in her ears.

"Doesn't look Italian either, if you ask me. Could you imagine the business we'd lose if people found out a cowboy took over? McQuade...what the hell kind of name is McQuade? German? A German making cannoli?"

Leaning closer to the window, Angel peered down. "I'm

seeing the guy, Dad, not marrying him," she mumbled.

The Stetson tilted. The roar in her ears amplified. Her heart hiccupped. Tanner, leaning against the side of a car, his booted feet crossed at the ankles, glanced up and grinned. Lurching back, she bumped into her father.

"Dammit, Angel, now look what you've done." Her father held his wine-stained shirt away from his chest and ran to the kitchen sink. As he dabbed at the crimson splotch with a wet cloth, he continued, "That Tucker—"

"Tanner." She edged back toward to the window.

Her father snorted. "Tucker. Tanner. What does it matter? He's a cowboy. And did you see those boots? He can't even walk like a normal man."

Turning, she waited for him to glance up from his shirt. "Tanner stalks just fine!"

"Stalks?"

"Huh?" She inched a little closer to the window.

"You said he stalks."

Seeing the roof of the car, she figured another couple of inches would get her close enough to see the top of his hat.

"Angel, is this guy stalking you?"

"I said walks, Dad. Stop putting words in my mouth just because you don't like him. And I happen to like his boots." As soon as her father returned his attention to cleaning his shirt she stole a peek out the window then scooted a bit closer, darting glances between her father and the window.

Rubbing viciously at the crimson stain, her father grumbled, "Cowboys may look good with those ridiculous boots, but they can't bake a tiramisu. And he mentioned a ranch back in Texas. What are you going to do? Leave New York? Me?"

"I'd never leave you or New York." Had she said stalked? Did hanging outside her apartment mean her cowboy was a stalker? Her stomach lurched again.

"You're wasting your time with him. Now Antonio came all the way from Italy just to meet you. The man's tiramisu sells out every day. And he'll stay here for you, not take you away."

Rising on her toes, Angel tried to nonchalantly glance out her window and see if Tanner still waited. A trill of fear and excitement skittered down her spine. "I really doubt he came for me. Remember, Dad, you told him all about Roselli's."

Seeing a bit of the Stetson, she spun away from the window and faced her father. He stared at her as if he'd caught her with her hands in the cookie jar.

"Looks like it might rain..."

"Are you even listening to me? Antonio—"

"Let's weigh what motivated Antonio to leave good 'ole Italy." She held her hands out to her sides, palms up. She glanced at her left hand. "You told him that Roselli's has been a favorite of New Yorkers for nearly a hundred years. A thriving, very profitable business. You told him that you had no sons to take over the reins of this family gold mine. You also told him that you had a single daughter whose husband would co-own and run Roselli's with her. Oh, and let's not forget, you offered him a job that pays twice what he made in Italy if he just came here to check me and Roselli's out."

Her left hand rose high above her head. Glancing at her right hand, she said, "Hmm...he saw a picture of me. A bad one, I might add. Anything else? Did fireworks go off when he looked at it? No?" Her right hand hovered below her waist. "Now you tell me again he came here for me."

Tossing the washcloth on the windowsill, her father shook his head at her. He draped his arm over her shoulders and led her away from the window. "Antonio is a good man. Whatever his motives for coming here, he's fallen for you. I see it in his eyes every time he looks at you."

"That's lust, Dad. Nothing more. You blabbed about me being a virgin and he, like any man, can't wait to be the first."

When her father shook his head, she gave him a rueful smile. "Don't lie, Dad. I heard you two talking by the ovens one day. You bragged that I was probably the only virgin in New York City. You even told him that you know I'm one 'cause you never give me enough time off to date."

"No, no, no, I said the bakery, running the bakery didn't give you time to date." Snagging her chin, her father kissed the tip of her nose. "Can you blame a father for bragging that his daughter isn't tainted like most women these days?"

"Tainted?" Angel had to smile back.

"Cowboys can't make pastries."

For years, she'd practically run Roselli's herself. And yet, as far as her father was concerned, the future of the bakery would someday rest in the hands of her husband. "*I'm* the pastry chef. When I marry, if I ever do, I'll stay the pastry chef." She met his gaze head-on. "Look, no matter how Tanner acted, we are not anywhere near marriage."

"Angel's honor?"

She nodded and drew an imaginary halo over her head.

Relief shone in her father's eyes. "Look, if you want to see this cowboy, Tucker…"

"Tanner."

"Well, if you want to see him, fine. But promise me that when your cowboy goes back to Texas, you'll give Antonio a chance. Angel's honor, Angel. When Tucker's out of the picture, Antonio's in."

Although his implying that she'd need his permission to see Tanner—or anyone for that matter—made her see red, she merely nodded. They rarely fought. She wouldn't allow their disagreements to go that far. Memories of her last fight with her mother always cooled her anger toward her father. Lately, though, she found it harder and harder to resurrect those memories.

Tonight she had no intention of keeping her father here longer by arguing. Tanner waited outside. Tanner and his callus-roughened hands and his wicked promise that he could bring her higher than she'd ever gone with good old Jack. Her earlier fear that he might end up being a stalker faded with the sudden memory of those hands scraping her nipples until they felt raw.

Gritting her teeth, she smiled sweetly, "Sure, Dad. Angel's honor. I'm real tired."

"Sure, you're tired. That man's legs are so long we all had to run to keep up with him. See, Antonio would have slowed his pace down for you."

Before Angel could answer, her father turned and, waving over his shoulder, left.

She rushed over to the window. The sun had set since she'd last looked out. A heavy downpour now drenched a maze of multicolored umbrellas hiding the identities of those below. The car Tanner had been leaning against no longer filled the parking space in front of her brownstone. Bumping her head against the cool glass, she uttered a silent curse. Obviously, her father's extended visit and the foul weather had chased Tanner away.

Telling herself she was better off, she poured another glass of wine and went to take a shower. Pleasantly buzzed by the wine, she turned the showerhead on pulsate and stripped. A glance in the mirror sent a nervous giggle up her throat and a flutter of pleasure down her stomach. Red blotches marked where Tanner's stubble had scraped the sensitive skin of her breasts. Something about the man made her feel and act wicked. It struck her that for the first time, she had no desire to explore the kinky sites she had grown addicted to on the internet.

Steam billowed from the shower stall behind her and wrapped her in moist heat. Like Tanner's embrace. Like when his breath had flowed over her skin earlier, warning where his hot, wet mouth would touch next.

Holding on to that memory, she stepped under the spray

of water and shut the glass shower door. It pelted her sensitive nipples, trickled down her stomach. Closing her eyes, she let her imagination take flight. Tanner's teeth nipped at her breasts, his lips marked a hot trail down her stomach, his scalding tongue tortured her inflamed clit. She reached for the soft washrag draped over the door railing, but recalling how rough Tanner's hands had felt, grabbed the net puff hanging from a hook instead.

Initially, she swept the soapy netting over her skin almost timidly. The subtle scratch awakened her nerves, her arousal. Nipples hardened, reaching out for more contact. Her clit swelled, her lower lips thrummed in anticipation. With eyes closed, Angel imagined Tanner's stubbly cheek skimming down her stomach, his calloused hands glancing over her inner thighs.

Spreading her legs in answer to the gruff order she imagined he gave, she increased the pressure of the netting. Another order, one that left no question that she obey or face punishment. Ever obedient, she raised her leg and propped one foot on the hot water knob. Her finger poked between her slick folds—Tanner's tongue tasting her as his stubble irritated her skin. She delved deeper. Flicked her clit. Tensed as she approached climax.

This time she would not pull away when the sensations grew too powerful. This time Tanner was in control, forcing her to continue.

A distant voice broke through her fantasy.

"Angel. *Figlio di una femmina!* You with that *bastardo*? *Lo ucciderò!*" Antonio's angry voice came from the direction of her living room. "You hear me? I kill him! Angel!"

Angel jerked her hand from between her legs, lost her balance and flailed her arms in a useless attempt to stay on her feet.

Something thudded against the door just as she realized that she was going down. Her soapy hands struck the glass shower door first.

Chapter Three

Tanner paced the hallway outside Angel's apartment. Something about Angel drew him. She was innocent yet wild. Meek yet strong willed. Traditional yet unconventional.

A woman who'd given her virginity to a vibrator.

Damn, she was everything he'd hoped for but never expected to find.

Rubbing the back of his neck, he wondered how he could go through with his father's demands. He needed a wife. Wanted more time with Angel than the will allowed.

Sure, Angel turned him on. But he had no idea what marriage to her would be like. One afternoon didn't tell a man a whole lot.

One year and his brother had ended up marrying a woman he loved but fought with constantly. And even if Angel turned out to be the perfect wife, her father had made it clear at lunch that his little girl had no intention of ever leaving New York City. She had obligations. To him. To their ancestors.

To Roselli's Bakery.

He'd seen the way Angel and her father had beamed with pride when they told Tanner the history of the family business. Man, you'd think *they* had carried that bag of flour across the ocean to start the first Roselli's Bakery in America. You'd think Mr. Roselli and Angel had carved the sign that still hung over the door.

He'd also seen the way both father's and daughter's eyes had misted over when they mentioned Angel's mother. Seen the way Angel's hand had slid across the table and covered her father's when he said that if not for his daughter, he would have had nothing to live for after his wife died.

Now, staring at the door to Angel's apartment, Tanner knew he should do the right thing. Any man with half a heart would turn around and forget he'd ever gazed into those doe eyes. Rolling the edge of his Stetson in his hands, he forced himself to turn away from her door.

"Angel!"

Antonio's voice, edged with more anger than Tanner considered safe, came from within Angel's apartment. A string of what sounded like Italian curses mixed with English followed.

Angel's sudden scream and the sound of glass breaking sent him barreling into her door. Pain ricocheted through his body. He slammed his shoulder against the unforgiving wood three times before the molding splintered and released the locks.

Landing face first on the floor, he scrambled to his feet and took off down the hall toward the door at the end, toward Angel's pain-filled moans. He flung open the door and took in the horrific sight.

Naked, Angel lay facedown on a bed of broken glass. Blood marred her olive skin and the white tile floor. Not a lot, but amount never mattered.

Tanner, tough ranch owner and rodeo rider, never could handle the sight of blood. Feeling the familiar waves of dizziness threaten to send him down to join Angel, he gripped the doorknob and ground his teeth until they passed.

Watching him as he swayed, Angel shifted.

"Don't move," he barked out. "There's glass everywhere. Just lie still and I'll get you out of here."

Leaning over her, he slid his hands beneath her chest and hips and lifted her straight up. She immediately turned in his arms until she nestled against his chest. Wrapping her arms around his neck, she buried her face in the crook of his neck.

The cold water from her body seeped through his shirt.

"Antonio's here," she whispered, her voice tinged with fear.

"I know. I'll take care of him as soon as I get you outta here." Keeping an eye out for Antonio, Tanner carried Angel to the living room and laid her on the couch. Stripping out of his wet shirt, he covered her then turned to search the apartment and beat the living crap out of the man who had hurt his angel.

The shrill ring of the phone made them both jump.

"Don't answer it." Tanner whispered, then, while it still rang, started to check in every shadowed corner of the room.

The answering machine clicked on.

"Come on, Angelina. Pick up the phone. Angel!" Antonio's voice filled the room.

Tanner looked at Angel. A blush stained her cheeks as she stared down at the answering machine and the flashing red "two".

"Well, I guess I won't find Antonio lurking under the couch," he said, grinning.

His grin vanished when a red dot appeared on his shirt right above her right breast. "You're bleeding."

"I fell…when I heard his voice," she mumbled, avoiding his eyes.

"Yeah, sweetheart," he said softly as he sat on the edge of the couch, "I figured that."

Lifting the shirt, he held her gaze. Angel's breathing grew ragged but she didn't move and she didn't stop him as he bared her body. Fine scratches covered her breasts, stomach and legs. Not many, but enough to make him dizzy.

"You're lucky." He dabbed at the scratches with his shirt. "This could have been worse."

He was a bum. A snake in the ground. The lowest, slimiest creature to grace the earth. Blood seeped from the scratches, a bruise already darkened her cheek and he could not stop his Long John from standing at attention.

Yup, slime.

But her legs were relaxed, her mound clean shaven and he wanted her more than he'd ever wanted anything in his life.

"You looked weird when you came in the bathroom." Her soft voice brought his gaze up to meet hers again. "Like you were going to faint."

Heat swept over his face. Long John slumped. His eyes dropped to the bloody splotches on his shirt. The room tilted. "Did I?"

"Yup. Just like you do now, cowboy."

Angel's fingers touched his cheek. They burned into him, steadied him and shook him at the same time.

She took the shirt from his clenched fingers and wiped away the last of the blood. "You can't take the sight of blood, can you, Tanner?"

"Never could." He chuckled and closed his eyes. "Crazy, considering I brand cattle without a problem."

"A lot of men faint at the sight of blood. I can't imagine how you can brand those poor animals, though."

Opening his eyes, he leaned over and kissed her scrunched-up nose. "It's not that bad."

She glanced down at her exposed breasts. Pressed the edge of his shirt over a particularly nasty nick. "So how did you end up in my bathroom? I thought you'd left."

"I was about to when I heard you scream."

"So you were planning on reneging on our deal."

Her eyes lowered toward his bare chest, darkened. Lingered there.

Tanner leaned farther down until he felt her nipples tangled in his chest hair. "I never renege on a deal." Her cheeks pinked. "How do you want to run this rodeo, Angel mine? Do I stand by and watch you and Jack Rabbit? Or do I go first?"

That sweet blush swept down her neck and chest even as her tongue moistened her lips. "Jack died." She lowered her lids and shrugged.

"You...you already used it? And broke it?" God, could his cock hurt any more?

"No." Angel giggled. "I dropped it. I guess you get to go first."

Tanner heard the slight hitch in her voice. It didn't matter how many times she'd felt that cold plastic enter her. She'd never had a man. And like any virgin, he figured Angel was scared.

Damn, he was scared. "There should be candles. And music. And a bed of rose petals," he murmured.

Angel smiled, her eyes soft as they focused on his. "That doesn't sound like a rodeo to me."

"This is your first time, Angel." His first time had been behind Clancy's Hardware store in the middle of a freak storm. Where he'd taken a woman never mattered before, but it mattered now.

For some crazy reason, it mattered with Angel.

Glancing over his shoulder at the broken door, he released a loud sigh. "Come on."

He lifted her into his arms and tried to ignore the feel of her naked body against his. Striding to her room, he lowered her to the bed then drew up the sheet.

"But—" Angel's shock and disappointment ate away at his resolve.

Grinding his teeth, he straightened. "Stay here. I'll clean up the glass and see if I can fix that door."

"Tanner?"

Ignoring the plea in her voice, a plea he probably imagined, he strode from the room and the sweet enticement of Angel Roselli.

He returned over an hour later. Cleaning her bathroom hadn't been easy. Every drop of blood nearly sent him to the floor. Her door required a new lock and molding. Having neither, Tanner had gone to the phone to order what he needed. A square post-it above the phone with the word "Super" and a phone number saved him the money and labor. Now, with Angel's bare feet safe from glass and her apartment once again intact, he planned on saying his farewells.

Temporary farewells.

An hour outside the bedroom of a naked woman more than willing to spread her legs has a way of stripping away every moral restriction a man may believe he set up. An hour smelling the lingering scent of jasmine, cinnamon and fresh baked bread made Tanner decide that maybe, just maybe, he could coax this lamb away from her daddy. He imagined Angel standing on the porch of his house, waving as he rode in from a hard day in the saddle. Shit, he'd probably toss her over his shoulder and carry her up to their bedroom every damn day.

When he peeked into the room, Angel's doe eyes were trained on the doorway. The glow from the streetlight outside her window cast the bed in a pale, amber glow. She sat up. Cast a timid smile at him when the sheet slid down and pooled in her lap.

Sitting there like that, with her body aglow and her breasts bared, she looked like one of the ladies at the Pleasure Ranch back home. Unlike them, she wasn't used to welcoming men into her bedroom. Her fingers trembled against the sheet, like they itched to pull it up.

Oh, he'd definitely found an angel. An angel with dirty wings.

"Well, cowboy, ready to enter that rodeo?" she asked in a sultry voice that did him in.

Tanner had wanted her to have the right atmosphere for her first time. Couldn't remember exactly what he'd planned.

As far as he was concerned, the atmosphere in her room right now seemed perfect. She raised her arm and held out a shaky hand.

"Darlin', what do you say we start the rodeo tomorrow night?" he murmured as he crossed the room and took her hand in his.

She stuck out her lower lip. Not a full-blown pout, just enough of one to draw his balls up so tight they nearly shot up to his stomach.

"Oh, I expect to take you, Angel mine. In about two minutes." He laughed when one of her sleek brows went up. "I'll *start* in about two minutes. But being this is your fist time, I think I'd better save the heavy artillery I'll need to beat 'ole Jack for another night."

"I like the way you think, Tanner McQuade." Angel sucked her lips between her teeth and held his gaze as she pulled the sheet to the side. "Now take off those pants and convince me I'm right in letting you be my first." She drew in a deep breath and let it out on a sigh. "Well, my first man, at least."

Tanner undid his jeans and dragged them down over his hips, watching Angel's face take in just how long Long John really was. He'd scared a few women with his size and wondered if he'd scare Angel right out of the room. Her doe eyes grew wider with every inch exposed. She gasped when his cock sprang free and rose up to greet her. "Now don't worry, Angel. I'm gentler than a hen with her chicks."

"Oh Tanner. I didn't know I'd nabbed a deluxe model." Her eyes twinkled. "Definitely the deluxe model."

He sat on the edge of the bed and yanked off his boots.

The phone rang.

"Don't answer it," they both said in unison then laughed.

Tossing his socks on the floor as the phone continued to ring, Tanner reached out and dragged Angel onto his lap. His lips had just touched hers when the answering machine clicked on.

"Angel? Baby, you there? I don't feel so good."

"Daddy?" Angel leapt off his lap and sped out of the room.

Part of him wanted to run after her and drag her back before she had a chance to pick up the phone. The knowledge that it just wouldn't be right and the pain in his stomach and groin hogtied him. When Angel returned, her face lined with worry, he forgot the pain, forgot the frustration.

Rising, he crossed the room and gathered her in his arms. "I'm sure whatever's bothering him will be nothing serious. We'll get him to a hospital—"

"No, no hospital. He's just…well…I think he drank too much when he was here," she mumbled against his chest.

Still hard, still wanting and needing her more than normal, he smoothed her curls and kissed the top of her head. "Then we'll go over and—"

"He'd die of embarrassment if I brought someone over." Tilting her head, she gazed up into his eyes. "When Dad drinks, he thinks about my mother and starts crying."

Nodding, Tanner kissed her nose. "Sure, I get it. He wouldn't want me to see him bawling."

They dressed quickly, silently. Tanner felt like a snake again when he wondered if the old man had purposely gotten drunk just to throw a wrench into their evening. From the look on Angel's face, she had no doubts that her father was drowning his sorrows in a bottle. Her lips quivered when she had to take off her bra for the second time and untwist it. She looked up with shimmering eyes when he took the bra from her hands and proceeded to help her dress.

"He'll be fine, Angel. It takes time to get over losing a loved one," he explained in a hushed voice.

"She died ten years ago, Tanner. I don't think he'll ever get over it. That's why he's so set on finding me a husband." She raised her arms through the sleeves of the shirt he pulled over her head. "Ever since Mom died, he hates being in the bakery. It brings back too many memories. I guess he figures if he marries me off and hands the business over to my husband, he could spend less time there."

"I'll never get you to marry me and come back to Texas, will I?" His voice sounded harsher than he'd intended.

"Cut it out. I told you. That line is so lame." She ran her fingers through her curls as she glanced in the mirror over her dresser then rushed out the door.

Leaning against a railing on the Promenade long after Angel had entered the brownstone in Brooklyn Heights, Tanner gazed over the water at the glittering lights of Manhattan and told himself that Mr. Roselli couldn't have known they were about to make love.

* * * * *

Two days later, elbow-deep in pastry dough, Angel wondered if her father had purposely set out to sabotage her evenings with Tanner. True, her father occasionally allowed his melancholy to get the best of him then ended up calling her after knocking off a bottle of wine, but he never had more than a few bad nights a month. Well, bad enough for him to call. Last night made two in one week.

Two in a row.

She hadn't thought anything about it that first night Tanner had accompanied her to her father's, but when her father called for her again last night just as she and Tanner had once again started shedding their clothes, she found it hard to accept his interruption was a coincidence.

And usually she never spent more than an hour soothing her father. Last night he went on and on about how much he needed her, how much the bakery needed her. Well, if he'd wanted to ruin her chances with Tanner, he'd succeeded.

When Tanner had brought her back to her apartment, instead of asking to come in and finish what they'd started, he'd just kissed her on the forehead.

The forehead!

No one had to tell her what a kiss on the forehead meant. She'd never see her cowboy again.

She slammed her fist into the middle of the dough. "Sorry, folks, after one too many postponements, the rodeo just up and left town."

"*Scusè?*" Antonio looked out from the side of the towering wedding cake he was decorating.

"Nothing, Antonio. Just talking to myself."

"I have the ears. You talk to me?"

"No. I think I'll just beat the hell out of this dough."

"No, *mio* angel, we lost enough dough with the bad batch of yeast today."

He looked so taken aback, she had to laugh. A long curl slipped free of her pony-tail and fell into her eyes. Sighing, Angel blew a puff of air at the curl, but it only rose a fraction of an inch then landed back in her eye. "Damn."

"What is wrong, Angel? You look so sad."

The concern on Antonio's face surprised her. Those chocolate eyes held hers. She noticed that his dimples all but flattened out as he made his way around the table. The heat in the kitchen made her feel like a sweaty mess, but the sheen of sweat on Antonio's muscle-bound arms and shoulders made him even more enticing. The sight resurrected an image of Tanner yanking his tee shirt over his head last night, exposing his fine chest. Angel had enjoyed the sight for all of two minutes before the shrill ring of the phone had sent her and Tanner running back to Brooklyn Heights. She'd only known Tanner for two days, but the possibility that he'd given up on her hurt in the worst way.

"Angelina?"

She blinked.

"It's nothing, Antonio. Just feeling sorry for myself."

He squeezed out a chocolate butter cream rosette onto the tip of his index finger. "A rose, *bella* angel."

As he approached, the heat of his finger started to melt the cream. By the time he reached her table, the rosette began to slide off.

"*Mangia*. Hurry!" Swaying his finger from side to side in a wild attempt to keep the rosette from falling, he raised his finger toward her mouth.

Angel laughed and opened her mouth to accept the finger and rosette. The exquisite cream, another of Antonio's specialties, melted on her tongue. She closed her eyes. His finger remained in her mouth for just a second then grazed her tongue as it slowly slid free of her lips. When she opened her eyes, her gaze met his.

Standing so close she could feel the heat of his body, Antonio smiled. His dimples deepened. His eyes darkened.

Logic told her that she had to be nuts to turn down a hunk like Antonio, especially since she'd screwed up royally with Tanner. A hard glint in Antonio's eyes had always made her heart rate flutter with fear. And yet that flutter, that sliver of fear excited her. Drew her to him. Purposely holding her ground when part of her longed to back up, she licked her lips and smiled. "That has to be the best chocolate butter cream I've ever tasted, Antonio. What do you add to make it so decadent tasting?"

"Ah, now that is a secret. When you marry me, I tell you. *Cabite?*"

"I get it. The recipe is a bribe." Chuckling, she shook her head.

"Bribe? I do not know bribe, but if it get you to be my wife, then yes. It is bribe." He waggled his eyebrows. "Hold still, you have some bribe on your chin."

Enjoying Antonio's company for the first time since he'd arrived with her father, she held out her chin.

He peered closely at her face, frowned. Moved closer and,

placing his finger under her chin, tilted her face up.

"You're not planning on kissing me, are you?" She narrowed her eyes but felt her lips curve up.

"No. No bribe on your lips. But..." He closed the gap then licked her chin. A swift, glancing lick.

Their eyes met.

When Tanner had simply gazed at her, her body had stirred with anticipation. Nerve endings tingled. Exquisite flutters had erupted in her stomach then trickled up and down her inner thighs.

With Antonio, she felt nothing.

Not fair. So not fair. Antonio had a face and body she should crave. He was here. And Tanner? Well, Tanner was probably on a plane halfway to Texas by now.

"*Molto bella.*"

"I don't speak Italian, Antonio." Drawing in a deep, weary breath, she lowered her head and stared at her hands.

"You are Italian, but you do not speak your language?" He brushed his knuckles down her cheek. "You are an angel, but you do not believe in God."

"God?" She looked up, angry with him for assuming he knew her, angry with Tanner for leaving and so angry with herself for feeling nothing, absolutely nothing for this beautiful man with chocolate eyes and dimples she would sell her soul for. "What makes you think I don't believe in God?"

"You are the most beautiful woman I see in America, but you are not married. God bring me here for you and you do not believe I am the man to make you happy." He smiled. A crooked, dopey, contagious smile.

"My father brought you here."

"God led him to my home."

She smirked. "My father has visited his cousin in Capri every year since he came to America."

"God led him to me."

"You were working at his cousin's bakery!"

"Yes, that is true. God led me to the bakery." He moved closer. Grinned down at her.

"You live in Capri, Antonio. You're a baker. My father said *Un Poco Cielo* is the finest bakery there. Where else would a baker with your talents work?"

"Exactly." He tapped her chin.

She tapped his. "You just lost me."

"*Un Poco Cielo?*"

"A Little…damn, I know the name… A Little…"

"Heaven. You see? God led me to you, the woman I was born to make happy."

She had no witty reply.

When did he move so close that her nipples skimmed over the taut abs she could see under his tank top? The heat of his body warmed hers. Her gaze strayed to his biceps. Lingered on the bulging muscles.

Feel something, she silently told herself. *Tanner's gone. Feel something, dammit.*

"I want you, Angel Roselli," he crooned in a deep, hushed voice. "You understand? When you are ready, I will have you. And then I will make you very…" He leaned over and sniffed up her neck to her ear then whispered, "Very happy."

A tingle! She felt it. It wasn't the bevy of tingles and tiny electric shocks Tanner's mere gaze brought on, but it was definitely a start. A timer went off. Muscles trained over the years bunched to rush over to the ovens, but she remained before him, wanting, needing more than the mere satisfaction of seeing another tray of perfect ladyfingers. "Really? You sound so sure of yourself."

"I am sure."

His breath tickled her neck.

Tilting her head toward his mouth, she closed her eyes. "Tell me more."

"I am a demanding lover. I demand my lover has many...how you say?"

"Orgasms?" Another tingle? She couldn't be sure, but the word demanding had done something.

"Yes, orgasms. I do not stop and I do not take my pleasure until my lover has many orgasms." His lips trailed over her cheek. "I know what you like, Angel."

Although she knew he couldn't, that no one could possibly imagine what she longed to experience, his proclaiming that he did wove a web of decadent images and trapped her in a spell she had no desire to break free of. She turned her head, ready for this kiss. Ready for Antonio.

The bell from the front door chimed.

"A customer...I have to go." With a groan, she spun around and ran out to the shop. Stopped short.

Tanner leaned against the glass counter, a large white shopping bag hanging from his hand, a huge, shit-eating grin on his face. "In Texas, bakers break for lunch."

Her body sprang to life. Every erogenous zone she knew of throbbed. Untying her apron, she pulled it over her head, tossed it on the counter and forced herself to casually stroll up to Tanner.

She could feel Antonio watching from the kitchen, feared he'd come out and cause a scene.

She wouldn't blame him if he did. In the mirrored walls, she caught sight of the flirtatious smile on her face as she walked up to Tanner. No, she wouldn't blame Antonio one bit. "We break for lunch here. What are you offering?"

"I found a place around the corner that serves these rolls that look like donuts." He raised both brows. "Bagels. Ever try them?"

She laughed at the odd way he said bagels, drawing out the first syllable and sounding like a sheep. "Yeah, I've tried them. That's an awfully big bag for a couple of bagels."

"Well, the thing is, they had every kind of cream cheese you can imagine in there. I bought a few."

"A few. You wouldn't happen to have strawberry cream cheese in there, would you?"

"If they had it, I have it." The shit-eating grin returned.

"You bought them all?"

"I didn't know which one you'd want."

So matter of fact. "Hm…well, listen, if you ever go to Tiffany's I want the strand of diamonds."

"A whole strand, huh?" One corner of Tanner's mouth rose. "I gather you've gone to this Tiffany's and already picked one out."

"No. My mother left me hers, but some jerk mugged me and ran off with it the first time I had the nerve to wear it." When his eyes grew somber, she regretted bringing up her mother. She scrunched up her nose and giggled. "Oh, hell, you'll never remember. Just buy all their jewelry. I'm sure I'll find something I like."

"I'll remember." He ran the tip of his finger around her neck. "I'll remember."

Long after his finger lost contact with her skin, the heat of his touch lingered. She cleared her throat. "So, anything else in that bag?"

"I noticed that you ordered that French coffee at the pub yesterday, so I brought you some of that too. So, where do we go?"

She glanced around. Noticed Antonio scowling from the kitchen doorway. Her stomach lurched. "I-I don't know."

"Where do you usually eat?"

"Usually I just munch on a sandwich between customers."

Antonio stepped into the shop. Opened his mouth as if to speak.

Grabbing Tanner's arm, Angel steered him toward the

door. "There are tables out front."

Outside, sitting across the white bistro table from Tanner, Angel couldn't stop smiling or feeling like she'd stumbled upon a treasure when she'd bumped into her cowboy. He made a show of holding up each container and announcing the kind of cream cheese it held. For more than half of them, he'd give her a "do you believe it" look. As they ate, he never took his eyes off her face. Horns blared, a constant flow of people streamed by and the humidity made it feel like it was at least ninety degrees. Somehow, with Tanner, Angel felt as if they were alone, as if a cool breeze caressed her skin. And for the first time in too many years to count, she felt carefree, giddy.

"So, I see the Italian Stallion is inside."

Giggling a little too loudly, Angel nodded.

Tanner scowled. "I don't like him."

She tried to hold on to her smile, hold on to the euphoria that had only a moment ago felt so real. "Really? I never would have guessed."

"It's not what you're thinking."

"You're not jealous?" She raised her brows.

"Well, yeah, but that's not why I don't like him." Tanner picked at his bagel. "I don't like his eyes."

"His eyes. Why? They're choco…brown. Nothing special." Shifting in her seat, she wished she'd taken the chair facing the window so she could see if Antonio stood at the window watching. The hairs rising on the back of her neck and the way Tanner kept glancing over her shoulder led her to believe Antonio not only stood watching, but she'd bet all the pastries in the display that he also had his face pressed against the glass.

Dipping his finger into the tub of strawberry cream cheese, Tanner scooped out a dollop and held it out to her. "My mother always told me that if someone's eyes are hooded, it means they're hiding something."

Angel lowered her eyes and stared at his finger. Her heart

tap-danced up her throat. Two fingers offered up in one day? Was finger number one watching? She leaned forward and closed her mouth over Tanner's finger. He stared at her mouth while she licked it clean. Moisture tickled her as it seeped out of her body and drenched the crotch of her thong.

"Damn, Angel, do that again and I'll drag you back to your apartment and continue where we left off last night."

Guilt washed over her. Although she just met Tanner, she felt as if she'd cheated on him with Antonio. She looked down at her half-eaten bagel. "Hooded eyes? Maybe he was born with them."

"No, he's hiding something."

"He's not so bad." Her stomach felt like she'd eaten her bagel whole.

"Yeah, well, just watch your step with him. Okay?" Tanner chomped down on his bagel.

They spent the next ten minutes in silence.

"So tell me, business slow today?"

His question shocked her. "Extremely. I don't think we had one customer. How did you know?"

He pointed toward the door with his bagel. "Well, I figured most customers would see the closed sign and just walk away."

"Closed?" Turning, Angel looked at the door. Sure enough, the side of the sign with "Closed" printed with large red letters faced out. "No!"

Jumping up, she ran to the door and fixed the sign. "I know I turned it around this morning. It's a habit. Do you have any idea how much business we must have lost? We usually have a line out the door before nine."

"Surprised you didn't notice then." Tanner brushed some crumbs off the table toward a couple of pigeons. "Why'd you think no one came?"

Recalling how distraught she'd been over his kissing her

forehead, refusing to admit to him that he had occupied her mind all morning, she merely shrugged, but she couldn't shrug off the ramifications of her blunder.

Sundays, their busiest days, paid the mortgage. Sundays mornings pretty much paid all the bills. The past couple of weeks, one thing after another plagued the bakery and knocked their profits for the month down another notch. This would take it down more than a notch. Her stomach churned.

"My father is going to freak out. I have to go, Tanner. I have to call our regulars and see if I can fix this."

"Need help?" With one swipe of his arm, everything on the table tumbled into the shopping bag. "I know how to bake bread."

Stunned, she hovered by the door. Although the offer tempted her, she couldn't imagine Tanner and Antonio sharing a kitchen. "No, thanks."

Tanner strode up to her and swept her into his arms. "Last night you looked so tired, I stopped myself from kissing you goodbye the way I wanted."

Snuggling into his embrace, she nibbled her way up his neck. "And how was that?"

"The way any red-blooded cowboy kisses the woman he plans on courting."

"Court—"

He bent her over his arm in one fluid motion that took her breath away. Gazing down into her eyes, he ever so slowly brought his lips to within a hairsbreadth from hers.

"A man could drown in your eyes."

Angel felt as if she were drowning. Her heart swelled, rose up to her throat. She wanted to say something witty, something that would match the power of his words, but her thoughts scattered when he nibbled on the corners of her mouth then spoke again.

"A man could grow addicted to these lips."

Any misgivings she might have had about Tanner's interest in her fled when his lips closed over hers and his tongue teased until she opened her mouth and gave him free rein. His sweet tongue delved in. Caressing each and every inch of her mouth, he kissed her until she whimpered with need. When he straightened, she wrapped her arms around his neck to stop herself from crumpling to the ground.

"When do you get off from work?" His gaze lingered on her lips.

Blinking, Angel tried to focus on his question. "Um..."

Once again taking possession of her mouth, his lips demolished any chance she had of remembering her name, much less the bakery's closing time. She had no idea how long they stood there kissing. If not for the blare of a horn, she probably would have let him kiss her for the remainder of the day.

When he pulled back, she felt like stomping her foot and demanding he keep kissing her. Instead, she gathered her wits and murmured, "Well, we close at six, but I usually spend a few hours baking and cleaning up."

Tanner scowled. "You said you got in before dawn. That's a hell of a long day."

"Well, someone has to do it." Uncomfortable by his reaction, she stepped out of his arms.

"And you're the only one? What about Antonio?" He nodded his head toward the door.

Angel didn't dare turn around for fear that she'd find Antonio standing behind the door. "Well, Antonio helps but my father wants me to oversee him as much as possible."

"Speaking of your father, why doesn't he help you out?"

"I told you. Since my mother died, most days he tends to stay away." More and more unnerved, she reached behind her for the door.

Tanner covered her hand with his and held the door in place. "Since your mother died? Ten years ago?"

It struck her that he seemed to remember everything she did and said. "Well, yeah."

"So you've been working these hours for ten years? Shit, Angel, no wonder why you're still a virgin. And your father just lets you slave and waste away in there?"

Slave.

The word struck a chord. Too many times she'd felt like one, ranted and raved to her empty apartment that she was one and would be one to the bakery for the rest of her life. Like her mother.

"Watch it, cowboy. You're crossing the line here." She shoved until he released his grip on the door.

"One more question."

Sunlight glinted off his golden hair.

"It better not be about my dad."

"How old were you when you started working in the bakery?"

She looked into his eyes, intense, disapproving eyes.

Memories flitted through her mind. Days spent playing in the bakery, learning how to fill cannoli, braid bread and count change instead of going to nursery school like the other children in her neighborhood. Years, rushing to the bakery to help while others went to Girl Scouts or friends' houses. Summers sweating in a hot kitchen while others tanned at Jones Beach or in Central Park. So many nights helping her mother bake and clean while the other teens went on dates and had sleepovers.

"I don't recall. Not that it's any of your business."

She didn't like the way he looked at her. The same way her mother would look at her when she'd cry and beg her father to give her a day off for friends. The same way her teachers looked at her when she'd explain that she had to miss out on after-school functions because she had to help at the bakery.

"You don't understand, Tanner. When you run a family business, you—"

"Sweetheart, I run a ranch, the largest in my neck of Texas. My ranch hands, every one of them, get time off for their families. For their lives. Every one. And I make sure I get off. No business, I don't care what it is, is worth slaving away your life."

His voice, though tender, held an edge of anger.

She wanted to tell him to go to hell. That he didn't understand.

She wanted to run back into his arms and cry on his shoulder and beg him to take her away from the bakery and the life, or excuse for one, she'd lived all these years.

"You don't understand. This isn't just a business. It's family. History. It is our life." Turning away from the pity etched in his face, she rushed into the bakery. Her bakery.

As the door closed behind her, she recalled how many times it sounded like a cell door slamming shut. Deep in her heart, she loved the bakery. There she could look behind the counter and see her mother, younger, healthier. There she could sit in the kitchen and recall eating her first slice of sugared bread while her mother braided her hair.

Lately, her memories included her mother sweating and swearing as she filled cream puff after cream puff. Memories of tears and arguments. Memories of herself standing behind the counter and wistfully watching young couples walking hand in hand past the window.

She'd never admit it to her father or anyone else who asked, but lately, like her mother, she hated wasting hour upon hour, day upon day and year upon year baking for or dealing with customers who knew and cared nothing about her life outside Roselli's.

Most days, she wished she could walk out those doors and never return.

The day dragged on. Her father dropped by, but only to

sit outside with his friends. Watching him laugh and chat and enjoy the bright sunshine, Angel longed to pound on the window and demand he come in and help her. Or better, that he take her place.

"You look so sad, *pico* angel."

Turning, she found Antonio leaning against the door. His shirt hung from his hands.

"Just tired, Antonio."

"Then go home. I will watch the shop."

Angel took in the sight of him. Narrow hips and waist flared up to a massive, muscle-bound chest. Perfect, white teeth, finely chiseled nose and jawline, disarming dimples and eyes too intense for words. His hair, nearly as black as her own, shone even in the dim doorway. "You can't bake and watch the shop, Antonio."

"You did before I came."

"Yeah, well, that's different. I was trained from birth." She heard the bitterness in her voice and wondered if Antonio had.

"Your Papa is here. He can help me. It is a beautiful day. Go." Tossing the shirt over his shoulder, he dazzled her with a sad smile. "You are too pale, *pico* angel. Your Papa, he is too dark. I tell him to come in and let you take the sun. *Si?*"

She turned. One glance out the window at her father, his skin a golden bronze, had Angel gritting her teeth. In a voice that sounded so like the angry child from her youth, she replied, "*I* have to work. Every day. Every night. He put in his time. Now it's my turn."

She never heard Antonio approach. His arms wrapped around her and drew her back against his bare chest.

"When you are my wife, *you* will sit outside." His lips brushed over the whorl of her ear with each word.

While his nearness still affected her so much less than Tanner's, his promise stopped her from breaking free of his hold. He'd spoken like this before. Sometimes with a voice tinged with anger while he questioned her father's demands on her time or her father's refusal to cut her hours.

She didn't need him to point out her father's failings, but his observations and comments fed the fire of her anger. Antonio probably didn't realize it, but since he'd arrived, he'd managed to create an ever-growing rift between her and her father.

"And if I'm outside, who will watch the shop?" She leaned her cheek against his biceps and watched her father stretch his arms over his head then tilt his chair back and hold his face up to the sun.

"I will hire someone."

Angel snorted. "We don't make enough to hire someone."

"Nonsense. I see the books. There is enough to hire three women to work the counter."

Angel stiffened.

The bagel soured in her stomach.

Outside her father laughed at something one of his friends said.

"You saw the books?"

Her father kept those books under lock and key. Even she had never received the privilege of knowing what lay between those covers.

"Yes. Your Papa, he show me."

The nubs on his cheek scraped hers.

"And there's enough money to hire help?"

"*Si.* That is why I do not understand why your Papa make you work so hard, like a slave. When you are my wife, you come in when you want. *Si?*"

Tears burned her eyes. "I never said I'd marry you."

"Go, *cara.*" Antonio kissed her temple and released her.

Blinking away her tears, she turned, rose up onto her toes

and kissed his cheek. "Thanks, Antonio."

In one swift move, she pulled her apron off and left the shop. Outside her father almost tumbled back when she slapped the apron down onto the bistro table.

"I'm taking the rest of the day off."

"Like hell you are."

"Like hell I am!"

He snatched the apron from the table and held it out to her. "Put this back on and stop acting like a child."

"No. I told you, I'm off." She could feel the eyes of his pals watching.

"Angel, be reasonable. Who'll watch the shop with you gone?"

"Hire someone!"

"We can't afford to—"

She jabbed her finger at her chest. "As the equal partner you always claim I am, I say we can. Or would you like me to check the books and see what we can and can not afford?"

Her father sank into his chair. Shoulders slumped. He shook his head.

Seeing him like that, she nearly raced to his side, but Antonio's revelation and his promise that he'd never allow her to waste her life away in the bakery hardened her heart. "If I feel like it, I'll be back the day after tomorrow. Hire someone, get in there yourself or close. I don't care."

"Close twice in one day?" Mr. Franco, her father's friend, looked at her and her father as if they were crazy.

Her heart sped up.

Her father pointed to the sign showing their times of operation. "What are you talking about? Roselli's never closes on Sunday!"

"Well, you were closed this morning," another of the men said.

They all nodded.

Angel considered running for home.

"What the hell are they talking about, Angel?"

Her father stood. Slumped shoulders straightened. His mouth thinned until she could barely see his lips.

When she didn't answer immediately, he banged his fist onto the table. Espresso cups rattled in their saucers.

Angel jumped back. "I don't know what happened. One minute the sign was turned to 'Open', the next it was turned to 'Closed'. Beats me how it happened."

"How long?" He grabbed her apron. Twisted it in his hands.

The child of a volatile man, Angel couldn't help but wonder if he'd remove his belt and whip her in front of his friends. She had to remind herself that those days were long gone, that his belt had not struck her since she'd threatened, at the age of twelve, to report him for child abuse. Still, her muscles tensed and her breath lodged in her throat. "All morning."

The apron fell to the sidewalk.

"All morning," he bellowed, causing passersby to stop and stare.

"I didn't do it. Maybe one of the first customers..." She trailed off. Remembered that not one customer had entered the shop all morning.

"How many customers came in before it was turned, Angelina Maria?"

Drawing up her own shoulders, she faced him. "None."

The red "V" erupted on his forehead. "V" for violence, the child within screamed. "How could you not notice that no one came into the shop? It's Sunday, dammit!"

Heat swept down her cheeks. Although she stared at her father, she saw the growing crowd from the corner of her eyes. "I was beat. You kept me up so la—"

"You were beat? You were beat so you didn't notice that we had not one customer on our busiest day?" Her father's voice grew louder with each word.

Spittle flew from his mouth and struck her in the face. Angel hadn't seen him this angry in years. Not since that day she'd almost called child abuse hotline. She could almost feel his fist sinking into her stomach as it had that day. Feel the welts from his belt rising up on her back.

Mr. Franco stood up and rested his hand on her father's arm. "Calm down. What's done is done."

Angel watched in shock as her father turned his anger on his friend. Shoving Mr. Franco's hand, he stared him down until the old man dropped back down onto his seat and focused his attention on his espresso.

Her stomach sank in when her father swung around toward her.

"Do you have any idea how much money we lost?"

Anger overshadowed fear. "No, Dad, I don't. Maybe if you let me see the books like you do Antonio, I would. Oh, I'm sorry. I forgot. I don't have the right to see them! I'm just your fucking slave!"

He stepped back as if she had struck him, raised his hand high above his head.

His friends backed away.

Someone from the crowd watching yelled, "Hit her!"

Angel froze.

The door to the bakery swung open.

Her father's hand came down toward her.

Angel, still too shocked to move, focused on the palm nearing her cheek. Just when she was about to close her eyes, she saw a massive hand grasp her father's wrist.

"Mr. Roselli! What you do?" Antonio, his face calm, his eyes hard, moved between Angel and her father. "No one touches Angel. No one!"

"Let go of me." Her father's cheeks flushed.

Years of protecting her father, of fearing she'd lose him too, washed away Angel's anger.

Still, she couldn't move or speak to help him. She could still hear Antonio's claim that her father had opened the sacred books for him, that all these years her father could have hired people to lighten her load.

"Angel." Antonio continued to stare at her father.

"W-what?"

"Go. You take as much time off as you want."

While he seemed to be helping her, his tone told her that this was no request. He was ordering her to take off. Somehow, Antonio had taken the reins of power from both her father and her hands.

Her father sputtered, winced.

"Antonio! You're hurting him." She grabbed Antonio's arm.

Still holding on to her father, Antonio looked at her then leaned down and kissed her nose. "I no hurt him like he hurt you. Now do what I say. Go."

Angel stared into Antonio's dark eyes. Her father could fire him and send his sweet, tight ass back to Italy, but that hadn't stopped Antonio from standing up for her.

He grinned, leaned down.

Antonio's lips just touched hers. "Later, *mi amore*."

For the first time, Angel's body reacted to Antonio like it did to Tanner. She wondered if he noticed. Wondered if somehow Tanner would notice her body's betrayal. Angel backed away from Antonio. Sunlight glanced off the window of the bakery and blinded her for a moment but not before she saw the raw desire in his eyes as he licked his lips. A shudder ripped through her body. Her clit pulsed. Nobody had ever stood up to her father for her. She glanced at her father then, ignoring the urge to demand that Antonio release him, she spun around and forced herself to walk away from the bakery, Antonio and her father.

When she arrived at her apartment, she found a note taped to her door, a note from Tanner asking her to call his hotel the minute she got home. Too confused by her conflicting feelings for Antonio and Tanner to deal with either one and free for the first time in years on a Sunday, she decided to take the day off from all her responsibilities. She taped the note back to her door and left. By the time she returned, the sun had set and she had to shift her shopping bags to one hand just to retrieve the note and open her door. Tossing the bags on her couch, barely missing her cat, she rushed to the phone and dialed the number of Tanner's hotel.

Tomorrow, she'd go back to the bakery and Antonio. Tomorrow, she'd try to figure out why she wanted Tanner, yet couldn't say no to Antonio.

Neither one held any claim to her.

Yet.

* * * * *

Four days later, once again standing on the promenade and waiting for Angel to return from her father's, Tanner wondered if he'd ever get to savor the pleasure of feeling Angel writhe beneath him. This was their sixth emergency run to the man's home. Chest pains, indigestion and dizziness overtook the man every time Tanner got close to touching Angel.

Every damn night!

He couldn't even get a kiss in without the phone ringing or the man popping in with one complaint or another.

Tanner wondered if a man ever ended up hospitalized for blue balls. If not, he had a feeling he'd be the first. He sure wasn't having any luck being Angel's first.

Tonight, he'd decided to call Mr. Roselli's bluff. Following Angel into the man's brownstone, he'd expected to find a lousy actor fooling a too-trusting daughter. Instead, he'd seen the man's gray complexion and immediately called an ambulance. The paramedics had given the man a shot and told him to see his doctor about changing his usual dosage. Tanner had glanced between father and daughter, totally baffled until Angel explained that her father was a diabetic.

He'd felt like a heel.

To make matters worse, the last few times he'd gone to visit her at the bakery, he'd found her laughing with or smiling at or standing close to Antonio. Oddly, the more Angel and Antonio got along, the more her relationship with her father seemed to deteriorate.

It shouldn't matter to him. Neither man wanted him in Angel's life or would accept her joining him when he returned to Texas, but Tanner believed Angel and her father had a bond he had believed he'd shared with his father until the reading of the will. He could handle losing her to her father.

But Antonio? Something didn't ring true about the man.

Antonio had hours to work on Angel, hours when she wasn't worn out from a day at work or too worried about her father's health or the odd mishaps at the bakery to do much more than sleep.

She worked from before dawn until way past dark. By the end of the day, she looked like a flower wilting beneath the hot desert sun.

Of course, after a quick shower and some food, she regained some of her energy. But then the phone would ring and they'd be back in Brooklyn Heights or the doorbell would chime and they'd hover over her father for one reason or another or the alarm would go off at the bakery and they'd be rushing downtown. Afterward, knowing her workday would start before dawn, he could never bring himself to do more than cuddle her in his arms and watch her sleep. She never sent him back to the hotel. Once she'd dozed off, he couldn't bring himself to leave.

Four nights staring down at that angelic face and not touching.

Four mornings cooking her breakfast as she rushed around half-dressed.

Four wonderful mornings sitting across the counter from her as she moaned like a woman in ecstasy over the omelet or waffle or pancake he'd cooked up.

He may not have made it past first base with Angel, but he sure as hell enjoyed every minute with her. Especially the mornings. But even they were short-lived. She barely had time to kiss him goodbye before leaving again to join Antonio at the bakery.

Every day he failed to win Angel over brought him one day closer to losing the ranch.

Now, waiting for Angel to join him on the Promenade, he considered running back to Texas with his tail between his legs. The idea of finding a wife in the city seemed hopeless. He doubted he'd find someone like Angel in the time left. Doubted he'd get her to agree to marry him in time.

But he couldn't leave her. First and foremost, something about the mishaps at the bakery made him fear for her safety. Gas leaks, constant false fire alarms, the sign on the door flipping over to "Closed" every morning. And then just last night, all the refrigerators stopped, and hundreds of dollars worth of pastries and fixins spoiled.

Angel had laughed when he'd asked if she or her father had any enemies.

He stared down at the black water separating him from Manhattan.

It had to be Angel's father. The old coot probably knew just how to make his sugar drop or rise enough to scare Angel. And those mishaps at the bakery? Tanner had no doubt that his future father-in-law had a hand in those too. Just another way to keep Angel out of Tanner's arms each night.

Tanner slammed his fist on the railing. "You want a war,

Mr. Roselli? Well, you just got yourself one."

Ten minutes later, when the sound of Angel's heels striking the sidewalk met his ears, he was already in position. Leaning back against the railing with his legs crossed at the ankles and his Stetson down low over his eyes, he waited, knowing he looked like every woman's fantasy of a real cowboy.

He hadn't lied when he'd told Angel her weakness stemmed from the boots. He'd just left out that it also had to do with the hat. And jeans. And Clint Eastwood.

Ladies loved cowboys. Especially those not living amongst them. To city girls—well, city girls outside the Western states—cowboys were the fantasy men portrayed in the movies. Back home, the city girls saw John Travolta and trailer parks. When they saw a cowboy coming toward them, they crossed the street and themselves.

But Angel probably saw Clint Eastwood or some hot Marlboro model. To Angel cowboy probably meant one hundred percent rugged, raw male.

Tanner crossed his arms over his chest and prepared to woo Angel Roselli right out from under her father's nose. He listened to her approach. When he felt she was close enough, he lifted his finger and shoved the brim of his Stetson up. Greeting her with a lazy grin, he uncrossed his legs and stood up.

"If you ain't the prettiest girl in New York City," he drawled.

* * * * *

Angel had felt like a wrung-out washrag when she'd left her father's house. Seeing Tanner leaning against that railing, looking one hundred percent cowboy, ignited the embers that always burned in his presence. His stance, the way he'd tipped his hat back and the sight of those boots did all sorts of strange things to her body. She felt as if the past few hours had never happened. "I bet you say that to all the girls back home."

"No, can't recall ever telling a filly back home that she was the prettiest girl in New York City." Tanner reached out and hooked her by the waist.

She gasped when her chest slammed into his.

"And I certainly wouldn't have if I'd first laid eyes on you."

His drawl, thicker and richer than normal, twanged her nerves in all the right places, but she realized that he was acting a bit too Texan. Narrowing her eyes, she tried not to smile. "Wait a minute. What is this?"

The past four days had been a mixture of heaven and hell. Practically living with Tanner, she found herself growing used to waking with him beside her. For two people who had yet to make love, they sure slept together a lot. It amazed her that more foreplay filled their first day together than the last few. She wondered if women suffered from an ailment similar to blue balls. If not, she had a feeling she'd be the first.

A constant ache deep in her womb grew more unbearable every night they ended up merely sleeping together. She had no doubt that her father's complaints were legitimate, yet she couldn't help but wonder if the man had her apartment rigged with cameras or body temperature alarms.

Seeing Tanner lounging against the railing, she was tempted to ask if they could sneak off to his hotel room and, forgoing any foreplay, just screw their brains out.

Watching his lids hover halfway over his eyes, she felt as if he were playing some kind of role. "What's up, Tanner?"

"Nothing, darlin'."

"Darlin'?"

He stepped back, dragging her with him, then leaned against the railing. Spreading his legs, he led her between them. "What do you say you take tomorrow afternoon off and we find ourselves a couple of horses?"

"Horses? In New York?" she asked, covering the sudden surge of fear the mere mention of horses always brought on with a giggle.

Tanner leaned over and kissed her neck until she practically fainted from the shivers running down her back.

"That's right. You don't get out much. There *are* horses in the city, Angel. In Central Park." The rich timbre of his voice vibrated against her neck. "I hear tell a man and woman can find a secluded spot and not be found for days."

His hands slid over her buttocks and pressed her mound into the hard ridge of his erection.

Tilting her head back when his mouth made its way toward the front of her neck she murmured, "The closest I've ever gotten to a horse is sitting behind one in a buggy."

"That could be arranged. But I think you'd enjoy it more if you had your legs spread wide and your sweet pussy planted on a saddle." Tanner's hot mouth moved to the hollow of her throat. "I could sit behind you and help you along until you got the hang of it."

Liquid heat seeped from between her aching lower lips. "I don't know. I'm terrified of horses, Tanner. I could spread my legs in a carriage. They have enclosed ones with blankets."

"That's the best idea I've heard in a long time. So tomorrow you call in sick and we take a carriage ride through the park." Tanner shifted.

Raising his head he stared into her eyes with those dark blue jewels.

"Kiss me, Angel mine."

He'd started calling her that after only one day, and Angel found that she considered herself his more and more. Rising up onto her toes, she brought her lips to his. She expected to hear a phone ringing then remembered they were outside and, in her haste, she'd left her cell phone home. As if he too realized that they were safe from any intrusions, Tanner deepened the kiss and, lifting her, spread her legs wide and planted her astride his lap.

A whimper rose up her throat when the hard ridge of his cock ground into her. Needing more, needing so much more, she wriggled and squirmed. He continued to devour her mouth while he grabbed her hips and ground her pussy up and down the length of his cock again and again. Her cries when she felt the stirrings of an oncoming orgasm sounded desperate even to her own ears. When the orgasm hit, it struck with a gentle force that left her even needier than before. She reached down between them and tugged at the button on his jeans.

Tanner raised his mouth from hers and slid his hands up her thighs. "Calm down, Angel. You're playing with fire."

"Take me, Tanner. Take me here. Take me right now. I'm so sick of waiting."

"Outside?" Tanner let out a weary sigh and shook his head. "I'm gonna hate myself in the morning, but there's no way. With our luck, your first time would end up including a night in jail for a public display of lewd behavior."

Angel dropped her head on his chest and groaned. "You're right."

"Come on." Tanner slid her off his lap. "You have to be up in a few hours."

Chapter Four

Leaning over the glass counter in Roselli's the next afternoon, Angel blew a puff of air up at the curl tickling the bridge of her nose and glanced up at the clock for the tenth time in the last five minutes. If all went according to plan, Tanner would arrive shortly and take her out of here for an afternoon buggy-ride through Central Park.

The bakery and petite, black-clad older woman biting down on a cannoli on the other side of the counter blurred. Blinking until her lids remained up, Angel struggled to stay awake.

The recent rash of late-night emergency visits to her father's apartment was taking a toll on her. Feeling the heat of Tanner's body blanketing her while she struggled to sleep during the few hours left of the night didn't help. The man either had the morals of a saint or had yet to come out of the closet about his sexual orientation. Judging by the hard-on poking into her all night and the pinched look on Tanner's face every time he insisted she needed sleep more than sex, Angel figured she'd found herself a saint.

She didn't want a saint.

She wanted a man who took, a man who saw the hunger in her eyes and fed it until she passed out. She wanted a man who tore down any walls her upbringing may have built and introduced her to all the decadent, kinky ways to pleasure her body she'd seen on the internet and read about in the books stored in the tiny Palm Pilot she kept hidden in her purse. A man who would tie her down and torture her senses until she begged for release. A man like Drake, the Master in *No One But Madison*, the book she'd just finished before meeting Tanner.

She believed she'd found a man like Drake when Tanner slid her vibrator between her legs in the restaurant that first day they'd met.

Obviously, she was wrong. But if she even contemplated giving up Tanner, her heart ached.

"I've fallen for a saint," she muttered, resting her chin on her arm. "Damn, dumb luck."

On the other side of the counter, Mrs. Catalino licked a glob of cannoli cream from the corner of her lips. "*Scusè?*"

Angel straightened, then with a weary sigh leaned her arms over the cool glass. "Nothing. So, how many, Mrs. Catalino?"

"No, no. Again the cream is sour."

Gritting her teeth, Angel smiled. "No, Mrs. Catalino, the cannoli cream is not sour. I made it fresh this morning."

Mrs. Catalino pursed her pale lips. Wagging a wrinkled finger at the front window and the empty lot across the street, she snapped, "Ever since they knock down Guiseppe's, the cannoli cream tastes sour."

Raking her hands through her hair, Angel tried her best to maintain the smile she'd plastered on her face the minute Mrs. Catalino had entered the shop. They'd had the same argument again and again since the city knocked down the building across the street and exposed Roselli's front window to the noon sun. One week of sour pastries and the woman was convinced Roselli's would never make decent cannoli cream again. "We tinted the windows last month, Mrs. Catalino."

Taking another bite of the cannoli clutched in her hand, she swallowed then made a spitting motion. "Toey! They no taste right, I tell you."

It occurred to Angel that Mrs. Catalino had been coming in two to three times a week for a taste of the so-called sour cannoli and no longer purchased any. She narrowed her eyes as the woman popped the last of the cannoli into her mouth and shook her head.

"I come back tomorrow. Maybe then you have good cannoli cream. Hm…" Brushing powdered sugar off the front of her dress, she bent over and eyed the sfogliatelle. "Maybe I try—"

"Now wait just a minute." Angel straightened and placed her fists on her hips.

She couldn't believe Mrs. Catalino had scammed her into giving her free pastries all these weeks. The woman had to be seventy. God, she'd wet-nursed Angel when her own mother had to help at the bakery. Word had spread that their pastries weren't what they used to be after a few customers had witnessed Mrs. Catalino's taste tests.

"I wasn't born yester—"

"Ah, *buon giorno*, Signora Catalino. How is the prettiest woman in all of America?" Wiping his hands on the white apron slung around his lean hips, Antonio strode out of the kitchen. "Have you tasted my espresso tiramisu?"

Stains covered his wife-beater, macho-man muscle shirt. Not that any normal female would actually notice them for more than two seconds, much less mind. Muscles in all the right places glistened from the sheen of sweat coating his bronze skin. Midnight black hair and bittersweet-chocolate eyes on a flawless face also tended to take a woman's mind off his shirt. Well, unless she pictured herself licking the butter cream and chocolate icing off it. And when he smiled like this, baring perfect white teeth and those damn dimples, no woman in her right mind would recall one single stain, much less the color of his shirt.

Mrs. Catalino smoothed her hair back toward the tight bun at the nape of her neck. "Oh, Antonio. Come here and give an old lady a kiss."

Angel groaned when Antonio puffed out his massive chest and winked at her before making his way around the counter. As he leaned over to kiss Mrs. Catalino's cheek, Angel couldn't stop herself from leaning forward.

Damn, the man had a fine ass. She raised her eyes to snag a peek at the biceps that always bulged as if he'd just worked out.

Oh, yeah, Antonio definitely had a fine body.

"Angelina, when you are done, get Signora Catalino a slice of my espresso tiramisu to taste, no charge."

Meeting his bittersweet-chocolate eyes in the mirrored wall, Angel groaned again. "Antonio, she's already had a napoleon and a cannoli on the house."

"And she will have my tiramisu on the house." His eyes narrowed.

"Listen, I decide who eats free here." Still holding his gaze in the mirror, Angel felt her body stir to life. Anger, fear and arousal gave her the burst of energy she'd needed all day.

The face her father and most of the young women who entered the bakery felt put Antonio Banderas to shame hardened before her eyes. She'd seen that look too many times in the last few days. Something in his eyes made her stomach lurch.

The power he reeked of affected her in another, most unwelcome way. Angry with herself for finding Antonio's domineering ways a turn-on, she met his glare with one of her own.

"Angelina," he said in a low voice laden with an unspoken threat, "get Mrs. Catalino a piece of my tiramisu."

"No, no, Antonio. Tomorrow. The sour cannoli gave me *agita*." Patting his arm, Mrs. Catalina turned to leave.

"Then you bring it home for tonight. Angelina. Now." Antonio glared over Mrs. Catalino's head.

Angel couldn't believe her ears. "Excuse me? I must be hearing wrong. I could have sworn you just ordered me—"

"Angel."

Turning, Angel saw her father standing in the doorway to the kitchen, a small white box resting in his outstretched hand.

Still shocked that he'd spent the last hour chatting with Antonio in the kitchen and even helping with some of the baking, Angel could only stare at the box.

"Dad, you don't understand."

"I understand perfectly. Give this to Mrs. Catalino."

Opening her mouth to argue, she clamped it shut when her father swiped his forearm over his brow and let out a sigh. Snatching the box from his hand, she plopped it on the glass countertop, then stalked past him into the kitchen.

Mumbling to herself, she strode up to the pastry table and gave a mound of dough a vicious punch. As usual, it helped. A little.

Ever since Antonio had arrived, her father treated her like an underling. While she and Antonio had grown closer, it irked her that he acted like he already owned Roselli's.

Sliding the dough across the floured table, she grabbed another bowl. Lifting the cloth, she removed another risen mound and pictured Antonio's face peering up from it before slamming down her fist.

"Ah, Angelina, you are an animal in the kitchen," Antonio purred as he trapped her against the edge of the table and ground his erection into her lower back.

"Back off, Antonio," she ground out between clenched teeth. The cologne he drenched himself in burned her nostrils. Today, with the temperature in the kitchen climbing into the nineties, the cologne did little to cover up his body odor. Wrinkling her nose, she added, "And take a shower. You're chasing away the customers."

"You fight, but I know you want me." Grabbing her wrists in an iron grip, he nuzzled her neck. "I see you looking at me."

She twisted her arms, but he wouldn't let go. "I'm warning you, Antonio, let go or lose the jewels."

"You do not fool me, Angel." Releasing her wrists, he grabbed her shoulders and turned her to face him. "Why do you not admit we are good for each other?"

For all his talk, she saw the glint of anger in his eyes. Her heart stuttered when he caught her chin and forced her to tilt her face up to his. As he lowered his head, she leaned back and fought to turn her face away, but his fingers held her in place.

"And, *mi amore*," he whispered against her lips, "You will never contradict me in front of the customers again. Do you hear me?"

Before she could answer, he crushed her lips in a bruising kiss. She gritted her teeth, refusing his tongue entry into her mouth.

Lifting her with one arm while the other still kept her from breaking their kiss, he sat her on the edge of the table and wedged himself between her legs. Feeling possessed, overpowered, she fought for control. The hard ridge of his cock ground into her clit. Sensations she didn't want to feel left her gasping for air.

His tongue slid in and swept away all memories of his overblown ego, ulterior motives and short temper. Angel didn't notice where his hands were until one had worked its way under her shirt and kneaded her breast.

She may have been revolted, but her nipples were so sensitive and the feel of a hand finally doing something about it held her captive. The invisible wire between the nipple he now twisted and pinched and the clit he continued to torture with his erection vibrated and pulsed.

The feel of his other hand slipping under the waistband of her jeans snatched her out of his control.

Silently telling Antonio that she'd warned him, Angel wrapped her arms around his shoulders and slid off the table. Balling up her anger and shame, she slammed her knee into his groin. A string of English and Italian curses met her ears as she bolted around his huddled body and fled to the safety of the shop.

Her father sat outside at one of the bistro tables with a

couple of his cronies. Skidding to a halt by the door, Angel glanced in the mirrored wall. Swollen lips and the beard-scratched skin around them gave away too much information.

Lately, her father looked too pale. Only this morning he'd complained that his heart wasn't as strong as it used to be and he feared he'd die before he ever saw his Angel walk down the aisle, before he ever held a grandchild in his arms.

Seeing her like this would make his day. Hearing that Antonio forced himself on her just might send him to the hospital.

Swiping away a stray tear, she spun away from the door.

Antonio leaned against the counter. "I forgive this. You are virgin, Angelina, so I forgive," he said, his voice cracking.

The tinkle of the bell over the door sent her heart straight up to her throat. Trapped between whoever stood behind her and Antonio, she snuck a peek in the mirrored wall.

Her eyes widened.

She clapped her hand over her telltale lips, but it was too late.

* * * * *

Tanner stared at the hand covering Angel's mouth until she lowered it.

"Angel?"

Still refusing to turn around, Angel opened those just-kissed-swollen lips then closed them and lowered her eyes.

His stomach soured. Every muscle in his body wilted.

Until a teardrop slid free from beneath her spiked lashes and trailed down her cheek. Until he saw a pale pink imprint in the shape of fingers on her face.

"You son of a bitch."

He lunged for Antonio.

The way Antonio wobbled around the counter

momentarily stunned him until he remembered his first kiss with Angel. Another sign that the bastard had forced his kiss and God only knew what else on Angel.

Seeing only red, only the blood he intended to spill, he failed to notice Antonio's arm swinging back. The man's fist met him with a blow to his stomach, but Tanner, having been in too many brawls to enter a fight soft, barely felt it.

His fist connected with Antonio's jaw.

Ignoring Angel's screams and pleas to stop, he landed a half-dozen punches before the sound of glass shattering and Antonio's startled face brought him out from the red haze of fury engulfing him.

"Mary, mother of God, what the hell is going on?" Mr. Roselli rushed through the door followed by a small group of elderly men.

Lying in the display atop broken glass and crushed pastries, Antonio whined, "This, how you say? This *figlio di puttana* throw me..."

Continuing in Italian, he moved to rise then winced and flung his arm over his face when some small glass fragments showered down from the jagged edge of the destroyed counter above him.

Angel and Mr. Roselli rushed over and tried to help him up.

"What'd you just call me, you Italian piece of horseshit?" Tanner glared down at Antonio. Well, he tried to glare. He could feel his left eye swelling shut. "Angel, what'd he just call me?"

Angel scowled at him and followed her father and Antonio into the kitchen.

"What the hell did he call me?" Tanner yelled, feeling a bit like a mad bull bellowing in the middle of an empty pasture.

"How you say? How you say?" Antonio's strained voice came from the kitchen as Tanner bent over to pick up some of the glass.

"Son of a whore. That is it. You are the son of a *puttana*."

Tossing the glass across the shop, Tanner made for the kitchen. No man got away with insulting his mother. He came up short in the doorway when Angel's petite body blocked his way.

Her soft voice cut right through his anger. "Don't you think you've done enough damage for one day?"

Seeing those marks on her flawless skin almost sent him in for another round. Tears pooled in her eyes. Tears and disappointment.

"Listen, Angel, I know what went on in here before I arrived."

"So you figure you have a right to beat the crap out of any man who kisses me? And wreck my shop in the process?"

"He didn't just kiss you and we both know it." Tanner nodded down at the portion of her white tee shirt that hung over her jeans.

"What I do with whomever I want is none of your business," she ground out. Her hand shook as she tucked the shirt back into her jeans.

"You're right, Angel." Tanner gingerly grasped her arm and led her into the shop. Glass crunched beneath their feet. He held on to her arm in case she slid and whispered, "But I can see those marks on your face."

Her fingers rose to her lips. Chagrin filled her eyes.

"No, Angel mine, not those." He brushed his fingers over the marks that told him just how forcefully Antonio had held Angel's face, just how much she'd fought. "These. I'd have beaten the shit out of him even if I didn't know you. No man has a right to force himself on a woman."

Angel's face lit up for a moment before she slumped. "I kissed him back."

Tanner could have sworn a quake had hit New York the

way the floor shifted right out from under his feet. Realizing he'd snatched his hand back from the feel of her skin, he shoved it in his front pocket.

"I see," he said, unable to think of anything else to say, anything else to do.

"No, I don't think you do, Tanner. I don't even understand, but...I..." Her voice cracked then died out.

Like a spineless coyote running with his tail between his legs from a yapping mutt, he spun around, stepped over the glass and left Roselli's bakery and Angel.

He swore he heard the clink of Angel's golden halo breaking in two.

Then again, that may have been his.

* * * * *

Sitting on her couch that night, Angel forced the mouthful of choco-fudge mint ice cream down her throat. Whipping another tissue from the box on the end table, she wiped away the tears streaming down her cheeks and watched Clark Gable turn his back on Scarlett O'Hara. She always watched *Gone with the Wind* when life got her down. Her mother had loved the movie. Watching it was as close as Angel could ever get to crying in her arms.

She tossed the damp tissue onto the pile covering the couch and shoved another heaping spoonful of ice cream into her mouth.

"Creeps," she muttered. "They're all creeps. I'm better off without him."

Flicking off the TV, she stood up and padded over to the kitchen. Washing out the dish, she blinked away the tears and told herself to get a grip. "What kind of name is McQuade, anyway? Or Tanner for that matter?"

The dish slid from her hands when the phone rang. Grabbing the remote before it rang again, she took a deep breath, said a silent prayer, then said aloud in a soft, emotionless if breathy voice, "Hello?"

Her father's voice almost sent another wave of tears to her eyes. "That cowboy of yours cost me a fortune. And Antonio had to get stitches in both his hands."

"Both?" She couldn't care less if Antonio had a hundred stitches. The jerk had ruined everything.

"And he won't be able to work for at least a week."

The idea of a week without Antonio ordering her around or trying to seduce her brought a smile to her lips. "That's too bad."

"And they can't get me a new display for three days, so on top of everything else, I'm losing three days of business. Another lost Sunday. You know that's the biggest day of the week. Another fight like that and we can kiss Roselli's goodbye."

"Yeah, well, I don't think you'll have to worry about that, Dad." Her eyes burned. Cursing, she squared her shoulders. "Tanner's gone."

"Back to Texas?"

"I don't know. Just gone."

"Well, good riddance. That boy was nothing but trouble. Lurking around all the time. Sticking his nose where it doesn't belong."

Angel could almost feel Tanner's nose nuzzling her neck the way it had while he'd slept behind her. She bit her lip hard, but the room still blurred. "I have to go, Dad. I'm beat."

"Sure, honey. You go to bed early."

Just before her finger touched the off button she heard him yell her name. She made her way to the bedroom as she brought the phone back up to her ear. "Yeah?"

"About tomorrow. Since this whole fiasco with that cowboy was really your fault, I, well, I told Antonio that you'd come by his place and help him out."

"What? You didn't." Angel dropped down onto the bed. "Well, forget it. I—"

"Come on, Angel. Give the guy a break. He can barely unzip his own fly to take a piss without help. Not that I expect you to go that far."

"I should hope not!" Angel's stomach knotted. Any minute he'd mention that she was all he had. Any minute the guilt that had eaten away at her since her mother's death would have her giving in to his every request. "Why can't you do it?"

"I haven't been feeling up to par myself lately. Come on, Angel, do it for your lonely old dad. You're all I have."

Clenching the phone, she swallowed the retort lodged in her throat.

She'd had an argument with her mother only moments before her heart attack. That guilt, that horrible feeling that she'd somehow killed her mother, had her breaking out in a cold sweat whenever she so much as considered of standing up to her father.

And he knew it! Why hadn't someone warned her that day beside her mother's casket that breaking down and announcing that her mother's death and her father's tears were her fault would give her father the perfect weapon? That he'd use it again and again? That knowing he used it would not stop her from giving in?

Therapists didn't help. Discovering that her mother had a diseased heart didn't help.

"I really can't, Dad."

He coughed.

Bile filled her mouth. "Dad? You all right?"

"Please, Angel. The man is alone. I know how that feels. Alone and hurt."

The buzz of her doorbell propelled her off the bed. Her heart stilled then beat a little faster.

"That your bell I'm hearing?" her father asked, suspicion lacing his voice.

"I, uh, ordered pizza. I really have to go," she murmured, rushing down the hall to the door.

"All right, Angel. So tomorrow…"

Half listening, she said, "Yeah, sure. Bye, Dad."

At the door, Angel held her breath before peering through the peephole. Tanner's distorted face frowning back at her nearly sent a squeal to her lips. Smoothing down her hair, she opened the door and met him with a stern look.

"Howdy, miss." Tanner grinned sheepishly. Wringing the edge of his hat between his hands he raised one brow. "Heard an Angel lived in these here hills and had to come take a look fer myself."

Giggling, Angel shook her head. "A real angel? No such thing would dare set foot in what I've heard some people call the city of sin."

"Now that's Las Vegas, sweet thang." His eyes lit up the way she'd remembered, the way she missed in the short time since he'd left Roselli's.

Stepping back as if to close the door, she met his gaze. Held it. "There are no such things as perfect angels, Tanner. Placing that title on a woman is just not fair."

He palmed the door with one hand before she could shut it. Stepping over the threshold, he hooked her chin with the other hand and tilted her face up. "I know, Angel mine."

"You've been here less than a month."

He brought his face closer to hers. "I know."

"I was shocked. And more than a bit frustrated from our, uh, nights together."

"I know exactly how you feel." His lips skimmed over her damp cheek. "You taste good."

"You probably wouldn't have reacted any differently."

The door slammed shut.

Tanner brought his lips to hers. She felt them quirk up.

"While I like to consider myself a modern man and I'm so hard for you these days I'd probably shove my dick in anything available just to make the pain stop, I highly doubt I would have kissed that man."

So relieved that he'd come back, Angel laughed, ran the tip of her tongue over his lower lip and whispered, "I'm available."

He plopped a sweet, way too short kiss on her lips then strode around her. Shocked, Angel watched him pace the length of each wall. She opened her mouth to ask him what he had in mind when he suddenly bent down.

"This," he announced as he stood up, holding the end of the phone wire in his hand, "stays out until we're done. Promise?"

Happier than she remembered being since before her mother died, she nodded.

"Now go take a long, hot shower." He strode with a determined look on his face for the apartment door.

"Excuse me?" Thinking that once again her cowboy would back out, Angel wanted to stomp her foot and demand he give her what she wanted this instant. "Listen, I know this isn't the way you keep saying you want my first time…"

"Now who said it wasn't? Picked up a few things on the way here." He winked over his shoulder at her then opened the door. "Left them in the hall."

"In the hall? In New York City?" Gnawing her lip, Angel watched him disappear around the doorjamb. She pictured her cowboy returning empty handed. "Listen, Tanner, I don't need anything but you to make it memorable."

"Get in that shower, Angel, before I come in there and carry you in."

Though the idea of him tossing her over his shoulder and sharing a shower with her turned her on to no end, his next words sent her scurrying to the bathroom before he returned.

"You have some chocolate stuff all over your face. And tear tracks."

When she caught sight of her face in the mirror over the sink, she burst out laughing. Yes, she had a smudge of ice cream here and there. And so many lines from her tears, she doubted he fell for her nonchalant act when she'd first greeted him at the door.

Shedding her clothes, she stepped into the shower.

"Angel?" Tanner poked his head in the door just as she was about to draw the shower curtain. His gaze trailed down the length of her body, setting fire to every inch it touched.

Mist billowed into the room, but she still saw the desire in his eyes when they rose up to meet hers. "Come to join me, cowboy?"

Shaking his head, he chuckled. "Much as I'd love to, darlin', I'm kinda busy out here. Just came to ask where you keep your cell phone."

"My cell..." Realizing that tonight Tanner was taking no chances, she felt her body weep. "In my bag."

"That's what I figured." He shoved her bag toward her. "A gentleman never goes through a lady's purse." Shuddering, he added, "God knows what lurks in those things."

Laughing, Angel turned off her cell phone and handed it and her bag back to Tanner. The door slammed shut. Stepping under the hot spray, she took the quickest shower she ever had. Even so, it took her at least twenty minutes to shave. She conditioned her hair twice, scrubbed her body with sandswept coconut butter, removed chipped nail polish from her toes, then stared in the floor-length mirror and wondered what her cowboy saw in her.

Her hair curled and frizzed before her eyes. Her breasts, no bigger than apples, bore red blotches from a little too much scrubbing. Too short, too lacking in the hip department, she looked more like a young boy than a woman as far as she was concerned. She raised her eyes and stuck her tongue out at herself.

Huge, light brown eyes took up most of her face. She scrunched up her nose. Yup, it would look much better smaller. Running her fingers over her jowls, she recalled how the men in Italy during a visit had complimented them. "Yeah," she muttered, "tell Americans that big jowls are hot."

A soft knock on the door made her stomach flip.

"Angel mine, you ready to find out what it means to ride all night?"

Tanner's voice grew huskier with each word. It seemed to reverberate throughout her body, wrap invisible ropes around her waist and draw her toward the door. Opening it, greeting a fully clothed man without as much as a towel covering her, she wished she were taller, curvier, prettier.

Seeing the look on his face when he took in the sight of her, she wondered what he saw that she did not. The man took the meaning of wolf and put a whole other twist on it.

"Come here, darlin'," he crooned, holding out his hand.

When she hesitated and glanced over her shoulder at herself in the mirror, he stepped inside the small bathroom. Lifting her up as if she weighed no more than a child, he tossed her over his shoulder and carried her down the hall into her bedroom. Raising her head, Angel gasped.

Nearly a hundred candles lit the room. No matter where she looked, flames flickered. On the windowsill, the dresser and nightstand. Some were even scattered on the floor.

"Oh, Tanner."

Lowering her so that her body slid down the length of him, so that she felt every inch of his clothes scrape over her bare skin, he wrapped his warm hands around her shoulders when she finally stood before him.

She expected him to draw her into a kiss, an embrace.

He turned her around until she faced her reflection in the

full-length mirror. This time the sight held her gaze for an entirely different reason. Framed in the antique mirror with the glow of dozens of candle caressing her body, she looked feminine, maybe even pretty. Naked with Tanner fully clothed behind her, she looked decadent. His big hands slid down her slender arms then took hold of her wrists and raised her hands up and around the back of his neck.

"Keep them there, darlin'. Now hold on and watch."

She met his gaze in the mirror.

"No. Watch my hands."

The soft strains of music filtered into the room along with the scent of vanilla. For all of ten seconds, she wondered how he knew her favorite scent.

Her thoughts scattered when his hands moved down her arms so slowly she nearly screamed with need by the time those rough palms finally met her hips then moved up and grazed over her ribs.

"Do you like this? Being naked while I'm still dressed?" The feel of his lips brushing the sensitive whorl of her ear as he spoke sent a tremor through her body.

"Yes." Her voice was so deep it sounded alien to her ears.

Calloused hands scraped her stomach, hips, legs. Entranced, she watched it all, willed them to go where she wanted them most.

"You're at my mercy, you know," he murmured in her ear. "Spread your legs for me."

His clothes scratched her inflamed skin as she shifted her feet wider apart.

"More," he ordered, rubbing his stubbly cheek over her temple.

Tanner's gruff voice shocked her. Meeting his gaze in the mirror sent a trill of excitement and a little fear down her spine. Naked hunger shone in his eyes, burned her and demanded she obey. Gasping against the onslaught of desire that look wrought, she spread her legs wider and wider each time he shook his head, each time those rough hands slid close to where she longed for their touch then moved away.

"Arms up, Angel."

Blinking, Angel realized she had released her hands and lowered her arms. As she reached up, Tanner straightened and grasped her wrists. He pulled her arms up higher and higher until she had to rise up onto her toes.

This time when he skimmed his hands down her arms, he brought them over her breasts. The ache beneath his coarse palms and between her legs grew unbearable. Leaning her head back against him, she closed her eyes and let the wonder of his touch engulf her. A slight stab of pain shot through both her breasts.

"Ah, ah, Angel. Open your eyes and watch."

Looking at the reflection, she watched in amazement as he pulled and squeezed her nipples, sometimes to the point of that sweet pain, sometimes only to send trill after trill of pleasure shooting down her stomach. The pain deep in her pussy sent a whimper to her lips.

"Tanner, please, I can't take any more."

His smile turned lethal. "Tell me what you want, Angel mine."

Heat flared over her cheeks. Shifting her hips, she pushed back against the ridge of his erection. "You know what I want."

"No, I don't." He kissed along her hairline, leaving a trail of heat to her ear. "Don't move."

After he lowered her arms, he stepped away. When he returned with a chair, Angel was sure she'd died and gone to heaven. *Dear God, could the man read her mind?* Her legs had just about given out. The bed would have been better, but at this point she'd take whatever she could get. When he sat in the chair and started to rub those coarse hands over the globes of her buttocks, the jelly legs barely holding her up dissolved completely. As if he knew just when she'd lost the ability to stand, Tanner grabbed her hips and pulled her back onto his lap.

"Now don't forget, Angel mine, I want you watching."

Tanner shifted until his knees rose slightly between her legs.

She and Tanner looked like they belonged in a museum. He was so handsome in the candlelight, with his bronze skin and blond hair. The white tee shirt, worn jeans and boots with actual spurs packaged her cowboy just right. God, he even had his Stetson on.

Shadows flowed and trembled over her body. Where no shadows dwelt, an amber glow seemed to rise from deep within and shimmer around her. She looked like an actual angel sitting on his lap.

He spread his knees apart, taking her legs with them. Watching, Angel saw the candle in front of them cast more and more light on her glistening flesh. Unable to look away, she followed his hands as they skimmed over her legs, her inner thighs. Still he didn't move higher. Instead they pulled her legs even wider apart until she felt her inner lips open. They looked so swollen. Liquid seeped out from her onto his jeans. Moaning, Angel tried to shimmy down toward his hands but he held her in place.

"Say it," he said in a soothing voice. "Tell me exactly where you want me to touch you next."

"I can't."

"Pussy. Say it, Angel." His thumbs traced circles closer and closer. "It's a beautiful word."

Minutes ticked by, torturous minutes with his thumbs glancing along the crease between her outer lips and her thigh. Unable to take it any longer, she pled, "Touch my pussy, Tanner. It hurts so much. Touch my pussy, please."

"God, I love hearing you say that."

Finally, he slid his fingers along her moist flesh. She felt her hips jut up to meet his touch. Every time her eyes closed, he stopped until she opened them.

"I bet you're tight. Are you, Angel mine?"

Too busy watching his finger delve into her, she didn't answer.

"Too tight for two?"

Frantic, Angel shook her head, then nodded, then shook her head.

"You're losing me. Yes or no?"

She met his gaze in the mirror and spread her legs wider.

Another finger entered her. Watching them slowly glide in and out, she dug her nails into his arms. So close to coming, she struggled for control. She'd had multiple orgasms with her vibrators, but man and machine were so different.

By the time he snagged her clit between his fingers and tugged, Angel had hovered on the brink of an orgasm too long and shattered in his hands. Through hooded eyes, she watched herself buck and writhe on his lap, watched him lift her and stand while she still floated down to earth. When her wits returned, she found herself sitting alone on the chair and Tanner kneeling before her.

Staring at her with eyes that seared, he removed his hat and tossed it across the room. "Don't forget, Angel. Keep watching."

He shoved her legs wide, spread her open.

Lowered his head.

Looking in the mirror, down at his head buried between her thighs, at the candles surrounding them, she tried to take in all he did for her while his wicked mouth shot her right back to the brink of ecstasy. His tongue scorched her clit, laving it, flicking it until she shoved her hips forward.

Pleasure so intense it bordered on pain ricocheted through her body. A hunger she had only read about created an undeniable ache deep within her core, an ache that gnawed at her control and had her wailing with despair when he lifted his mouth and turned his head to nip at her inner thigh.

Raising his head, he bestowed the most devilish grin then burrowed into her pussy and sucked her clit deep into his mouth. Needing something to hold on to, she sank her hands into his hair. When he trapped her clit between his teeth until she yelped then left it to delve his tongue into her, she flung her head back, noticed rose petals strewn over her bed then tumbled into another, mind-blowing orgasm.

Maybe she passed out.

Maybe she only lost touch with reality.

Either way, Tanner had somehow carried her to the bed and spread her out atop the rose petals without her knowledge. Lying there, she nearly cried while he slowly undressed without taking his eyes off her face.

Before lowering his jeans, he whispered, "Memorable so far?"

She couldn't speak past the lump in her throat. Merely smiled and nodded.

"Now remember, Angel. I've been big my whole life, so I know how to handle it and not hurt a lady. But this is your first time—"

"Tanner, actually Jack had the pleasure of breaking me in." She giggled when for a moment a scowl passed over his face.

"Oh, right. The vibrator." He lowered his pants. "Well, then, say hello to Long John."

She'd already seen it, felt it at night pressing against her butt. His size still impressed her a little, still scared the living daylights out of her. "That can't be normal."

"I'm normal all right." Chuckling, Tanner climbed onto the bed.

Angel spread her legs. Crawling up between them, he nestled his hips between her thighs. She tingled where his skin met hers. The hairs on his thighs tickled her as he shifted and sank his hips deeper.

The fat head of his penis nudged open her lips.

"I did turn off your cell phone, right?" Tanner glanced over his shoulder.

Chapter Five

❧

Tanner closed his eyes and silently let out a string of curses. Sometimes, in a rodeo, you have the ride of your life. The bell rings and that bull is still banging the shit out of your ass. You racked up so many points, you'd bet the ranch that no one can beat you. Thrown before the bell too many times to remember, you can't wipe that shit-eating grin off your face. You're going to finally grasp that damn brass ring, rip it right out of the bull's nose and hang it on the shiny championship buckle.

Another rider breaks out of the gate, but you're not worried. He's a rookie. He'll hit dirt way before the bell.

Nothing is gonna stop you this time. You're already on your horse and itching to make that victory lap, dammit.

But the rookie hangs on.

And the bell rings.

And your horse rears.

And your ass hits the ground with a bone-jarring thud.

And your balls shoot right up to your throat and strangle the curses rising up with them.

"Ignore it," Angel's voice—soft, determined and sounding like she might have a pair in her throat too—broke through the haze of anger drowning him and pitching him back in time. "Tanner, please, ignore it."

Her moist heat had just planted a kiss on the head of his cock when that doorbell rang. Any other time, any other woman, and he would have plowed in. But, shit, this was her first time. Blinking, he struggled to maintain his hard-on. Almost succeeded.

The damn doorbell rang again.

"Son of a bitch!"

Shoving himself off the bed, he stormed down the hall to the door. Peering through the peephole, he saw a wiry teen holding a bouquet of roses. Red roses. At least two dozen.

Flinging open the door, Tanner barked, "Hand em over."

"Uh...uh...a r-rose b-by," the boy stuttered. His eyes darted down then up into Tanner's eyes. Awe filled his face. "Y-you A-an..."

"Spit it out!"

Crimson stains covered the teen's face as he glanced down then squeezed his eyes closed.

Tanner didn't need to look to know his cock twitched as it wilted. He felt it. And he didn't need some kid witnessing Long John's slow death. Reaching out, he yanked the roses from the boy's trembling hands. "Come back tomorrow for your tip."

Slamming the door, he scowled at the white envelope stapled to the tissue paper wrapped around the roses.

He'd heard the bedroom door slam shut, knew Angel wouldn't know if he peeked inside. A thorn stabbed into his palm. Glancing down the hall, he stared at the closed door then drew in a deep breath and brought Angel her roses.

Long John breathed his last breath when her gaze fell to the roses and her face lit up.

"You didn't," she squealed taking the bouquet in her hands as if it were made of glass.

A candle on the nightstand, one of the dozens he'd painstakingly set up around the bedroom, sputtered out.

"No," he muttered, "I didn't." Turning away, he licked his fingers and started dousing the candles lining her dresser.

"Oh...I wonder...Tanner?"

The touch of her hand on his arm shocked him. Yeah, it was that damn rodeo all over again. Some kid comes in and takes that brass ring, yanks that buckle right out of your hands.

"Open it."

"It doesn't matter who sent them."

"Just open it, Angel."

Raking his fingers through his hair, he stepped away from her touch, from the hunger clawing at his insides since the day he'd bumped into her. From the frustration sucker punching him every time he came close to feeding that hunger.

From her father. The bakery. The Italian Stallion.

"Or maybe you already know who they're from."

"I have an idea."

The sound of tissue paper crackling brought him around to face her. Angel twisted the bouquet between her hands. Petals floated down and joined some already lying around her bare feet.

"Now why'd you go and do that?"

"Ouch!" Wincing, she brought her hand up to her mouth and sucked on her palm. The ruined bouquet fell to the floor. "I know who sent them and I don't want him or them. Now will you please come back to bed and finish what you started?"

Another candle sputtered out.

Her lower lip trembled. "'Cause I can't take this, Tanner. I swear. I'm so twisted up inside from wanting you, I'm afraid I'll start screaming if we don't...don't..."

Tears filled those fawn-colored doe eyes and still he couldn't move. The sight of her standing there naked while the firelight caressed her every curve immobilized him. She glowed, shimmered as if she really was an angel.

And damn if it didn't scare the shit out of him.

A tear trailed down her cheek, dripped from the side of her chin, landed on her breast. Another followed. He watched it merge with the first and glide down to her nipple.

"Get your ass in that bed, Angel, before someone else comes calling."

Her face lit up, but rather than returning to the bed she leapt at him. Before he knew what hit him, Tanner had his angel in his arms. She rubbed against him like a cat and kissed his neck until Long John saluted and lust took control. His legs wobbled.

"I told you to get into bed."

"You ordering me around, cowboy?" she asked in a voice that would shame the ladies at the Pleasure Ranch. Holding on to his shoulders, she hoisted herself up and swung her legs around his hips. "I don't follow orders, you know."

"Really?" His voice cracked. Feeling that moist heat so close to his dick did him in. He grabbed her ass with both hands and shifted her until he hovered at heaven's gates. "You take bribes?"

She nipped her way up to his lips. "No, I just take."

With a strength he wouldn't have figured such a tiny thing possessed, Angel shoved herself down over his cock until her mound nestled against his base. Her warm, sweet breath whooshed out of her mouth and filled his lungs. Her lids dropped, nearly shielding her eyes, but he still saw those fawn-colored orbs darken.

An odd feeling came over him. Buried to the hilt, her warmth embracing him, seeping through him, he could only compare it to slipping into his own bed after a week-long cattle run.

Her inner muscles clenched around his cock and drew it in deeper. Surrounded by Angel, buried so deep in her that he lost sight of himself, Tanner felt something deep inside shift, and he knew, without a doubt, that he'd never be the same.

Kissing her, taking her tongue into his mouth, he carried her to the bed. When they hit the mattress the scent from the rose petals surrounding them mingled with the scent from Angel's arousal still clinging to his lips. Feeling happier than he had since his father's death, he chuckled against her lips.

"God, you feel good, Angel mine." Raising his hips, he broke their kiss and stared into her eyes. Her inner muscles gripped him almost painfully when he slid back into her pussy. "Damn, woman, where'd you learn that?"

"I may be a virgin, but I'm well read." Angel raised her head and bit his lower lip.

He burrowed deeper, shifted back and forth to torture her clit. "Later you can show me what you learned from your books."

Her gasps and soft moans rocked him. His mind wrapped around every inch where her skin met his. Nerves he never knew mattered tingled from her touch. Picking up speed and force with every thrust, he fought for control. Her body writhed beneath his, but every time he'd rise and try to keep his weight from crushing her, she'd pull him back down.

"I won't break, Tanner."

Still he held back. She felt so small beneath him.

"Dammit, Tanner. Let go," she demanded, scraping her nails over his back.

Control slipped. "You don't know what you're asking for. I'm…too…" He sucked in a deep breath and held his climax at bay. Her body tensed beneath him.

"I took Jack all the way to the rabbit, damn you."

Tanner shook his head and grinned. "That much?"

Her warm hands cupped his butt. "I like it hard and rough."

"Hold on tight, Angel mine." Tanner grabbed her wrists and drew them up over her head. "This is how *I* like it." Bending over, he trailed kisses and nips down her neck. Continuing until a hard nipple bumped his lips, he clamped down and bit until she moaned and arched her back. Torturing one hard nub then moving to the next, he withdrew almost completely from her heat. Sweat shone over her skin, dampened the dark curls framing her face.

When she sobbed for release, he slammed into her with more force than he ever had before, like he'd always wanted to but never dared. Angel screamed but her hips rose up on the next thrust as if she feared he would go easier.

Losing touch with everything but Angel, he silenced her screams with his mouth and thrust into her again and again. The moment her body started convulsing around his, he came with a force that shook him to the core.

Never had he come so hard and long. Never had he felt so sated yet hungry for more. Never had he wanted to stay buried in a woman forever. Filling her with his seed, he slid his hands from her wrists and weaved his fingers between hers. He kissed her eyes, cheeks, nose and mouth. Swallowed the soft moans that accompanied her return. Took her air into his lungs when she sighed and stretched beneath him.

The plaintive mewl of her cat broke the spell, freed Tanner from the webs binding them together and reminded him that Angel bore all his weight. Reluctantly, he shifted to rise.

Her slender legs wrapped around his hips. "No, don't move."

Giggling, Angel caressed his back until he felt himself grow hard inside her. Her eyes opened, held him captive.

"Your eyes are lethal. You know that?"

She rolled her eyes. "Where do you get these lines, cowboy?"

Stunned that what they'd experienced hadn't left her as awed as he, Tanner cupped her cheeks. "I've never given you a line, Angel. Never," he said, his voice betraying the anger and disappointment he could feel churning in his stomach.

"Oh yeah. And you came here for a wife."

Shrinking down faster than a prairie dog charging down a burrow for safety, he backed out of Angel's heat and rose from the bed. Unmindful of his nakedness, he went to the window and gazed out at the street below. "I did."

"Please, Tanner, don't ruin this. I don't need the promise of marriage to go another round."

Turning, he sat on the windowsill. Crimson petals clung to Angel, adorned her breasts and inner thighs. Her damp, flushed skin glowed in the light of the few candles that had not gone out. His anger dissolved. "I'd give my favorite horse for a camera right now."

"Like I'd ever let someone take a picture of me naked."

"I'm not just someone, Angel."

"No?"

"I am now and will always be your first. That makes me special."

Laughing as she scooped up some petals from the mattress and brought them to her nose, Angel drew in a deep breath. "I'd say a lot more than being my first has made you special, Tanner."

She rolled over and stretched like a cat awakening from a long nap. Now practically covered with petals, she demanded much more than a mere camera. Tanner had no doubt that an artist, one who commanded the highest price, would pay him for just one look.

Unexpectedly, the memory of her standing in the bakery after his fight with Antonio arose and her voice saying the words that had filled him with unexplainable rage slithered into his mind.

She'd kissed Antonio back.

Suddenly, his angel shared the bed with another. He closed his eyes, but when he opened them, Antonio still lay beside her, mocking him.

"Come back to bed, Tanner." She raised her hand out to him.

He took a step. The bedroom became Roselli's bakery. Tanner saw Antonio grabbing Angel and forcing her to kiss him. Watched as she melted into that kiss even as Antonio's fingers bruised her tender flesh.

"I like it hard and rough," he heard his angel whisper in his ear but when the bedroom came back into focus, he saw that she was still lying on the bed waiting for him.

"Did you just say something?" His throat closed, choking off his words.

Angel rose up onto her knees and wiggled her fingers. "I said come back to bed. I want more."

"You like it rough and hard, Angel mine?"

A slight frown flickered across her face. Her tongue darted out to moisten her lips. "Is something wrong?"

"Tell me why you kissed him." As soon as the words left his mouth, Tanner wished he'd never uttered them.

Angel's hand dropped to her lap. "Oh, I see."

"Forget I just said that."

"*My* forgetting isn't the problem, Tanner."

Rose-petal-covered legs slid over the edge of the bed. If he had a rope, he might have lassoed her and tied her to that bed. Every muscle tensed from the need to stop her, to push her back down onto the mattress and obliterate the memory of Antonio's kiss from her mind. He knew he would never forget her admission. He would always see her lips swollen from another man's mouth. Her face flushing as she touched the marks from Antonio's fingers.

Her toes touched the floor. She glanced at him with cold eyes and rose.

"Get back in that bed." At the sound of his harsh order, Tanner felt his cock stir back to life.

Angel's hand rose to her chest. "E-excuse me?"

"I'm not through with you. Get back in that bed." Exquisite pain shot through his cock when her hand trembled as she backed toward the bed. "Now!"

Angel leapt onto the mattress then spun around and

stared at him. Like a deer frozen in the headlights of an oncoming car, she didn't move when he approached.

Lifting a curl from her shoulder, he twirled it around his finger. "I think I've figured you out, Angel."

"Tanner..." Her breasts rose and fell as she drew in one deep breath after another.

He watched the curl unfurl then fall back down to her shoulder. Grabbing her ankles, he dragged her to the edge of the mattress. He shoved her legs apart. When he let go, he saw her thigh muscles flex.

"Don't move," he whispered, his voice soft but threatening.

"Listen, Tanner, this isn't you."

He took her arms and positioned her hands on the mattress behind her. Sitting like that, with her pussy exposed and her chest arched, she looked almost like the ladies at the Pleasure Ranch. Well, the ones who knew what he liked.

"Actually," he said, turning away, "it is."

He dressed, glancing at her and repositioning her legs whenever they looked as if she'd inched them closer together. At the door, he turned around. "I expect to find you like this when I get back."

"When you get back? Where are you going?"

Angel watched the door close. She listened to the clunk of Tanner's boots as he walked down the hall. When the door to her apartment slammed shut, she nearly bolted from the bed.

Instead, she softly called, "Tanner?"

Straining to listen for some sign that he remained in her apartment, she gasped when she heard the sound of him slamming the front door outside.

The warm air flowing through the open window had felt refreshing. Now goose bumps rose up on her arms and legs. Tears burned her eyes as she wondered why she still remained exactly as he'd placed her. A candle on her dresser went out. A tear slid down her cheek when the one beside it followed suit.

One by one, the flames succumbed to pools of wax.

"This is ridiculous," she said to herself when only the light from her alarm clock and the streetlamps held the darkness at bay.

Still, she couldn't move.

Sweat trickled down her back as she wondered if she'd allowed a madman into her bed. Her heart beat so quickly she thought she'd pass out.

"A sane woman would lock her door," she muttered. "A sane woman would never have let a stranger bring her to orgasm with her vibrator…in a public place."

The sane part of her told her to jump up, lock her doors and have the police waiting with her for Tanner's return. The part of her that led her to search out websites she never would admit to knowing even existed kept her rooted to the bed, kept her legs open and her eyes on the door. Tanner had somehow uncovered the truth behind her response to Antonio's kiss. Heat flared over her face as if everyone now knew of her decadent fantasies.

By the time she heard the sound of his boots striking the concrete steps and the unlocked front door opening, the agonizing fire deep in her pussy dwarfed the pain in her cramped muscles. The moisture dripping down her labia and over her anus had tortured her. Her frenzied heartbeat strummed along every erogenous zone she knew of and some she hadn't. She glanced down at her legs. Watched them quiver from the strain of keeping them apart.

Had they closed at all?

Would he notice?

She spread them wider a moment before the bedroom door opened.

Holding a shopping bag in one clenched hand and a rolled-up length of rope in the other, Tanner leaned against the doorjamb. "So, I was right, wasn't I?"

She didn't answer. Couldn't. She'd kept this part of herself hidden far too long.

His eyes burned with hunger, shone with triumph.

"Have you ever been tied up?" With a flick of his wrist, the rope uncoiled and snapped against the hardwood floor. "Answer me."

"No, I..." Her voice cracked.

"Ever surf the web?"

"Doesn't everyone?"

"I'm talking about the sites on bondage, Angel. Ever check them out? Look at the pictures? Get all horny picturing yourself tied up?"

Annoyed that he still remained in the doorway, she cleared her throat and hissed, "Yes."

"Okay, lie down, Angel."

Trills of excitement swept through her body as she slid back on the mattress and did as he ordered.

"Spread-eagled," he barked out, sending her heart into her throat.

As she spread her legs and raised her arms above her head, she silently prayed her instincts were right and Tanner could be trusted. Keeping her eyes trained on him, she watched him push off from the doorjamb and cross the floor to her bed. Without looking at her, Tanner set the shopping bag on the floor then tied her wrists to the bedposts. She shivered when the rope slid around one ankle, moaned when she felt it enclose the other. Came when he cinched it tight, spreading her legs almost to the point of pain.

Through her lashes, she watched him watch her climax. Shame swept over her when he chuckled and dipped his finger into her convulsing pussy.

"That's my naughty Angel," he crooned then sucked her come from his finger. "Sleep tight."

Angel nearly choked when he turned and headed for the door. "Wha-where are you going?"

"You need your sleep. Tomorrow I have big plans for you."

Yanking on the ropes, she yelled at his back, "Tomorrow? You can't leave me like this!"

"I'll be right in the living room if you need anything," he yelled over his shoulder.

"Tanner, wait!"

"If you have to pee, let me know. I'll bring a pot."

"A pot? A...a..." Watching him walk down the hall, Angel twisted her hands and feet. "This isn't funny. Come back here."

But he didn't come back. She waited and cursed herself for allowing him to bind her. Soon his soft snores broke the silence. The prospect of what he had planned kept her awake for hours.

When she opened her eyes, sunlight blinded her. Stretching, she realized her legs and one of her arms were free. Fingers slid under the rope still wrapped around her other wrist as she squinted up at Tanner.

"Morning, tiger," she purred, glad that tomorrow had finally come and he hadn't turned out to be a serial killer.

"Get up, quick," Tanner whispered, "your father's about to break down the door."

The pounding she'd somehow failed to hear now seemed deafening.

"My father?" she squealed and wrapped her arms around his neck as he lifted her off the bed.

Their eyes met. Her cheeks burned when he smirked.

"So now I'm a tiger?"

Before she could answer, Tanner crushed her lips in a quick kiss that took her breath away. Plopping her on her feet, he lightly smacked her butt.

"Get something on and let him in. I'm not here. Get it?"

"You're not?" she asked as she raced to the closet. Rubbing her butt, she yanked her robe off the hook on the closet door and put it on.

"It's just after dawn, Angel. You want to explain why I'm here? Just close the door and get rid of him." He slid behind the bedroom door as he opened it.

Cinching the belt on her robe, Angel closed the door behind her and ran down the hall.

When she flung open the apartment door, her father's fist glanced over the wood and nearly hit her in the nose.

"Dad! What are you doing here so early?"

Panting in a frightening way, he scowled. "What am I doing here? You don't answer your phone or cell phone all night and you ask me what I'm doing here? Where have you been all night?"

Her heart skipped a beat. Beads of sweat covered her father's forehead, so like the sweat that had appeared on her mother's forehead when her heart attack had struck.

Ten years. Would she ever get over that day?

"I was sleeping."

"Sleeping. Since when do you sleep through the phone ringing?" Pushing past her, he stormed into the kitchen and turned on the faucet.

Angel closed the door and tried to come up with some excuse. "I was really tired."

Holding a glass of water, her father leaned against the sink and stared at her as she tried to walk as casually as possible to the couch. He coughed then downed the glass of water. "You were so tired you didn't hear the phone. You expect me to believe that bull?"

Sitting down on the couch, she curled her feet under her. Felt something dig into her ankle. A flash of heat swept over her face when she realized that Tanner had untied the wrong knot in his haste and she'd left her room with rope tied around one of her ankles.

"Y-you can't come over here and break down my door every time I don't answer the phone, you know," she murmured as she tucked the length of rope hanging over the edge of the couch under her robe.

Her father slammed the glass on the counter.

Angel jumped. Her stomach dropped. "Dad, relax!"

"Where were you? Out with that cowboy? Were you lying when you said he'd left?"

The mention of Tanner somehow calmed her. Angel squared her shoulders. "I think I'm a little too old for this, don't you?"

"A daughter, a *good* daughter, is never too old for her father to expect her home by dawn! That Tucker—"

"*Tanner* has nothing to do with this."

He walked over to her phone's base. Her mouth went dry when he grabbed the cord and pulled it until the jack slid up onto the top of the end table.

"So you were tired. Your mother and I didn't raise our daughter to be a—"

"I think you should leave before one of us says something we'll regret."

He plugged in the jack then stared at her. "I was worried."

He looked so forlorn. So damn lonely.

"Dad, I haven't had a decent night's sleep all week." Rising, she went to him. Stopped short of hugging him for fear he'd catch some scent of her and Tanner.

Realized she now stood in the middle of the room with the rope trailing behind her. "I just needed to sleep."

She took his arm and led him toward the door. A subtle tug on her ankle sent her heart slamming against her ribs. She didn't dare look down to see if her father stood on the rope.

Trying to hold his gaze with a bright smile, she cupped his cheek. "And I'm still beat. Can we talk about this later?"

"Don't forget to go see Antonio."

Antonio.

Domineering, take-without-asking Antonio. Even with Tanner's rope dangling from her ankle, even with Tanner's scent filling her lungs, she could almost feel his fingers pressing into her cheek.

A flutter of pleasure shocked her. She needed to see a therapist. Maybe two. At least two before spending another moment alone with Antonio.

"What am I supposed to do? Play nursemaid?" *Play?* The flutter returned with a vengeance. Snatching her hand away from her father's face, she stepped back and nearly lost her balance when her father's foot on the rope held her right leg in place.

"It's the least you could do. You brought that cowboy into our lives, after all." He glanced down. His brows furrowed.

"Oh." Angel giggled and feebly tried to tug the rope free. Heat flared over her face.

Her father let out a low rumble that sounded frighteningly like an animal growling. "Tell that cowboy I'll teach him the New York meaning of street justice if I ever see that on you again."

Muttering about cowboys and daughters turning on their father, he stormed past her into the hallway.

Angel watched until he disappeared down the stairs before she closed the door. Pulling her robe away from her chest, she drew in a deep breath. She reeked of sex. Of Tanner. Her eyes burned. Judging by the look on her father's face as he left, he'd never think of her as his angel again.

If this didn't give him a heart attack…her hands shook. No. She wouldn't, couldn't run after him. Not with nothing on except her robe. And she could not run down Madison Ave. with a rope tied to her ankle.

She sniffed. Groaned.

Tiptoeing, she got a towel and made a dash for the bathroom. As she shut the door, she heard her bedroom door creak open. By the time the doorknob on the bathroom door jiggled, she had already turned on the shower and slid under the comforting spray of hot water.

She heard the clink of metal a moment before the door swung open. Peeking out from behind the curtain, she took in the sight before her. Tanner stood naked in the bathroom, his cock jutting out toward her. She drank in every inch of his fine body. When he turned to drape the towel he'd brought in over the towel bar, she winced. Scratches marred his back.

"I believe in preserving water whenever I can," he drawled, winking.

"Preserving is good," she said then let out a long, tremulous breath. "He saw the rope."

"I noticed it wasn't tied to the bedpost, but you'd already left the room. You okay?"

Unable to voice just how much it hurt to know that she'd tarnished her father's image of her, she nodded.

He slid the curtain aside and gazed down the length of her body. "Not sore from last night?"

Feeling as if he touched her wherever his gaze alit, she shook her head and backed up until the spray of water washed away the warm tears sliding down her cheeks.

"He saw the rope, Tanner."

Tanner stepped into the shower. The silken head of his cock grazed her thigh. "I hate to say this, but I think we need to put off our plans for today and spend some time with your Dad. I wouldn't want the man to hate me."

"I think it's too late for that."

"It's never too late to make amends, Angel."

"You don't know my father. Maybe I should try to catch up with him and try to explain."

"You're a grown woman, Angel. He doesn't see it because you never act like one with him."

"Excuse me? I do too." She looked at the water swirling around the drain. "You don't understand."

"And you treat him like he's a…a…damn, all I can think of is the way an overprotective mother might treat her kid. Like he'll break."

Angel dragged in a deep breath. "Tanner, for ten years we've only had each other."

Calloused fingers gripped her nipples and tugged her closer until she felt his hard cock press into her stomach. "Well, now you have me. Time to throw away your toys and show Daddy his girl's all grown up."

Angel pouted and rose up onto her toes until she felt the heat of his cock blanket her clit. "My toys?"

Tanner's deep, rumbling laughter filled the bathroom and vibrated through her. "Don't worry. I have some I think you might like."

Feeling more empowered than she ever had before, Angel told herself her father would survive another day. She licked a drop of water from Tanner's chin.

"How about you show me why I don't need my toys."

A few minutes later, just as Tanner pressed her against the tile and brought his mouth to hers, the doorbell rang again.

"It can't be my father."

The old fear returned. It was the police. The paramedics.

Shoving aside the shower curtain, Tanner stepped out and handed her a towel. "Wanna bet?"

Chapter Six

"I figured, since I was already in the neighborhood, I'd go with you to Antonio's."

Angel plucked a lock of wet hair from her cheek and tossed it to the side. "I'm not going."

"He's helpless and it's just as much your fault as that cowboy's. Now get dressed and do what's right."

Once again standing in the living room while Tanner hid in her bedroom, once again thwarted in her attempt to rediscover the pleasure of Tanner's touch, Angel wanted nothing more than to shove her father out of her apartment and lock the door.

Instead, she clenched her fists and snapped, "What do you expect me to do? Hold him while he takes a leak?"

Crossing himself, her father stared up at the ceiling. "Your mother must be rolling over in her grave, hearing you talk like that."

"Dad, stop turning Mom into a saint. She wasn't religious and she cursed like a truck driver!"

"Angel Roselli, don't you dare speak ill of your mother."

Tears glazed his eyes like they always did when he or anyone mentioned her mother. Usually, the sight broke her heart. Usually, she'd do anything to make him smile, but this time, Angel felt her anger rise.

"I was not speaking ill of her. I loved that she didn't care what people thought and that she spoke her mind. The only thing that bothered me was the way she never let on how much she hated the bak—"

She shut her mouth, almost biting her tongue, but her

father's face told her he'd heard the unspoken word.

"She...she hated the bakery? She never complained to me. How was I supposed to know she hated Roselli's?" He dropped down onto the couch and stared out the window.

"No, she didn't. I was just mad. I-I...I'll go get dressed. Okay?" Running from the room, Angel mentally slapped herself for revealing the one secret her mother had ever told her. The bedroom door flung open just as her fingers touched the doorknob.

Tanner grabbed her wrist and dragged her into the bedroom. Slamming the door, he stared at her with eyes filled with rage.

"You are not going to that man's apartment." His voice, though low, left no doubt in her mind that he expected no argument.

"What the hell is going on here? First my father orders me around and now you?" She shoved past him and went to her closet. Rummaging through her sundresses, she purposely searched for one that would annoy both of the men bullying her.

"You've been following your father's every order since I've met you. The man is no better than a snake. No, a pimp! He's willing to offer you up to that creep just so he can have a baker for a son-in-law."

"Don't you dare call my father a pimp. He has been there for me since my mother died." Her voice cracked.

She could still hear her mother's weak voice whispering in her ear moments before she died. A revelation that she'd hated wasting her life in Roselli's Bakery. A plea that Angel not allow her father to chain her to the bakery, that she not spend all her time elbow-deep in dough.

She'd managed to get Saturdays off. Not an easy task considering how busy weekends were, but she'd insisted until her father finally agreed. Weddings and other catered affairs managed to draw her into the bakery two to three Saturdays a month, but she didn't mind. Tears burned her eyes. She didn't.

"How many men has your father welcomed into your life?"

Angel jumped at the sound of his voice coming from just over her shoulder. "That's none of your business."

"No? Then tell me this. When we first met, your father and Antonio arrived to take you to your 'father-daughter' lunch, right?"

She knew what he'd ask next. She'd asked herself the same thing. "I don't want to discuss this, Tanner."

Tanner slid between her and the closet and crossed his arms over his chest. "Who manned the bakery, Angel? Did he close it so Antonio could woo you over lunch?"

She opened her mouth to defend her father. Closed it when she could find no other reason for Antonio's appearance that day.

"Did he ever close it for you? For your prom? A birthday? A date with a guy you were crazy about? Oh wait, that's not possible. You told me yourself that you put in too many hours to date. So tell me, did he ever close the sacred Roselli's Bakery for you?"

"Get out of my way." She refused to look him in the eyes. Knew he'd see the impact of him voicing her own doubts and complaints about her father putting her second to the bakery.

"I'll take that as a no."

"You can take it any way you want, cowboy. I'm—"

"Listen, Angel, I will not allow—"

"Not allow? Not allow?"

How she wished they were alone in the apartment and she could scream at the top of her lungs. Instead, she snatched the sundress she'd worn the day she'd met Tanner and felt a surge of power when his eyes narrowed and focused on the scant dress.

"You have no right to tell me what I can or can't do. Who

do you think you are?"

Tanner's brows arched then furrowed so close together over the bridge of his nose, they nearly met. "I'm your first, that's who I am. And I'll be your last. Now march out there and tell your father you're not going."

"First, Tanner. Not last. First. Some women can't even remember the name of their first, so don't go making more out of this than there is or thinking you're special! Maybe I want a chance with Antonio. Maybe I want a chance with the next man I meet!"

His massive chest rose and fell like a lava bubble rising higher and higher with each burst of hot air, a lava bubble ready to burst and scald anyone foolish enough to linger and watch.

Backing away, she untied the sash on her robe. "Turn around."

"What?" A muscle along his jaw twitched.

"I have to dress. Turn around."

"Like hell—"

"Angel?"

Her father's soft voice set her into motion. Flinging her robe off, she tossed it onto the floor and slid the sundress over her head.

"I want you out of here when I get home, cowboy," she whispered then ran for the door before he could reply.

As the door closed behind her, she realized she forgot to put on underwear, but she would rather leave the house commando than return to her room and Tanner. Taking her father's hand, she followed him down the hall.

Outside, as she and her father hailed a cab, Angel felt a cool breeze flutter up her legs. The memory of Tanner's lips planting butterfly kisses on her inner thighs last night nearly sent her running back into his arms. She might have if a cab hadn't pulled up.

Staring out the window as the cab pulled away, she saw the curtain in her bedroom window move. Would he be there when she returned?

She doubted it.

The silence in the cab grated on her nerves and allowed Tanner's accusations against her father to replay over and over in her head. To make matters worse, since her slip about her mother hating her role as the baker's wife, a wall now stood firmly between her and her father.

She'd heard the first bricks fall into place when he'd caught sight of the rope tied around her ankle. She might have broken through that wall, might have reinforced the bond they'd formed over the years alone, but she had seen her father's face harden when she'd mentioned her mother, had seen the mortar land between each brick, solidifying the wall.

Lines of worry she'd never noticed before made her father look so old. In the silence, his breathing seemed more labored. Over the last month, he'd somehow lost control of his sugar intake and had too many close calls. One mishap after another at the bakery, including cannoli cream that always soured for no apparent reason, kept him on pins and needles. Now she had to add to his woes with that slip.

"You okay, Dad?" She reached out and laid her hand on his.

Shuttered eyes focused on something over her shoulder. "I knew. I always knew."

She barely heard his admission, knew without asking what he meant. "How could you? You said she never complained."

A sad smile, the tremulous curve of lip while tears shimmered in his eyes, told her all she needed to know.

Her mother had complained. Memories arose, memories of late-night arguments between her mother and father, memories she'd buried over the years.

He let out a wheezing breath. "She wanted out of the city.

When she was in labor, she cried and begged me to sell the bakery. She knew she'd have no time for you. I didn't even give her that. One night, you woke up from a nightmare. When your mother went to comfort you, you cried and cried for Mrs. Catalino. I never saw your mother so heartbroken. I almost sold that damn bakery then."

Angel squeezed his hand. What else could she do? Years of hearing how that bakery had made it through generation after generation, years repeating that the bakery came first had ingrained in her the same love and hate for the family business. She cupped his furrowed cheek. "And be the Roselli to topple the empire? I don't think so."

Her father's large hand covered hers and held it in place. "I knew you'd understand, Angel. You always understood."

Not true, but she kept silent.

"Don't you see, Angel? Antonio understands too. That man wrote me a year ago asking to come and work for us, to help us with, in his words, 'the great Roselli Bakery'."

"You said he asked after seeing my picture."

The cab pulled up to the curb in front of the run-down tenement Antonio called home.

"Huh? Oh well, when I went to Italy last fall, he did. Then he wrote." Her father stepped out of the cab and held out his hand. "Give him a chance, Angel. His tiramisu can push Roselli's back to the top of the list and knock these damn gourmet franchises right off the block."

"How'd you meet him?" She took his hand.

"Hm...he worked in your cousin Sergio's bakery. In Capri." Her father chuckled. "Treated me like a goddamn celebrity!"

A tall, voluptuous woman with black hair, light brown eyes and pouting lips nearly shoved Angel to the ground in her attempt to claim the cab. A babble of Italian filtered out through the open window as the cab pulled away.

Coughing from the strong perfume left in the woman's

wake, Angel frowned at the back of the cab until it merged into the traffic bottlenecked at the corner. "That was odd."

Walking to the steps leading to a basement apartment, her father swatted his hand in the direction of the street. "What, that woman? She just wanted to make sure she got the cab."

Wrinkling her nose from the smell of urine, she waited on the bottom step as her father rang the doorbell.

"Dad, she spoke to the cabbie in Italian. And no one else seems to be looking for a cab."

The door opened with a whining creak. The smell of garlic and Antonio's musky cologne mingled with the woman's perfume. Her stomach churned. Looking bedraggled in a gray tattered robe, Antonio stood in the doorway of the dark apartment and stared at them as if they were strangers. He rubbed a bandaged hand over his stubble-covered jaw and frowned.

"I'm not really up to company at the moment."

Angel felt her mouth drop open. Not really up to company at the moment? While his accent was still as strong as before, it appeared Antonio had picked up quite a bit of English in a very short time. "Have you taken a cl—"

"Antonio, my son, you look terrible!" Her father wrapped his arm around her waist and brought her out from behind him. "Angel insisted I bring her over to help you out."

Eyes that a moment earlier had looked more wary than welcoming lit up. "She did?"

Her father gave her a slight shove through the doorway. Antonio held the screen door open, leaving little room for her to pass by and ensuring that her bare arm rode the waves of muscles covering his chest. The strange woman's perfume followed them into the apartment and seemed to overpower any other scent.

The hum from the fluorescent lights hanging from frayed wires drew her attention up to a water-stained ceiling. Turning, she continued to stare at them, counting, trying to keep her mind off the feel of those muscles and of her dress skimming over her bare butt.

One glance down told her that Antonio's gaze strayed to the slight bumps of her nipples. His attention unnerved her. Reminded her that she wore no underwear and left her wondering if he wore any under his robe. She returned her attention upward and counted stains on the ceiling. A move she considered safer than dealing with a beautiful, half-clad, muscle-bound Italian who knew just how to look into a woman's eyes.

A move she regretted the moment she slammed into Antonio. Firm, rippling muscles crushed her breasts. Arms of steel encircled her waist. The hard ridge that told so much pressed into her stomach.

A face that would make any woman swoon blocked out the ceiling.

The scent of the perfume the woman at the cab wore wafted up from Antonio's body. Angel wrinkled her nose. "I saw a woman when we pulled up."

Antonio stared into her eyes a moment before answering. "My cousin."

"She's beautiful. You never mentioned a cousin."

"Are you jealous of my cousin?" Breaking out in a deep, dimpled smile, he lowered his head until his mouth almost met hers.

Forcing herself to remain still, Angel laughed. She found Antonio handsome with his chocolate eyes, chiseled face and dimples, but she couldn't care less whether he had one or one hundred women. "Should I be?"

"I can see it in your eyes. You do want Antonio, but we must wait. Your Papa must go," Antonio whispered.

She would have laughed or yanked free of his embrace or even snorted, but he shifted ever so slightly. Rock skimmed over nipples still tender from Tanner's mouth. That ridge nudged a little deeper into her stomach and bathed it with heat while his hands skimmed down her back, over her buttocks then back up her hips to her waist. The look on his face told her that he knew she wore the sundress and nothing more.

"*Mi amore*, you *do* want Antonio."

"L-look, An—"

Lips traced the whorl of her ear. The moist tip of his tongue flicked the sensitive skin behind her ear reminding her of how Tanner's tongue had tortured her clit. Thoughts scattered. Pleasure tingled in a sweet circle around her clit.

Silently cursing her wayward body, Angel pushed free of his arms. "I-I really can't stay...I really must meet...the...ah...man coming to repair the display."

"No, you stay with Antonio, Angel."

Struggling to break free of Antonio's hold, she glanced over her shoulder at her father and sent him a look she hoped he'd understand. "No, Dad, I really have to go. Look at the time."

Winking, her father backed toward the door. "I'll take care of everything. You just take care of Antonio here."

"Dad, wait."

Her father turned and with a brisk wave over his shoulder left. The moment the door shut, Antonio let out a low, rumbling growl. Tanner's words rang in her ears. She felt like her father had just given her up as a sacrifice to the god of bakeries.

Angel felt something deep in her heart twist. Ice-cold fingers wrapped around it and squeezed. If only she could hate her father. If only she could walk away and never look back. Be free to go where she wanted, do what she pleased. Say and do everything she'd been bottling up all these years.

"I know you are ready, *mio pico* tigress, but I must shower. Have some of the wine in the cabinet next to the, ah...*frigorifero*? It is from my grandpapa's vineyard."

Angel could only watch as he took off his robe, revealing

every beautiful detail of his finely sculpted body. Well, not every detail. But the ten-man tent in his boxers had her wondering if Tanner's Long John had just met its match.

Those damn tingles started up again when he turned and hopped out of his boxers as he strode down the hall.

Wondering how a man could have a butt that didn't jiggle in the least, she made her way around the narrow island. The kitchen was no more than a few cabinets, a tiny sink, toaster oven and narrow refrigerator. Glancing at an open wine bottle on the counter, she went to the cabinet he'd mentioned and found a half-filled, blue wine bottle. She grabbed one of the two tumblers in the drain board.

Watching the deep burgundy wine fill the glass, she tried to wipe the sight of Antonio's body from her mind. She succeeded but only after downing a whole glass of the worst homemade wine she'd ever tasted.

She frowned down at her empty tumbler, glanced at the bottle of merlot on the counter, then gritted her teeth and refilled her glass with Antonio's grandfather's wine. As she took another sip of the bitter wine, she saw Tanner's face when she'd told him he meant nothing to her and should leave. "Damn cowboy. Had to go and ruin everything by acting like such a jerk. One time and he thinks he owns me."

Clenching the glass in her hands, she stared across the living room at the feet of the people walking past the window. Shoes of every kind and size held her attention for all of five minutes before thoughts of Tanner once again took over.

He'd said that he'd come here for a wife. She laughed. Glanced around as if someone had seen, then cursed. Even if she believed him, the idea was ridiculous. She could never leave New York. Her father. Roselli's. Even if she could, Tanner would return to Texas long before they had enough time to discover if they were even meant to spend the rest of their lives together.

No. He was her first. Nothing more.

The sound of the shower caught her ear. Imagining Antonio's body with water streaming down it, she groaned and took a gulp of wine. If she remained here, he would be her second. Guilt struck followed by anger.

"No way I'm going to fall for the first guy I spread my legs for."

Taking the blue bottle and her glass to the lumpy, floral couch, she plopped down and sipped as she listened to Antonio's surprisingly good voice belt out an Italian ballad. Holding her glass up in the direction of the bathroom, she nodded. "Not when there's prime meat like you around."

Sitting in Antonio's apartment in nothing but a scant sundress, recalling the way he'd kissed her at the bakery, she wondered why she didn't just get up and leave while she could. She didn't have to be a genius to know that Antonio would take all he could without so much as asking. She sipped the odd-tasting wine, felt the warmth flow down her throat then fan out. A feeling of lethargy seeped into her arms and legs.

Fantasies too bizarre to admit to even Tanner, fantasies that had become all too unfulfilling when she had only her vibrators to share them with, filled the time she sat waiting for Antonio's return.

She had no doubt that Antonio wanted her. He would be rough, but she had no doubt that for the sake of his chance to become the next king of the Roselli Empire, he'd never harm her.

Her heart stuttered when she recalled how he'd dug his fingers into her face in the bakery.

No, he wanted to marry the queen of Roselli's. A sliver of dread slid down her spine. She touched her cheek. Her fingers trembled. Lifting the glass, she took another gulp, calming her nerves.

Antonio would take and demand, and she had to know if living a fantasy would feel as good as imagining one.

By the time she heard the shower stop, she had downed half of her third glass and relived every decadent fantasy plus some new ones. She convinced herself that Tanner had moved way too quickly toward commitment.

After years with only her hand on the controls of her toys, she longed to lie back and give that job to someone else. In the bedroom. Only in the bedroom. Antonio and Tanner apparently wanted that right in and out of the bedroom.

Still, she could think of little else than running back to her apartment and begging Tanner to stay. Her body had spent the last few minutes recalling every touch and now strummed with desire, but her heart ached from wanting Tanner. With Tanner, she would find it harder and harder to deny him anything. Like her father. She'd leave one prison and move into another.

Antonio was safer. He wanted to rule her, but she would have no problem standing up to him. He couldn't hurt her.

At least not the way Tanner could just by leaving. He was probably at LaGuardia right now waiting for a plane back to Texas. Her throat closed. Gritting her teeth, she stopped herself from bolting out of the apartment and running all the way to the airport.

"Control freak," she reminded herself, then greeted Antonio with a dazzling smile. Angel shifted over to give him room on the couch.

Wearing only snug-fitting sweat shorts that revealed his impressive size, he winked then poured more wine into her glass. "So, you like my grandpapa's wine?"

"It's delicious. I drank way too much already." Giggling, she realized she was drunk and wondered what the hell she was doing. Knew exactly what she was doing. With the a little help from an old winemaker in Italy, Angel was finally letting go. "But don't get any ideas. I can hold my wine."

Leaning over, he brushed his lips against hers and murmured, "We'll see, *mi amore*."

So what if she had no intention of marrying Antonio or her cowboy? She was young, no longer a virgin and so damn turned-on. Leaning forward, she reached for her glass. The room swam but only enough to give her pause. Growing up on wine, she rarely felt the effects so soon.

"This wine is del...del...really good. I brought out a glass for you." Glancing down at the coffee table, she frowned. "I could have sworn I did."

Antonio sat down beside her. The soft cushion sank in, bringing her down with it into the crook of his arm. "No, no wine for me. Finish yours and then we will talk. *Si?*"

"I'm perfectly capable of talking and drinking." But she finished her wine and held out her glass. "So, what do you want to talk about?"

"Why you, *mio pico* tigress." Instead of taking the glass, Antonio refilled it.

His warm hand slid up her thigh, under her dress then stopped just short of touching the tender flesh that yearned for attention.

A tiny alarm went off in her head, but she couldn't seem to focus on it enough to pay it much heed. Too many others were ringing throughout her body. Fire alarms that demanded someone soothe a burning hunger she'd never experienced before.

Oddly, with so many wicked sensations rippling through her, she felt lifeless, limbless. Angel stared at the glass, glanced at Antonio. That power she had always found so irresistible shimmered around him. His dark eyes promised complete domination. Torn between her feelings for Tanner and her desire to live out fantasies she doubted Tanner would understand, she took a gulp.

"Tell me what you want, Angel. Let me fulfill your most secret fantasy." His lips took possession of her neck and branded every inch his.

Again, her fantasies. First Tanner, now Antonio. Fantasies

she had no right to experience, no right to even imagine. Fantasies a little too much wine and a man like Antonio could bring to life. "My fantasies? Aren't we moving a little fast?"

"I see the wild woman hiding behind this angel. You want so much. Tell Antonio. I give you everything."

A tiny mewl escaped through her lips when his hand lifted her leg and draped it over his bare thigh.

"I don't have any fantasies."

His thumb drew an ever-widening circle on her inner thigh.

"Your dirtiest fantasy. One you wouldn't dare reveal. Everyone has fantasies, Angel. Why not live them?"

As she leaned her head back onto his arm and gave him more access to her neck, she let out a rueful sigh. "I can't."

"*Si*, my little *puttana*, you can. I understand. You want what all women want."

She felt his hand rise from her thigh and would have grabbed it and brought it back if she'd had the energy, but her arms wouldn't follow directions and his mouth chose that moment to move down over her collarbone.

Something fluttered over her breasts. Something soft, almost like a feather. His lips followed, finding bared skin no matter how low they meandered. His moist, hot mouth covered her nipple. Her bare nipple. The warm breath enticing her other breast told her that what she'd felt skim down her breasts earlier was her dress. She couldn't imagine how the man had untied the halter without her feeling it. Teeth grated over nubs still tender from Tanner. Gritting her teeth against the wave of guilt almost sending her running back to Tanner, she told herself that he had only used her to fill in his time in New York. That the man beside her offered more in the way of a future.

She closed her eyes saw Tanner's dopey grin when he had said he was looking for a wife. Yeah, right. Angel let out a snort.

Antonio raised his head. "Angel?"

"Don't stop," she spat out, angry that Tanner had managed to worm his way into her finally living out her fantasy.

Antonio chuckled then kissed her until she nearly passed out from lack of air. His lips left hers. Something cool replaced them.

"Here, take one more sip. Then I will let you tell me how to please you."

Angel opened her mouth to tell him to wait, to slow down.

That little alarm grew shriller, but before she could say anything, the warm liquid filled her mouth. It tasted slightly different. Delicious but now with a bite to it she couldn't place. The more she sipped, the closer his hand came to her weeping pussy.

She stopped.

His hand stopped.

She grabbed the glass, raised it to her mouth, felt some wine splash onto her breasts.

Realizing she was drunk, she considered leaving, but Antonio licked the wine from her breasts, suckled it from her nipples and, dammit, she couldn't deny that she wanted this. No control, no way to flick the off switch if the sensations Antonio awakened or the intensity of her orgasm frightened her. Angel and the wine had placed her fantasy in Antonio's hands.

A sharp nip on her nipple shocked her.

"Spread your legs for Antonio," he ordered in a husky, demanding voice that left no doubt she would soon get to live her most decadent fantasies.

She spread her legs apart.

"Finish your wine, Angel. All of it."

Again, an order rather than a request as if he knew just

what she wanted, what she craved.

Swallowing the last of the wine, Angel felt his hand shove each of her legs aside until her thigh muscles hurt. He resumed his assault on her breasts, nipping and biting as his hands yanked her dress out from under her and shoved it up to her waist.

Fingers caressed, pinched and kneaded her inner thighs and mound, always moving closer to her moist flesh, always veering away just when she was sure she'd finally find relief. Loud moans filled her ears. More of the bitter wine filled her mouth. God, she'd never wanted a man or wine so much.

Antonio offered her every decadent fantasy.

The wine offered blessed relief from her guilt.

She greedily sucked down every drop. Cried in despair when his hand once again denied her.

Fingers suddenly took possession of her nipples. Antonio's gorgeous face hovered over hers. Pain shot up through her breasts, shocking her with its intensity. She opened her mouth to dispel any notion he had that her fantasy included pain, but before she could utter a word, his deep voice wove another web of desire that immobilized her.

"Tell me your most secret fantasy or I will stop."

She tumbled back to last night she'd waited, tied to the post, for Tanner's return. She could almost feel the ropes scraping her skin every time she writhed in anticipation of what he would do to her. Last night, Angel had been sure Tanner would bring her fantasies to life, but she had been denied the pleasure of his dominance.

"Bondage. And I don't want...any control." A sob choked off her words. "I'm so tired of being in control."

"Are you sure, my little whore? You may go now and never live out your fantasy. If you stay, then I will use you in ways you can not imagine and you will have no say, no more chances to leave. So, do you want to stay?"

"God forgive me, yes."

The room shifted. She closed her eyes.

Another slight nipping pain shot through both of her nipples and ricocheted down until it ended with a tingle between her legs. She awaited Antonio's next move but when none came, she opened her eyes. At first she wondered who had covered the stained ceiling with clean white paint, but then, bit by bit, the room came into focus and she realized she was once again tied, spread-eagled, to a bed.

But not her bed. Not her room.

Not Tanner.

Her dress gone, her freedom gone, she still could not work up enough energy to fight her current situation either mentally or physically.

Because of the wine?

No. Because she had no desire to escape whatever Antonio had planned.

Squirming against the restraints, she looked around the sparsely furnished room and found Antonio bending over the bed, his hand between her legs. Something wet and cool covered her skin and delved deep inside her pussy. Mere seconds later a burning itch consumed her. Raising her head she watched in horror as he dipped a round pastry brush in a bottle and slopped the clear liquid over and into her anus. Her nipples, snagged and pulled by a thin rope tied to the bedposts, were the next introduced to whatever he had in that bottle. The itch created a web deep inside her, a web of undeniable need.

She would have said something. Asked him if she'd passed out. More likely begged him to stop what he was doing and soothe the burning itch, but a ball strapped to her mouth kept her silent. Tears filled her eyes and blurred Antonio's triumphant expression when he finally looked up at her. Tears of frustration. Of need.

This scene, in all its immoral entirety, turned her on almost as much as the solution he continued to paint over every erogenous zone. Jutting her hips up when he moved his head lower, she groaned and silently pled for his mouth, but he continued to sweep the brush over her again and again.

The burning intensified, became unbearable.

"Ah, so you are awake." Antonio stared down at her. "I checked out that tiny computer you keep in your bag. Do not look so surprised. You would always look up from it with red cheeks. So, my little angel is not an angel after all?"

The room seemed to blur behind Antonio. Every scene from every book played out in her mind and fed the fires coursing through her body.

Antonio chuckled. "I knew you would ask me to tie you up."

Ask?

Raising her head, she watched his disappear between her legs. She could feel his warm breath waft over her most sensitive skin. Instead of extinguishing the fire, his breath only served to fan the flames and plunge her into a mindless whirlpool of need.

The ropes bit into her flesh as she struggled to raise her hips high enough for one touch of his tongue. Something trickled down her wrist. She glanced up and discovered the ropes had broken her skin. Blood dripped onto the stark white pillowcase.

She didn't care. Nothing mattered but blessed relief. When he moved away from the bed she followed him with her eyes and dropped her hips to the mattress.

"You like toys, my little *puttana*?"

Angel almost swallowed the ball when he held up a large black bag bearing the logo of her favorite store.

"I am very good at hearing. Especially when you go out back at the bakery and chat with your friends about all your favorite toys."

His eyes gleamed.

A sliver of fear skipped down Angel's spine. Something was wrong, terribly wrong. Antonio did not look like a man driven by desire. And he kept glancing over his shoulder. At what? Tossing her head from side to side, she tried to see what kept drawing his attention but could find nothing in the little bit of the room she was able to catch sight of.

She wanted Tanner. With Tanner, somehow she knew she would fear nothing. She trusted him.

Antonio's hand slid into the bag. "The problem with toys is that they really don't listen. A man, you can say stop and he just might. If he believes you really want him to." Withdrawing a new, larger, fatter multifunction vibrator than the one Angel had broken, he turned it on with the flick of the switches. "But if I put this vibrator to work, I bet even if I removed your gag and you begged it to stop, it would just keep on going and going until you passed out."

Watching him cover the vibrator with gel and some of his solution, Angel's struggles grew more frantic. She just couldn't decide if she struggled to get away or get closer to whatever he had planned. The sweet sound of that buzzing worked on her body like the bell worked on Pavlov's dogs. The head of the vibrator nudged her anus. Fear stilled her struggles. Shaking her head, she yelled, but the gag only let out a gurgling groan.

Inch by burning inch, the vibrator stretched her tender flesh. Sweat broke out on her body when the strange, unsettling sensations followed its path until Antonio released it and straightened.

"In to the hilt. You're going to make such a good wife, Angel." He reached into the bag again, then after rummaging through it, cursed and dumped its contents between her legs. Angel barely noticed. Vibrations filled her anus and only served to exasperate the burning itch of the solution.

The sound of tape ripping and then the feel of Antonio taping the vibrator to her excited and terrified her at the same time.

No control? No pulling her vibrator out just when the pleasure reached that unbearable peak?

God forgive her, but she wanted this. She'd deal with the wife bit later.

Taking his time, repainting her with the solution whenever her squirming and moaning subsided, he placed vibrating butterflies to her clit and nipples. Then he turned on something she couldn't see. When he shifted it on the bed, she felt the head of a powerful vibrator nudging less than an inch into her then receding. After a few more nudges, she pulled against the restraints to slide down the mattress. Every nudge promised full penetration and amazing vibrations. But it would always leave her too soon.

"Have you ever tried a fucking machine? It is very expensive. I bought the largest one." Antonio pulled a vanity stool up to the foot of the bed. Looking at his watch, he nodded. "I think I'll just sit here and watch. An hour. No more, no less. Can you wait an hour, Angel?"

The nudges drove her mad. She shook her head, raised her hips.

Antonio frowned. "Keep those hips in place or I'll make it two hours."

She dropped her hips.

"Close your eyes. Enjoy every sensation." Again an order barked out.

She closed her eyes.

"I'll be right back. Do not open your eyes, Angel. You don't want to make me…"

His voice faded as the first orgasm hit, rose higher and higher, past the point where she'd normally shove her vibrators away, past the point Tanner had brought her to. Past the point of caring when he strode in the room and found her eyes open.

Before she could react to what she saw behind him, another orgasm hit with bone-jarring force. And another.

"Luigi, you'll have to forgive my fiancée, she's very naughty." Antonio walked over to the dresser.

A tall, young man standing in the doorway licked his lips.

Her mind shut down for a moment before filling with one lewd image after another. As if he read her mind, Luigi's grin broadened and propelled Angel into yet another orgasm.

Something clicked. A low whirring sound followed, but she couldn't tear her eyes from Luigi. Sending a pleading look at Antonio, she yelled against the gag. Shame heated her cheeks. Desire sent more evidence of her arousal pouring from her pussy.

Antonio blocked her view. Lifting the gag, he slid a straw into her mouth. "Drink," he whispered, "do not stop until I say to."

Wanting the wine to bank her desires, to block out the shame engulfing her and maybe even make her pass out before she degraded herself even more, Angel sucked and swallowed the bitter wine until only air entered her mouth.

"Good girl." He tossed the gag to the floor.

Both men stared down at whatever kept nudging into her pussy.

"Do you want to leave, Angel?" Antonio's voice boomed.

Luigi reached down between her legs. The vibrating head delved an inch deeper. The fire returned. The itch magnified.

Emphatically shaking her head from side to side, she closed her eyes. God forgive her, but she couldn't say no. Not when every nerve in her body demanded she go on. Not when this might be her only chance to experience pleasures she'd only imagined.

"We can do what we please? Me and Luigi?"

She moaned, nodded her head. Closed her eyes tighter. The ropes on her nipples grew even tauter. Other than the strange whirring, no one made a sound. Hot mouths covered her nipples. While they set fire to her body, they sucked away the solution and soothed her at the same time.

Chapter Seven

ಸಿ

Tanner remained by the window long after the cab carrying Angel and her father turned the corner. Unable to give up and leave, he paced the length of the apartment. Gut instinct told him that Angel was heading for trouble. Gut instinct demanded he charge down the street like an idiot, lasso his wild angel and drag her back home.

Back at the window, he rested his forehead against the glass. "Damn you, Angel Roselli."

A while later, he called her cell phone.

"Angel, ah, can not talk right now."

Tanner dropped the phone at the sound of Antonio's voice. Snatching it before it hit the floor, he yelled, "Put her on the phone, Antonio."

"Sorry, cowboy, she is impatient for me."

"You're full of shit."

"Hm…good, you listen. Then you understand."

A rustling followed. Gripping the phone, afraid to move and lose the signal, Tanner stood rigidly in the middle of the living room. The rustling stopped. Moans and a familiar buzzing set his nerves on edge. Antonio's voice almost sent the phone from his clenched hands again.

"Take off her gag," Antonio yelled.

Gag? Tanner's heart skipped a beat. And who the hell else was Antonio talking to?

The moans grew louder.

"You want Antonio to fuck you, Angel?"

"Yes, please. Oh, please." Angel's voice, raspier than he'd

ever heard it, weak, slurred and pleading, sliced into his heart. "I can't take it anymore."

Tanner's eyes burned. A sharp pain shot through his chest.

"You have to take Luigi too. No Luigi. No Antonio."

The moans continued. Swiping at a tear, Tanner prayed.

"No nodding! I want to hear you beg," Antonio's demand was not nearly as deafening as Angel's abject cry.

"Okay! I'll beg. I'll do anything you ask. Please, Antonio! It hurts so much!"

Hurts? "What the fuck are you doing to her, Antonio?"

But Antonio didn't answer. Instead, his voice sounded as if it came from a distance.

"Lift her up, Luigi. You get the back door. I'll take the front."

The groans that followed tore into Tanner.

"No," he yelled and flung the phone against the wall.

The phone shattered but Angel's groans seemed to fill the apartment.

He heard them as he ran out of the building. Outside, standing on the sidewalk as pedestrians stared and made a wide berth around him, he could still hear them. Tears blurred his vision. Angel, the Angel he knew, couldn't have wanted Antonio all this time. And what the fuck was another man doing there? Something was wrong. Her cry for Antonio battered him. Tanner halted at the curb.

Not a cry of ecstasy. She sounded more like someone who had been tortured. And her voice. Her slurred speech.

His stomach clenched. Bile flooded his mouth. He ran out into the street and stopped the first cab he saw by jumping in front of it. As soon as the cab swerved to a stop, Tanner rushed around it, yanked open the door and jumped in.

"What are you crazy? I coulda hit you." The cabbie turned with a scowl that quickly vanished. "You okay, pal?"

"I have to find out where someone went today. She took a cab."

"We don't give out that info, pal."

Reaching over the back of the driver's seat, Tanner snarled into his ear. "She's in trouble, *pal*, so call your dispatcher and get me the address."

Twenty endless minutes later, Tanner stepped out of the cab and rushed down the steps to Antonio's apartment. Through the window, he could see Angel lying on the couch. Her eyelids fluttered then closed, her hand hung down to the floor and her hips rested on the arm of the couch. Standing between her legs, Antonio slammed into her then stilled, his face twisted from climaxing. Tanner took in the scene without stopping and slammed his body into the door. After two tries, the door swung open before he hit it. If years of wrangling cattle hadn't strengthened his legs, he would have tumbled into the apartment.

"I knew you would arrive sooner or later." Stepping back, Antonio grinned, "Oh, I do not think she can do another, cowboy. But come in. Try. Luigi is almost done. I am done. Empty."

Tanner balled all his rage into his fist and sent it flying through Antonio's perfect teeth. Blood splattered. The man now standing between Angel's legs charged, skidded to a halt, then bolted down the hall. Stepping over Antonio, Tanner started after him. A weak moan brought him to a halt.

Angel rolled over into a ball. The hem of her dress rode up and revealed pink handprints on the back of her thighs. Rope burns encircling her wrists and ankles seemed to spread until the entire room swirled beneath a sheer crimson veil.

Muscles Tanner never paid much mind tensed to the point of cramping. Balling both fists, he snapped his head in the direction of Antonio. Still huddled on the floor, Antonio staunched the flow of blood from his mouth with the bottom of his tee shirt. Blood dripped from the saturated material onto the floor and ran in thin rivulets down Antonio's neck. Not enough. No amount of blood would calm the rage consuming Tanner.

He charged, a wild bull thirsting for blood, letting nothing come between him and his crimson target.

A soft whimper from the couch brought him to a screeching halt. Every muscle, every ounce of his being demanded he continue and beat Antonio until...until...

"As soon as I get Angel out of here, I'm coming back and then I'll kill you, you sonofabitch!"

"She wanted us, you fool! She begged us to fuck her!" Antonio staggered to his feet.

Tanner rushed to Angel's side. "Angel? Are you okay, honey?"

Her eyelids fluttered open to mere slits. Lips only he should have ever kissed curved into a soft smile. "Tanner? I..." Her smile faltered, her eyes closed. Another, heartbreaking whimper.

Blinking away the tears blinding him, Tanner bent over Angel and slid his hands under her. She barely stirred. Lifting her as gently as he could, he cradled her against his chest and left the apartment.

He clenched his teeth against the grief consuming him, but her whimpers resumed and shredded his control. Standing in the street with Angel's limp body clutched in his arms, he sobbed uncontrollably as he watched one cab after another slow down then speed off.

"Please! Someone help me," he bellowed after every approaching car.

"Take me home, Tanner."

Angel's soft whisper sent him into the middle of the street. Cars swerved. A minivan halted with its bumper a hairsbreadth away from his legs.

"Please," he choked out through the lump strangling him.

"She's...sick. I need to get her to a hospital."

Angel jerked so suddenly, he nearly dropped her. "No! No hospital!"

"Get in," the young woman in the passenger seat yelled.

Nails dug into his arm and shoulder. "Take me home. No hospital."

The side door of the minivan slid open. A little girl peered out.

"Oh God, no hospital." Angel's hands cupped his face and forced him to meet her gaze. "Please."

Tanner stared down into her terrified doe eyes only a moment before nodding.

* * * * *

Opening her eyes, Angel squinted into the sunlit room. A loud thumping beneath her ear and the warm skin under her cheek triggered a whirlwind of decadent images. Fear held her in its grip. What had she done? What had Antonio? What more did he have planned?

Careful not to move too much, she peered through her lashes at her surroundings.

One by one, the familiar furnishings and floral wallpaper of her bedroom allayed her fears and gave her the strength to raise her head and prove that she snuggled against Tanner in her own bed.

Meeting concerned blue eyes, she released the air trapped in her lungs.

"You all right, Angel mine?" Tanner tucked a stray curl behind her ear.

Nodding, she rested her chin on his chest and struggled to keep her eyes open. "Just a bad dream."

Tanner frowned then leaned forward and kissed her forehead. "That's right, honey. Just a bad dream."

"I'm so tired."

"Go back to sleep, Angel mine." He brushed his knuckles down her cheek while the fingers of his other hand caressed her shoulder.

His gaze never left hers.

Her heart stuttered. That same burning gaze had warmed her soul whenever she had caught her father looking into her mother's eyes. Needing to be sure, she held his gaze and struggled to keep her eyes open.

A mere blink later, she opened her eyes and discovered she now had the bed to herself. The images returned, haunted her, demanded she accept them as reality, but logic and the fact that she lay in her own bed and a deep-rooted ball of fear insisted they were remnants of a nightmare she had no desire to examine.

The sound of glass shattering shot her out of the bed and down the hall. Before she reached the bedroom door, her mind absorbed every twinge of pain from every tender spot on her body. By the time she entered the living room and found Tanner sitting on the couch while images of her wedged between Antonio and Luigi unfolded on the TV, she knew she had lived her nightmare.

Tanner's strangled sobs met her ears and mingled with the screams resounding in her mind, screams demanding release.

She must have screamed out loud. Tanner leapt to his feet and made his way to her in two long strides. His arms, so strong yet trembling, drew her into a crushing embrace.

"Don't look, Angel. Don't listen."

His hands covered her ears, but she still heard every moan, every word. Holding his hands tighter over her ears, she struggled to keep from throwing up or screaming or running back to her room and hiding under her blanket until someone told her that this too was just a bad dream. But she recalled every detail of how her fantasy swirled out of control.

How pleasure turned to pain and desire to shame. She'd wanted to lose control, wanted to live out so many of her darkest fantasies, but Antonio and Luigi had used her in ways even she had not known existed. And all the time, Antonio had reminded her that she'd asked for it, begged.

"He'll pay." Tanner's lips brushed the back of her hand as he spoke. "If it's the last thing I do, I make sure he goes to jail for raping you."

Rape? Her heart slammed into her ribs then plummeted to her stomach.

Rape? She heard Antonio asking her over and over if she wanted to leave, if she wanted him, demanding she ask. She recalled every thought that had raced through her mind when she had first arrived and downed the odd-tasting wine.

Rape?

Struggling against Tanner's hold, she finally let loose the cry that had lodged in her throat. "No!"

Breaking free, she staggered to the coffee table and snatched up the remote. Pressing pause, she froze an image of herself on her knees, her hand stretched out before her, a hungry, frenzied look forever on her face. Jabbing the remote toward the screen, she stared at herself. "Does that look like a woman getting raped?"

"He drugged you." Tanner's hand wrapped around the remote.

Before he could take it away, she yanked the remote free. "I know that. I've drunk enough wines in my life to know when one doesn't taste right! And I can hold a hell of a lot more wine than I drank there! My God, Tanner, I'm Italian. I had wine before I got my first bra." She sucked in a shaky breath.

"That's rape in my book and in any judge's book too."

Tanner reached out to her, but she jumped back before he could touch her. Before her heart led her to lie or do something, anything to keep him.

"Angel, you were drugged."

"I knew!" She felt her face crumple. Hearing the warbled words forced through her sobs only heightened the horror of her admission. "I knew, Tanner. I knew it was either spiked with grain alcohol or something potent. I drank it anyway. Deep down inside, I knew from the first sip."

"You don't understand. When I got there, you couldn't stay conscious long enough..." He backed away, sank down onto the couch. "You...you...knew?" He looked at the TV. Stared for eternal seconds then lowered his head. "You knew he was going to drug you? To use you?"

Self-loathing immobilized her.

"Well?" His harsh bark shocked her into motion.

Rushing up to him, she knelt before him and covered his fisted hands with hers. "I started drinking the wine and knew it tasted a little odd and hit me way too fast. At first, I didn't think drugs. I don't know what I thought he'd done but I knew something wasn't right and I almost left, but...but...by the time I really understood what...I figured why not?"

"W-why not?"

"Don't you see? I could live out my fantasies with Anto...and..." Words failed her.

Condemnation filled his eyes.

"Don't look at me that way."

"And what?" His mouth barely moved.

"I...I've always..." Angel swallowed and stared at the fists trembling beneath her hands. "I wanted—"

Fists unfurled, slid free and, cupping her face in an iron grip, forced her to meet his eyes. "Antonio? You wanted that Italian piece of shit?"

"No! Not Antonio. What he had to offer."

"What the hell are you talking about, Angel? What could he offer that I couldn't? A good raping? Your father's approval? His fucking tiramisu recipe? What the hell could he offer for you to stay and get raped?"

"No control!"

His hands slid down her cheeks and fell onto his lap. "No control?"

Fortified by some unexplainable force that insisted she make him understand, she stood, took his hand and practically dragged him to her room. Dragging her pillowcase full of toys out from under the bed, she dumped the contents on the floor. "Meet my previous boyfriends."

Vibrators, dildos, bullets and anal plugs littered the floor between them.

"So you like toys. What the hell does that have to do with you purposely offering yourself to that creep?" Tanner kicked away a long, fat dildo.

"Control." Sinking down to her knees, Angel stared at her toys. "*I* always decided when to stop, how high to go or what to do. *I* always pulled them out or shut them down when my orgasms reached what *I* believed was just shy of too much to handle."

"You're losing me."

"I knew before Antonio even told me what he planned that for the first time I might know what it felt like to leave the controls in someone else's hand. To go higher than I could ever bring myself." Picking up a bullet, she shoved it back into the pillowcase.

"First time? What about us? That slip your mind?" He squatted in front of her and helped her replace every toy. "What about me, Angel? Did you fake those orgasms?"

"No!" She pushed the bag under the bed and stood. Unable to face him, she sat on the bed and stared down at her hands. "But I have some wicked, unacceptable fantasies, Tanner. Things I could never have asked you to do."

"Like tying you up? Or did you forget about that?"

She stared at his feet. It struck her that another man

would have been long gone. Another man would not have cared why she did what she did. "Not merely tying me up, Tanner. Tying me up and taking every liberty you wanted with me. You wouldn't have done that. You would have been too concerned about whether or not you were hurting me."

"You're damned right. I would have never left those marks on your ankles and wrists."

Smiling though she wanted nothing more than to cry, she rubbed the raw skin on her wrist. "No, you wouldn't have. But Antonio didn't make these marks, Tanner. I did."

She felt him grab her shoulders and force her to stand, but she couldn't bring herself to look up. She'd find disgust in his eyes.

"You made these marks? Dammit, Angel, that only proves my point. You were so drugged you don't even remember what happened."

"I did it! I struggled so hard that I made those ropes cut into my skin."

"Because you wanted to get free!"

Needing him to understand, to see her eyes when she shattered his ideal of who she was, she raised her head. "Because I wanted more. Because they were leaving me with nothing but toys buzzing inside me. Because I...I...wanted them to take control of my body and show me how high I could go. I had such an awful, burning ache—"

"I washed you, Angel. You were covered with shit that burned the heck out of my hands. Your skin was red wherever I found that stuff." He lowered his head and stared into her eyes. "I saw him shoving a fucking brush dripping with it up your...your..."

"It doesn't matter!" Wrenching free, she backed into the bed. "Don't you get it? I liked it! God forgive me, but I liked every minute."

She hated herself, hated Antonio for releasing fantasies that should have remained locked in the recesses of her mind forever. Hated Tanner for refusing to see just how this degraded her.

"You liked it because of what they did?"

She could only nod.

"So, this had nothing to do with you liking Antonio or desiring him more than me?"

She laughed, sobbed. "I won't lie and say Antonio doesn't have a killer body or gorgeous face, but no, it had nothing to do with him. It had to do with me and my need for a therapist." She turned away. "So run back to Texas, cowboy. You came to the wrong place if you're looking for an angel."

Endless minutes passed. Every sound she never noticed before—the cars in the street, the air conditioner, the dripping faucet in her kitchen—now seemed deafening. Tanner's eyes seemed to bore into her back. Her lungs burned for want of air, but she daren't speak for fear that she'd beg him to stay.

"You, Angel mine, have a terrible memory," Tanner murmured in her ear then trailed kisses down her neck. "I told you that first day, I'm in search of an Angel with dirty wings. One who doesn't mind sins of the flesh. I have quite a few nasty fantasies, myself, just waiting to break free."

Ever so slowly, she turned to face him. "I'm damaged goods, Tanner. Antonio didn't wear a condom. For all we know, I could be pregnant or infected."

He took her hands and led her to the bed. "Sit."

Tears filled her eyes, but she could still see that look and feel it warm her soul.

"I don't care either way."

"But—"

"I don't care. We see what happens and then we deal with it, together."

Kisses stole every tear.

Lips of satin glanced over hers. "Now, Angel mine, I have to tell you that none of my fantasies include sharing you with anyone. Is that a problem?"

She slid her arms over his shoulders and gazed up into those baby blues she knew she'd never get enough of. "That was one fantasy I think a girl should only live out once."

"I like it rough. You?"

He looked so serious she giggled and rubbed up against him. "Rough works for me."

"We already know that ropes work for both of us. And I like nothing better than chasing a filly, bringing her down and proving who's boss."

Tingles of pleasure spiraled through her stomach. "Can I talk dirty?"

"Oh, that might force me to take out my whip."

The tingles shot down to her pussy. "You have a whip?"

"Darlin', I'm a cowboy. Remember?"

"What kind?"

"You name it. I got it."

"Shit, Tanner. You cowboys sure know how to charm a lady into bed."

His rich laughter filled the room. Sweeping her up into his arms, he carried her to the bed. "We don't charm them into bed, Angel mine, we just take them there."

The setting sun cast the room in amber light. Angel watched Tanner undress and wondered how she ever found Antonio's body impressive after seeing the perfection of her cowboy.

"Are you planning on making love to me, Tanner?"

"Darlin', I plan on making love to you every second in your presence. But tonight, I think I'll just hold you. That solution about burned you raw."

Not exactly a profession of love, Tanner's words and the way he then joined her and kissed her like she was made of porcelain made her wonder if maybe, just maybe, she could convince him to stay in New York, could convince him to give up his ranch and help her run the bakery.

If not, she'd enjoy every minute they had left and worry about farewells when it was time for him to leave.

She awoke to darkness and the touch of lips on her inner thigh. Fingers smoothed something slick and cool over her clit. The cold ointment gave way to heat. The black shadow of a man arose from between her legs. Angel's muscles tensed. Antonio?

Chapter Eight

A mewl of fear slipped free from Angel's trembling lips. Had she dreamed that Tanner had charged through Antonio's door and rescued her? Angel closed her eyes. Her heart slammed against her ribs. Holding her breath, she awaited Antonio's next move. Shame heated her skin. The mattress dipped between her legs. She could almost hear Luigi snickering, smell his sweat. The sound of her heart beating faster and faster boomed in her ears.

"Talk dirty to me, Angel mine."

Tanner's voice, hoarser and more demanding than she'd ever heard, vanquished the image of Antonio hiding behind the shadow that shrank back down between her legs. The nip of teeth where seconds earlier lips had pressed so tenderly set her pulse racing. She had been so wrong about Antonio. She had an inkling that her Italian Stallion might take her a bit farther than she desired or that he might enjoy being in control a little too much, but she had never imagined Antonio would purposely harm her. How could she trust Tanner? How could she trust any man? Her eyes burned.

She moved to touch Tanner but ropes cinched around her wrists and the headboard held her arms high above her head. A slight tug of her legs told her that Tanner had also ensnared her legs to the bed. "I-I don't think I can do this."

Tanner rubbed his stubbly cheek against her inner thigh. "You don't have to do anything, Angel mine."

Another nip startled her, higher than the last. This time his teeth held on and dug deeper until the sting made her flinch and her soft cry broke the silence embracing them.

"Please, Tanner. I really don't think I can. I don't know if

I'll ever be able to again."

She felt his lips curve into a smile as her skin slid free of his teeth.

"You know, darling, back home we learn how to ride a horse before we can walk. And when we fall, our mamas brush the dirt off our asses then put us right back on those horses. Hell, if they took us in the house and let us relive that fall over and over in our minds, we'd never ride again. Now you just ended up on the wrong horse." He flung her legs over his shoulder then grinned up at her. "Ready to hop back in the saddle?"

Angel stared down the length of her body. "You'll go slow?"

"Not likely. Trust me?"

After a few fortifying breaths, Angel nodded. As if her pussy understood, it gushed in anticipation.

"Brought some of my own toys, Angel mine. Close your eyes and tell me what you feel."

Angel closed her eyes.

A sharp bite to her thigh startled her.

"No nodding. I want to hear your voice. Understand?"

She started to nod then stopped herself. "Okay." A nip to the crease alongside her pussy sent a jolt of sweet pain up to her stomach. "I said, 'Okay!'"

"When you answer me, you will call me Sir." His teeth grazed over her clit. "Do you understand?"

Angel nearly giggled as she softly murmured, "Yes, Sir."

"Welcome to my fantasy, Angel. One I have lived and am in complete control of. One you will accept as your reality from the time the sun sets until it rises."

The strength and determination she heard in his voice sent thrills of pleasure ricocheting throughout her body. Like the bumpers of a pinball machine, every erogenous zone in her body pinged and lit up in response. Had she found the man capable of taking the fantasies she'd hidden in shame? Her time with Antonio had nearly extinguished Angel's burning hunger to explore the darker side of her sexuality. Tanner's voice and all he promised reignited that hunger.

"I'll have no control?" She cringed when her voice cracked from the lingering fear Antonio had planted when she first dared to offer herself into another's hands.

Tanner spoke against her quivering pussy. "You will always have the final say in how far I go, how far I take you. But Angel, you must trust me...completely. Trust that I may not listen to your pleas if I know that only pleasure dwells beyond the point you may feel is too far."

She absorbed his words as his tongue delved deep into her pussy. He would stop if she wanted, but only if he felt she had a valid reason? "I...I thought there was a safeword or something that I could say to make you stop and you had to listen."

"Pick one. A word you will only use when you feel I have crossed the line between pleasure and real pain."

Angel stared down the length of her body at Tanner. His gaze, clear and free of anger or condensation, met hers. "So, if I say...hm...ravioli—"

"Ravioli?" He dropped his face down to her shaved mound.

"I don't see why you find that funny." The vibrations of his laughter rippled through her pussy. "I read that a safeword had to be a word you would never say during a scene. Ravioli is perfect."

He raised his head and stared up at her for a moment. "You're sure? Ravioli?"

"Yes."

"Just remember, think twice before you speak. Once you say it, I'll stop and you'll never know what you missed. I'm not a vibrator you can toss aside if you're scared of the power of your orgasm."

Annoyed that he understood her a little too well, she snorted. "I get it. Now can we get started?"

A nip preceded a harsh reminder. "You forget your manners, Angel mine." When she stared down until he raised his head and scowled up at her, he added, "Sir."

Angel sighed. "Damn, Tan...ah...Sir. Is Sir really necessary? It's kind of silly, you know?"

Like a grizzly preparing to release a terrifying roar before devouring his prey, Tanner rose up onto his knees and towered above her. "Silly?"

Before she realized what he planned he untied her and draped over his knees. Her shock immobilized her as he shifted her body and his legs until her clit rested on one of his knees.

"Tell me, Angel mine, how many times should I spank you for calling me silly?" His knee started moving up and down.

Stunned, she mumbled, "You're spanking me because I think calling you Sir is, well, funny?"

She pushed up and turned to smile up at him but caught sight of his hand swinging down toward her ass. His other hand splayed over her lower back and held her in place. Angel screamed in shock at the sting of his palm. For the first time, she doubted her fantasy. "Oh, shit, wait, no."

But Tanner let out a loud bellow, "And still no Sir?"

Again his hand came down, this time lower, closer to her exposed pussy. The sting sent tears to her eyes. She opened her mouth to plant a vicious bite on his thigh in retaliation but clamped her teeth on her lower lip when heat fanned out from the site of his first smack over the latest and so close to her pussy. The vibrations of his knee sped up, taunting her clit as it mimicked her favorite toy. Angel closed her eyes when she felt Tanner's finger slide over her moist labia then encircle her clit.

"You like this, don't you?"

She grinned and nodded. Another smack, harsher than the other two, sent a new wave of heat. Before she could say or do anything, Tanner covered her ass and thighs with spanks. Her skin burned. Her pussy seemed to swell in anticipation of being the next target. And her clit! Tortured beyond imagination by his knee, her clit sent streaks of unbearable pleasure shooting straight up to her stomach. Muscles she didn't know existed clenched and coiled. Her mind told her that an orgasm hovered within reach, one that would be too out of control, too huge.

"I didn't hear an answer. You like this, don't you?" His knee stilled.

A sob slid from her lips. "Yes! Don't stop!"

"Manners, Angel mine." Tanner rubbed his calloused palm over her inflamed skin. "No manners, no pleasure."

Her muscles relaxed. Sweat mingled with her juices dripped down her inner thigh. Her orgasm, her ultimate orgasm, waned. And calling Tanner "Sir" made all the sense in the world. "Yes, Sir. Please don't stop, Sir!"

"You see? You call me Sir because I am the one in power here." Tanner gently patted her pussy as he talked and while each tiny smack in itself didn't have the power to create more than a feeling of skin hitting skin, the speed with which he patted her sped up and fed the flame. "That was a lesson, Angel mine. I know what you want, what you like. If you disappoint me, I will be forced to punish you. If you enjoy the punishment too much and still disappoint me, well, you won't be allowed to come."

The patting continued. Her muscles stalled, still clenched but neither relaxing completely nor recoiling in their journey toward release. "Okay, I understand, Sir. Got it."

A sharp slap to her pussy sent the air rushing from her lungs. "Do you need to be punished?"

Angel's brain shut down. "I'm not sure…Sir!"

Tanner's chuckle brought a smile to her lips. His nails

scraped a path up her inner thigh. She froze and held her breath. "I think you do. But if you take your punishment and thank me after each spank like a good little girl, I will let you come."

When his knee once again vibrated and his palm struck her, Angel nearly squealed with delight. She peeked over her shoulder. With hand held high, Tanner frowned down at her and arched one eyebrow.

"Thank you, Sir," she murmured, again feeling somewhat silly. Ten scalding spanks rained down on her already burning skin. Ten times she yelled, "Thank you, Sir." And when her muscles tightened to the point of pain and her mind lost track of where one spank ended and the next began, Angel couldn't speak. Writhing from the need to come, baffled that each time she nearly toppled into an orgasm her body seemed to retreat from that precipice, she soon noticed that Tanner's knee and spanking had taken complete control.

"Do you want to come, Angel mine?"

His lips brushing over her butt as he spoke surprised her, but her need to come kept her from demanding he stop screwing around. "Please, Sir. I don't know how you're doing it, but I'll call you Sir, I'll do anything you want. I can't take it anymore."

Something slid into her pussy. Something warm and hard. Her mind insisted no toy could feel so real. Angel raised her head and tried to see if another man had joined them. Tanner lowered his head in time to block her view.

"Keep your head down," he ordered in a voice that left no doubt that she would regret disobeying him. "Remember your manners and do not come until I tell you to."

A sliver of dread skidded down her spine. The spanking and vibrations of his knee against her clit resumed. And whatever Tanner had in her pussy now plunged in and out in time with each spank. Angel thanked him again and again. Her thoughts scattered, and still she thanked him.

She tried not to come. Her muscles wound so tight that she thought they would rip. She bit down on her lip until she tasted blood but in the end, Angel's ultimate orgasm burst upon her before Tanner gave her permission. Like shards of glass, pleasure pierced every inch of her body. Spasms converged upon each other. Her pussy clenched onto whatever still pumped into her. Something hot spewed into her vagina and trickled down her legs. She'd feel a hand spank her, another pinch her nipples, another graze her inner thigh. Too many hands for one man. Decadent images flashed before her eyes as her body still jerked and twitched. Deep in the recesses of her mind, she knew that if this had occurred with one of her toys, she would have flicked the switch by now. But Tanner had no switch and he didn't stop or allow her to pull away until her screams died down and her body stopped convulsing.

Angel remained draped over his knees for a few minutes while he smoothed sweat-soaked hair from her face. Realizing that she did trust him, she asked, "How did you do that?"

"What?" he asked in a soft voice as he lifted her into a sitting position. He kissed her forehead.

"Your hands were everywhere."

Tanner chuckled. "Cowboy magic. Ever see a cowboy hogtie a calf on the run? You learn to move your hands from one end of the body to the other in a split second."

"It felt like someone actually came in me." Too weak to move, she leaned against his chest and kissed his neck.

"Just a toy, Angel. Learn all your lessons, and you'll get to meet them all."

"I knew it wasn't a man."

"Really? How could you be so sure?"

She thought for a minute. Closed her eyes and smiled. "Because I trust you."

"Good. You can't have love without trust, Angel. Now go back to sleep." Lifting her into his arms, he gently laid her onto the bed then joined her.

"But what about you?" Angel snuggled back until he spooned her and his pants scraped her raw skin. "It doesn't seem fair that I came but you didn't."

His lips skimmed over the whorl of her ear. "Oh, there's plenty of time for me later, Angel mine. Now go to sleep."

Angel stared down at the calloused hand resting on her breast. As she took a deep breath, her breast rose and her sensitive nipple grazed Tanner's rough palm.

* * * * *

The shrill ring of the phone almost sent the coffee carafe flying out of Tanner's hand. Putting the carafe back on the burner, he picked up the phone and pressed "Talk" before it woke Angel. "Hello?"

The only reply he received was a whole lot of breathing. Clicking off the phone, he waited a few seconds then pressed talk again so there would be no more ringing phones or perverts interrupting Angel's sleep.

He sipped some of the scalding coffee from his mug then, with a heavy sigh, carried it to the living room. The task before him weighed heavily on his shoulders. He had no desire to watch Angel and the two men, but a mystery had begun to unfold today and he had to solve it before Angel ended up hurt or worse.

He couldn't figure out what could have motivated Antonio, a man obviously vying for Angel's hand and Roselli's Bakery, to do what he did then send the video to his victim. And why did he scrawl the word "Vendetta" on the manila envelope bearing the video? None of it made sense.

Scene after scene played out but nothing gave him any clue. He was just about to turn off the video when the screen flashed then showed Antonio and Luigi sitting on the living room couch with an unconscious Angel draped over their legs.

Antonio spoke first after making a point of running his

hands over Angel's breasts. "So, Mr. Roselli, what do you think of your precious daughter now? Will you call *her* a common whore? If she carries my child will you kick *her* out and tell her that because she was drunk she deserved what she got? Huh? Ring a bell, Mr. Roselli? No?"

He took the other man's hand and shoved it between Angel's legs.

Tanner jumped up. Coffee sloshed over the rim of the mug he held clenched in his hand. He had to use every ounce of energy to stop himself from leaving to kill Antonio. A stunning woman with black curly hair, light brown eyes and a slightly familiar face leaned over the back of the couch and kissed Antonio's cheek. Tanner glanced at the two men then back to the woman.

Antonio's face transformed, twisted with hatred. Soft lips thinned, eyes narrowed to mere slits and eyebrows formed a stark "V". The face women swooned over now would send any woman or man running. Antonio cupped the woman's face. "Meet your daughter, you bastard. Josephina Roselli Paradino."

The woman waved and smiled. "Hi, Daddy."

"Josephina and I grew up with Luigi's family. Why, you ask? Hm…" Antonio lifted Angel's arm, shook it until her hand flopped up and down, then laughed. "Like your sweet, pure daughter, my mother met a man, a certain baker from America, who had no qualms about taking advantage of a woman too intoxicated to make a rational decision."

"His English sure has gotten better overnight."

Tanner leaned forward and stared at the screen. He had no doubt he heard Angel, but she still appeared unconscious.

"You had to watch it?" This time he realized her voice came from behind him.

Turning around as he flicked off the TV, he saw no condemnation in her expression. What he did find unnerved him.

No emotion.

No anger that he witnessed what she probably wished to keep hidden. No shock over the discovery that she had a sister or that her father had apparently sired this woman on a woman too drunk to stop him.

Nothing.

"I had to see if I could find a reason behind what Antonio did. Angel—"

"Turn it back on." With shoulders squared and chin high, she strode up to the couch and sat down beside him. "If I'm paying for the sins of my father, I want to know each and every one."

"Maybe it would be better to hear your father's side of the story."

"His side?" She snorted. "Just what I'd expect from a man. Tell me, Tanner, if someone took advantage of your mother while she was drunk, maybe even helped her get that way, would you be interested in his side?"

He hooked her chin with his fingers and after a couple of tugs, succeeded in turning her face toward his. "You're right. I wouldn't. But you and I know that there have been women who turn to this story when they mess up and end up pregnant, especially if there is a stranger they can blame it on who's already left town."

A flicker of hope flashed across her face. "I hadn't considered of that." She glanced at the TV. Frozen with evil smirks, Antonio and the woman stared back at them. "No, Tanner, look at her. My hair and eyes. God, she even has the same-shaped lips as my Nonna. No, it's true."

"Maybe…" Tanner paused, searched for some way to bring the hope back into her eyes.

"Turn it back on, Tanner. Let's hear what my sister has to say."

When he hesitated, she reached over and pressed "Play".

Antonio chuckled and crossed his arms as if he knew they had tried to ignore him but couldn't.

"I was just a boy, but I remember my mother dragging me to your cousin's bakery when you returned to our village the next year. My sister," he reached up and cupped Josephina's cheek, "was the most beautiful baby. You wouldn't even look at her. When my mother told you that her husband had kicked us out and that you were Josephina's father, you laughed. You laughed! Your cousin came to the door and told you the baby had your eyes and, again, you laughed, you bastard. Then you told your cousin that my mother was nothing more than some drunken whore you met in a bar last year. A whore!"

Tanner watched, mesmerized as the face of a man bent on revenge crumpled and transformed into the little boy destroyed by one word.

"You called my mother, a woman who never strayed until you caught her scent, a whore!" Antonio buried his face in his hands. His shoulders shook.

Josephina leaned over and whispered into Antonio's ear, smoothed his hair back. Kissed his temple. When she raised her head, Tanner braced himself. Hard, uncaring eyes met his.

"My mother lived on the streets with us for two years. Every year she'd return to the bakery when you visited to beg you to help her. The last time, you shoved her out of the bakery and told her any woman who drank like some Bowery bum and spread her legs for the nearest man deserved to live on the streets."

Engrossed in the video, Tanner forgot that Angel sat beside him until he heard her strangled gasp. He wrapped his arm around her and drew her in close to his side, hoping somehow that would help. Her head falling down onto his shoulder and her hand resting on his chest stopped him from shutting off the TV and destroying the video.

"My mama," Antonio raised a tear-streaked face and drew in a deep breath, "my beautiful mama killed herself that night."

"Oh, no!" Angel turned away from the TV and pressed her face into his chest. "Those poor children."

"It doesn't absolve him of what he did to you, Angel."

Antonio's voice, hard, cold and unforgiving continued. "And now you must accept that your daughter, your perfect daughter you bragged would go to the altar a virgin, got drunk and let two men have their way with her."

"We gave her the chance to save herself." Josephina squeezed Antonio's shoulder. "Antonio insisted she have the chance you never gave my mother. But your daughter, who by the way Antonio discovered was not a virgin, chose to stay. She even asked Antonio to tie her up, didn't she, Antonio?"

Antonio held up a small recorder. "Maybe you have to hear her to believe us."

Angel's nails dug into Tanner's skin.

"Tell me your most secret fantasy or I will stop."

"Bondage. I don't want...I want...no control."

"Are you sure, my little whore? You may go now and never live out your fantasy. If you stay, then I will use you in ways you can not imagine and you will have no say, no more chances to leave. So, should I put you in a cab or tie you to my bed?"

Angel's moans resurrected the rage Antonio's tears had buried earlier.

"No answer? Then I will get you a cab."

"No! I'll stay. Please, let me stay."

Tanner felt Angel start to ease out from under his arm. He caught hold of her and firmly held her where she belonged. With him.

He almost laughed when he recalled that he'd come here looking for an angel. A wild woman in bed, but an angel he could trust, one who would never stray. That Tanner, the one who had believed in angels, would have left the minute she'd admitted she enjoyed what Antonio and Luigi had done to her.

That Tanner, if he'd dallied long enough to hear her plead for another man's touch, would have pushed her away and gone back home.

He held on to Angel and grinned. "We're a pair, Angel mine."

She glanced up, her doe eyes rimmed in red. "How so, cowboy?"

"I used to visit the Pleasure Ranch. What you'd call a house of prostitution. Can't tell you how many of those ladies got tied up. Hearing you just now? Damn, I felt like a little kid opening up a Christmas present and discovering he got just what he wanted."

Angel's face blurred as she moved in and planted a tender kiss on his lips. "Then I'd say we were made for each other."

"I won't bruise you like him."

"A few spanks won't bruise." She leaned back and pouted.

"Oh, I know a heap of ways not to bruise." He slid her onto his lap and leaned over to turn off the TV so he could show her just what he meant.

"No, Tanner. He's not done."

Glancing at the screen, Tanner watched the three whispering. "You're right. Something is up. We don't want to miss a word. This might be blackmail. You know, pay up or this goes to your father."

"Oh, no. That would kill him!"

Antonio nodded then smirked. "I almost forgot. See, I figure you are probably thinking this cowboy who keeps sniffing around Angel will save the day by marrying her. Don't be so sure she'll accept."

Josephina stepped out of view then reappeared holding some papers. "We did a little digging and discovered something we think you should know. Seems Angel's cowboy wasn't lying when he said was looking for a wife. What he failed to tell you was...he has to produce a wife by the end of the summer or he'll lose the family ranch. I have the papers to prove it. I'm very good at seducing men into giving me what I want."

Angel stiffened in his arms. "What did she say?"

Antonio stared out at them, his face sincere. "That's right, Angel. I have to say, I feel sorry for you."

"Fool," Josephina snapped and walked out of view.

Glancing over his shoulder then looking back at them, Antonio shook his head. "She doesn't understand like I do. You have been deceived by your papa. That is bad enough. Now, like my mama, a man I think you just might love has also deceived you. Add me and... Well, I don't think you'll be trusting anyone for a long, long time."

The screen turned blue.

Tanner's heart pounded in his ears. Words failed him. He couldn't call Josephina a liar. Couldn't even say that he hadn't deceived her the night they'd made love. Damn, he'd fallen in love with her that first day, but only realized it when he'd found her in Antonio's apartment. "Angel, I-I...love you. You have to believe me."

"He didn't mention any money."

"What?" Shocked by her words, he hesitated a moment too long.

She shot out of his lap and ran to the door.

"Angel!"

"He didn't ask for money!" She flung open the door and raced outside. "That means he sent it!"

Following her to the curb where she raised her arm and searched for a cab, Tanner grabbed her and spun her around. "What are you talking about?"

"My father!"

He barely heard her. He saw the difference in her eyes.

Felt the way she flinched from his touch. "What about your father?"

"Antonio must have sent him the video. Why else didn't he ask for money?" She opened the door and slid into the cab that pulled up to the curb.

When he moved to get in, she shoved his chest until he backed away, then slammed the door. "Angel."

"No, Tanner. No." She slammed down on the lock.

"Wait, you have no money." Reaching into his pocket, he took out his wallet and pulled out a couple of twenties. "Take this. And please, Angel, come back so we can work this out."

Angel grabbed the money from his hand. "There's nothing to work out."

"You have to at least give me a chance to explain." His heart stalled. He couldn't lose her. Not now.

Not ever.

"Explain? Explain why you lied to me?"

Her voice cracked. How he longed to open the door and gather her in his arms, soothe her.

But her next words stopped him cold.

"What did you tell me, Tanner? You can't have love without trust? You're no better than Antonio."

"I told you that first day that I came here for a wife."

She blinked. Stared into his eyes.

The cabbie cursed under his breath. "Can we get moving?"

"Just hold your horses!" Tanner yelled.

"Listen, buddy…"

"Shut up! The meter's on," Angel snapped then scooted closer to the window and frowned up at him.

Not an angry frown. A confused, thoughtful frown. One that filled him with hope. The muscles that had tensed to the point of pain relaxed a bit. He held her gaze. "You just didn't believe me."

Her eyes hardened.

"How could I? And if I remember correctly, you left out the fact that you only needed one to fulfill a will! You could have picked anyone off the street to trick into marrying you. I just happened to have the dumb luck to bump into you, didn't I?"

Again that crack in her voice. Or was that one his heart. It sure felt like it just split in two. "Angel..."

What could he say? Everything she said was true. He had come looking for a woman to marry. He would have done anything to save the ranch, even profess a love he didn't feel. And yes, if someone else had bumped into him and proven that she would satisfy sexually in a loveless marriage, he'd be on a plane back to Texas by now.

But he'd bumped into an angel, an angel who had managed to take his heart and warm it like no other woman ever had. An angel he couldn't imagine living without. An angel he no longer wanted in a loveless marriage.

One look in her eyes told him that this angel, if she ever did feel for him, no longer wanted anything to do with him.

He looked away when he felt the first tear trickle down his cheek. "It started out that way. But...but..." He turned, decided to let her see that the possibility of losing her had the power to make him cry in public. "Now I'm so glad I picked you, Angel, because I—"

"No! Don't you dare say it! Even if I was stupid enough to believe you, it wouldn't matter because you picked the wrong woman. I'll never leave the bakery or my father. You hear me? Never!"

He gritted his teeth until they felt like they would break, but still the words spewed out. "Why? Because your father's better than me? He fucking sold you for that bakery! And that bakery is nothing more than a prison! Unless it burns down, you'll spend the rest of your life locked in it! Or maybe that's what you want, Angel. Maybe life is just too fucking scary for you. Maybe it's just too fucking scary to admit you need me just as much as I need you."

"Need you? I don't need you! I—"

"That's right, you have your toys."

Angel gasped.

Tears streamed down her cheeks and still he couldn't stop. "Go! Run to Daddy. And while you're there, ask him who else he has lined up to pawn you off to so he can keep the sacred business running."

"You were going to take me away from my home to keep your sacred ranch," she screamed. "He wanted to keep me close to him. I'm all he has!"

He let out a weary sigh then slapped his palm on the roof of the cab and yelled, "Go! Get the fuck out of here!"

The cab swerved into the traffic.

* * * * *

Finding her father's apartment empty, finding a videocassette broken and the remains of the tape scattered around the living room, Angel sank to the floor. She'd lost everything. Everything.

A soft tap on the door jerked her to her feet. Explanations and a bevy of questions filled her mind as she rushed to the door and flung it open. She expected, hoped to find her father.

A young boy stood on the stoop. "My mom said I should watch from the window to see if you came by. They took your dad to...um...some hospital."

Her heart felt as if it stopped. She grabbed his arm when she realized he was turning to leave. "Which one? Where did they take him?"

"I don't know. We all just watched the ambulance take him away." Yanking free, the boy stuttered, "I-I g-gotta g-go."

A few frantic phone calls later, Angel stood in a crowded

subway and counted the seconds until she reached her father's side. She reminded herself over and over that the woman at the hospital had said he was fine, but still she felt like every second that passed was one less she'd spend with him before he died.

By the time she arrived at the hospital, her father had already been released. Another frantic series of calls turned up nothing. Angel went to the only place she could picture him going. The bakery.

This time she took a cab and searched the faces of the pedestrians filling the sidewalks for her father. A block away, she smelled smoke. Leaning out the window, she saw fire trucks blocking the street. A sick feeling lodged in her stomach. She tossed the cabdriver the last of the money Tanner had given her.

Running down the street, she shoved the people gathered around the barricades aside. When the last person blocking her view moved, she saw the flames shooting out the windows of the bakery and up the side of the building. A scream ripped free from her throat. Firemen aimed the hoses at the gaping holes where the windows displayed all the pies and breads she'd baked, but the fire appeared to grow more out of control.

Scooting under the barricade, she ran toward the bakery.

A cop who looked too young to be wearing a uniform of any kind stepped in front of her with his hands held out to his side. "Back behind the barricade."

"That's my bakery."

"Sorry, I have my orders."

Flakes of ashes fluttered down around them like snow. Smoke burned her throat and lungs. The firemen yelled incoherent orders back and forth. A loud bang from the back of the bakery and the blast of hot air hitting her face set her in motion. She moved to race around the cop.

He grabbed hold of her arm. "You can't go any closer, ma'am. They think the building might come down at any time."

"My father might be in there," she yelled, struggling to break free.

"Angel?"

At the sound of her father's voice, Angel spun around. A few feet down from where she stood, her father sat on the curb with an oxygen mask held to his mouth by an EMT.

"Dad!" She ran to him and squatted down beside him. Her eyes took in the sight of him, searched for burns. Soot blackened his hands and face, but other than that, he seemed fine.

She dropped to her knees and, wrapping her arms around him, leaned her head on his shoulder. "Daddy."

Sitting with him, she watched the place she'd called home for most of her childhood burn. Memories filtered through her mind. Happy ones mingled with those where she'd either yelled or prayed the bakery would burn down and set her free.

Tanner's words replayed in her mind. She knew he had only spoken the truth that the bakery had been a prison, but it had also been the only home she'd known. The brownstone where she'd lived with her parents had rarely had all three of them home at the same time. She'd hated wasting her weekends in the bakery, but at least there she had both her parents. And after her mother died, she felt her mother's spirit there. Even as her father's time in the bakery grew less and less frequent, she had only to look out the window to see him laughing and smiling with his friends.

A loud crack had the police shooing the crowd back and the firemen running for cover. Angel gasped.

The roof sank down, vanishing behind the walls of the building just moments before the walls tumbled to the sidewalk.

And still the fire raged.

"What happened?" she asked, coughing from the smoke and dust billowing around them.

"I...I..." Her father buried his face in his hands.

"Hush, Dad." She tightened her hold and kissed his damp cheek. Her eyes burned from the smoke.

They remained on the curb until the last ember had been extinguished, until the firemen and onlookers had all left. They watched the police set up the yellow tape warning all who passed not to enter the burned remains of Roselli's. They stared until no more smoke lingered amongst the remains and still they remained.

Her father's friends and some of the customers who had frequented Roselli's since Angel could remember hovered around them. Some of them offered their sympathy, some just stared like she and her father did as if they could still see the bakery with its gleaming windows and bright red sign. One by one, they all left until, eventually, only she and her father remained.

"Come on, Dad. Let me get you home."

He nodded and rose without a word.

They rode back to Brooklyn Heights in silence. Angel couldn't think of anything to say. This had to be the worst day she'd ever had. The fire had been the icing on the cake and left her incapable of producing a single, logical thought, left her incapable of even soothing her father. Bone weary, needing a shoulder to cry on, afraid to relax for fear she'd fall apart, she remained rigid.

While she helped him up the stairs, she remembered about the broken cassette and torn tape lying on the floor in front of his TV and wondered if he would say anything when he saw it. She needn't have worried. He headed straight for the stairs. Swaying, he grasped the pedestal and turned to face her.

"I'm sorry, Angel. I...I never should have left you there. I...I never should have put the bakery before my own daughter. Your cowboy was right."

"My cowboy? You spoke to Tanner?"

"He called me at the bakery. Told me not to look...well, it was too late by then. I told him so, said something stupid about you surviving. He went crazy. Told me it was all my fault. That I sacrificed you for the bakery. Said I should spend the rest of my life making it up to you." His soft hand cupped her cheek. "I told him to go to hell, but I knew he was right."

Before she could reply he started up the stairs.

He stumbled halfway up. Fell to one knee.

"Dad!" Angel took hold of his arm.

Brushing her hand away, he righted himself. Held his hand out behind him. "Please, I just want to be alone."

A lump she could barely breathe around lodged in her throat. "Sure."

She watched until she heard his door close.

That click seemed to release the tension that had managed to hold her up. She dropped down onto the step and leaned against the balustrade.

The phone rang. Pulling herself up, she made her way to the living room. The couch called to her.

The chance that she might hear Tanner's voice kept her moving, albeit slowly, toward the phone.

Her hand touched the receiver just as the phone stopped ringing.

Swallowing the sobs that nearly burst free, she went to the couch and sank into the soft cushions. Closing her eyes, she wondered if the caller had been Tanner. Wondered if he'd call again.

Then she heard him cursing her father and the bakery. Telling her that it should burn down.

"No...no, he wouldn't," she whispered into the empty room.

The silence mocked her. Demanded she accept that she would always wonder.

The phone started ringing again. Shutting her eyes, she

gave in to the sobs strangling her and rolled over.

Chapter Nine

Sitting on the stoop of Angel's brownstone, Tanner watched the Jeep pull up to the curb. He stood when the door opened to reveal Angel. He waited until she reached the steps.

"I heard. About the bakery."

She glanced up. Looked down the street at the departing Jeep. "Well, you got what you wanted."

"You can't believe that." He reached out to touch her.

Flinching away, she took the steps two at a time past him. At the door, she spun around and faced him. "Excuse me? Not two hours after you said the bakery should burn down, it does. That's too much of a coincidence in my book!"

"God, you don't think I did it, do you?"

"Why shouldn't I?" she asked, unlocking the door and disappearing into the front hall.

Tanner caught the door before it swung closed and followed her. "If anyone burned down Roselli's it was Antonio."

She didn't answer. Following her into the apartment, Tanner expected her to tell him to leave.

Instead, she went to the bathroom and shut the door. A few minutes later, he heard the sound of the shower. Going into the kitchen he poured himself some wine and put up a pot of coffee. Angel had looked more tired than he'd ever seen her.

When she entered the living room with a towel wrapped around her body, he had her cup already filled and mixed with milk and sugar exactly the way she liked it.

Without a word, she took the mug and sat on the couch.

"You know, Tanner, you're the only other person I could come up with when the fire marshal asked me if I knew anyone who might hold anything against my father or the bakery. Antonio apparently got his revenge through me. Why burn down the bakery?"

His stomach dropped. "You think I set the fire?"

A sad smile flashed across her face. "No. I'm guessing another gas leak. And deep down inside, I don't believe you could."

"Well, that's a relief." Joining her on the couch, he let out a long breath.

"You want to know why, Tanner?" She put the mug on the table.

The thin angry line of her lips had him tensing for a barrage of insults.

"Because you are a saint."

"Excuse me?" He laughed, stopped when her eyes hardened.

"That's right. You'd never give in to your emotions if it meant crossing some unseen line of right and wrong. You admitted that you were into bondage and domination and all sorts of kinky shit." She stood up and dropped her towel. Held out her arms. "Look at me!"

Bruises and cuts marred her wrists and ankles. "What the hell does that have to do with me burning down the bakery?"

"If you'd given in and taken me the way you and I wanted, I would never have gone as far as I did with Antonio."

"What?" He stood up. "You're blaming me for what happened between you and that sick fuck?"

"That's right." She closed the gap between them. "Tell me something, what do you want to do right now?"

"Now? I'd like to shake some sense into you."

Her nipples poked into his chest. Blood rushed down to

his cock.

She pressed her stomach into his groin. "Liar. You want to fuck me. But you won't. Want to know why?"

He grabbed her arms. "Because you don't know what you're doing, Angel. You're hurting deep inside and…"

"And you're a fucking saint." She wrenched free and turned.

Bending over, she grabbed the towel.

Lust ripped through him. At first he reined it in.

She turned, glared at him and planted her fists on her hips. "I don't even have to cover myself, do I?"

Apple-sized breasts jutted out at him. A cleanly shaven mound gave him a clear view of her clit. His cock felt as if molten lead filled it. He let his gaze meander back up to her face. Her tongue darted out to moisten her lips.

"Do I?" She sounded less sure and just as turned-on as he felt.

"You want me to lose control? You got it, lady." Taking the towel from her hand, he tossed it to the floor then scooped her up into his arms.

Angel gasped. "Wait a minute."

Lifting her over his shoulder he ignored the weak punches she landed on his back.

"Put me down."

"No, you're right. I want to fuck you. I want to tie you up and wipe out any memory you have of that animal touching you."

Her struggles ceased. "Tanner, I'm not so sure I can handle this."

He hesitated for all of two seconds before dropping her onto the bed. Her legs flailed and revealed that while she might be having second thoughts, her body wanted this. "That's just too bad, isn't it?"

"No, I mean it. It's too soon. I'm still tender." She rose up onto her knees and scooted to the other side of the bed.

Grinning, feeling so evil he could easily come just thinking about what he planned, he raised a brow at her. "I'd like nothing more than to put you over my lap and spank you until scream, so you'd better lie down and spread your legs, Angel mine."

"You wouldn't dare." She picked up a pillow and held it to her chest.

"You have five seconds to find out."

Her eyes darted from him to the door and back. Clutching the pillow, she backed up, bumped into the headboard.

"Time's up."

He lunged.

Catching hold of her ankles, he pulled her across the mattress. Her squeals rang in his ears. She fought, twisted and punched, but he had her draped over his knees and landed his first smack in under a minute.

This first one, controlled and way lighter than he ever had with the ladies at the Pleasure Ranch, left not a mark on her skin, but she screamed and squirmed to get away. "Are you going to lie down and spread your legs like a good girl, now?"

Glancing over her shoulder, she smirked. "What if I say no?"

He raised his hand.

She dropped her head. "Then no."

"I'd ask you if you were sure, but my saint days are over."

"Well, that's a relief!"

Tanner laughed and brought his hand down a bit harder with each ensuing spank. By the time Angel cried out that she'd do what he said, her cheeks were bright pink and her juices ran down her thighs. Lifting her, he turned her until she sat on his lap.

"I like this. You all naked and me completely dressed. Straddle me."

"I thought you wanted me to lie down?" She pouted but swung her leg over his lap.

Cupping one of her breasts, he lowered his head and sucked her nipple into his mouth. Just as she started to moan and grind her wet pussy down onto his cock, he bit down.

"Ow! What the hell was that for?" She rubbed her nipple. Scowled. Pressed down harder until he must have entered her, pants on and all.

"Next time I tell you to do something, you'll do it without any questions. Got it?"

Her lower lip jutted out as she nodded.

Tanner raised a brow. "Forgetting your manners?"

"Sorry…Sir."

"I want some more of that nipple. Hold up your breast for me."

Jutting out her chest, she cupped her hand under her breast and lifted.

The surge of power took over. This is what he loved. What he'd dreamed of.

Angel all meek and pliant while he did whatever he pleased.

Angel following his every order. He lowered his head. Held her gaze. Bared his teeth.

Her moan and her juices seeping through his pants did him in. Catching the nipple between his teeth he nipped and sucked, all the while holding her hips firmly in place. When her legs spread wider and her attempts to rub her pussy against his cock grew more frenzied, he lifted her off his lap and laid her on the bed.

"Spread them. Now!"

Her legs opened.

"Wider."

She complied with eyes dark with desire.

"Arms over your head, Angel. That's good." He reached under the bed and brought out the bag he had put there the morning he'd tied her up. He took out the rope, tied her arms and legs then pulled out the brand-new vibrator he'd bought. "This is supposedly the number-one-selling rabbit."

Her eyes widened.

Flicking the ears, he smirked. "You're familiar with these, but," he paused, turned the vibrator over and flicked the anal plug jutting out from the other side, "I don't think you've dealt with this one before. Or have you?"

She shook her head.

Placing the vibrator between her legs, he rummaged in the bag and withdrew a tube of lubricant. One look at her face told him she found the new vibrator more than appealing. Her tongue moistened her lips, her eyes lowered and a soft smile curved her mouth.

When he'd lubed the plug, he inserted the vibrator but left it in without turning it on. Sitting on the bed, he spoke to her without looking in her direction. "Someday, I'm going to tie you up to a tree and show you just how I became the state cat-o'-nine-tails champion." Her whimper and the rustle of her shifting egged him on. "I can whip an apple with enough control to knock it off a ledge without so much as a dent. Or slice through half of it without it moving a fraction of an inch." The rustling continued.

"Now I bet I could make you come and stripe your perfect little ass. Would you like that?" He rose and lowered his pants.

"Would it hurt a lot?" Fear laced her voice.

"Darlin', no more than that spanking you enjoyed so much." He flicked on the vibrator, slid all three knobs all the way up. Her gasp sent more lead to his cock. "Would you like that?"

"Oh...yes." Pink stained her cheeks.

"And someday, my sweet, innocent angel, I'm going to take you on a horse. You'll feel me plunge into you every time his hooves hit the ground."

The convulsions that overtook her body shocked him. Groans that sounded animalistic filled the room. Her hips shot up off the mattress. He pulled the vibrator out.

"No," she cried, pulling at the ropes binding her arms.

"Ah, ah." He wagged his finger. "I decide when you come. Shall we try again?"

Angel gnawed on her lip. Nodded. Sighed when he replaced the vibrator. After a few minutes his shirt lay on the floor with the rest of his clothes and sweat covered Angel's body. Her face showed the strain of her keeping her orgasm at bay. Leaning over, he licked each nipple. Her entire body tensed.

"Can you feel the vibrations in your ass?" he whispered in her ear. When she nodded, he barked, "Answer me."

"Yes!"

"And in your sweet pussy?"

"God, yes!"

"And your clit. Are those ears torturing it until you feel like you're going to scream?"

"Yes! Yes!" Her eyes squeezed closed.

Lying down alongside her, he suckled on her breast until he felt her body quiver from the strain of not coming. "When I bite down on your nipple, you may come."

He suckled some more, slid the vibrator in and out of her. Her cries drowned out the buzzing of the vibrator. He bit down. Angel screamed. Her body convulsed and trembled.

As soon as she started to calm down, he untied her, crawled up between her legs and pulled the vibrator out. Tossing it over his shoulder, he leaned over and dipped his tongue into her quivering flesh. Her sweet juices filled his mouth. Needing more, he covered her pussy with his mouth and suckled on her clit. Out of the corner of his eyes he saw her fingers claw at the quilt. Tremors overtook her body. Burrowing deeper with his tongue, he felt her inner muscle start to throb. He raised his head to tell her she could come.

Hands dug into his hair and drew his mouth back to her pussy. Grinning, he stilled.

"I think you've forgotten who is in control here, Angel."

Groaning, Angel let go.

Sucking her tender flesh into his mouth, he wondered how anyone could taste so good. Her thighs quivered.

He raised his head. "Don't come, Angel."

"I don't think I can stop it."

"Get on your knees."

Without hesitating, she swung her leg over his head and rose up onto her hands and knees. He knelt behind her. Took in the sight of her juices flowing from her pussy. "God, you're beautiful."

She glanced over her shoulder, smiled mischievously. "Is this the rodeo?"

"You bet it is." Grabbing her hips, he drove himself into that moist cavern.

A phone rang.

"Fuck!"

"You stop, Tanner, and I swear I'll tie you up and teach you the meaning of whipping!"

Pulling out until the head of his cock nearly cleared her swollen lips, he waited until she cursed then plunged in with everything he had.

Angel bucked back, forcing him even deeper.

He rode her until he felt as if he'd explode. "Come for me, Angel," he yelled.

Immediately she cried out and shattered in his hands. He

came with such force he swore he saw stars. Angel dropped to her belly and still they both continued to come. He thought it'd never end.

When they both finally calmed, he turned her over and cradled her against his chest.

When he awoke the next morning, Angel was gone.

* * * * *

Standing amongst the rubble with the fire marshal, Angel peered over his shoulder at the people milling around on the other side of the crime scene tape. She recognized some of the faces, but most were strangers who'd just come to see what remained of the city's oldest bakery.

The fire marshal, a burly man only a few years younger than her father, helped her step around the chunks of charred wood. Bending over, he picked one up. "Smell it?"

The faint scent of gasoline permeated the area. She'd spent most of the early hours of the morning with the police and fire marshal, refusing to accept that someone had purposely burned down the bakery.

"Like I said, we checked out this Antonio you mentioned. His alibi is ironclad. At the time the fire took place, he was in the emergency room. Someone knocked out some of his teeth. While someone else torched your bakery, Antonio was getting stitches in his lip and gums. You sure you can't think of anyone else who'd wanna burn the place down?"

Angel turned away. "I'm sure."

"Well, someone did." He tossed the blackened wood aside and rubbed his hands together.

Angel followed him to the Jeep he'd driven her to the bakery in. Her cell phone vibrated in her pocketbook. She ignored it. Had ignored it all morning. Like all the others, she had no doubt this one would display Tanner's number.

As they sat at a red light, the fire marshal stared at her

then reached into his jacket. "Listen, if you come up with anyone, give me a call." He handed her a business card.

Angel nodded and stuck it in the back pocket of her jeans. "I will."

"You know, sometimes it's the last person you'd suspect."

Her heart broke.

Later, sitting with her father, she asked him again if he had any idea who might have set the fire.

"Angel, I told you. It had to be that cowboy. I told you. He went crazy on the phone!" He poured a glass of wine then held up the bottle.

Shaking her head, Angel stood up. "I have to make a private call. I'll just be outside, okay?"

Staring at her a minute, her father nodded.

Just before she stepped out into the hall, she heard him ask in a soft voice, "You didn't go and fall in love with that cowboy, did you, Angel?"

She turned. Sitting beneath the glare of the fluorescent lights he looked so pale. So old and alone. "Don't be silly, Dad. I hardly know him."

Outside, she dialed Tanner's cell phone. He picked after the first ring.

"Angel?"

"Listen and please don't interrupt me. They found evidence of arson. Gasoline."

"Antonio. I knew it."

"No, Tanner. He was at the hospital getting stitches. You're the only other suspect."

"Angel, you gotta believe—"

"It doesn't matter what I believe! My father wants you arrested. I might be able to stop him from mentioning you to the police, but only if you're gone. You have a ranch to save. Go back to Texas, Tanner."

The silence on the other end lasted so long she almost hung up.

"Come with me." Tanner's voice shook.

"That will never happen."

"Why, dammit?"

"Because... I'll always wonder."

"If I burned down the bakery? Fuck, you know I didn't."

"I don't know anything anymore. I don't know if you want me to come with you because you love me or because you need a wife for the will. I don't know if maybe you lost it and did burn down the bakery or if some arsonist just randomly picked it."

Again the silence.

"If you believed I did it, you would have told the fire marshal."

"I don't know what's stopping me! Maybe it's because I blame myself for getting you so twisted that you'd do this."

"That makes no sense. Why blame yourself?"

"Why blame myself?" Angel laughed. A mirthless, hollow laugh. "You don't know me after all, do you, Tanner? It's what I do best. Either way, I can't leave my father. I won't."

"I do love you, Angel."

"Go home, Tanner. If you don't, I'll go to the fire marshal and turn you in myself."

She shut her phone and returned to her father.

Chapter Ten

ත

"So now what do we do?" Tanner's younger brother, Ryan, paced back and forth in the barn. Kicking a stray mound of hay, he cursed. "You fucked up, you know that? We have two days to find you a wife. Two days!"

"Forget it. I'm done." He flung the saddle onto Storm's back.

"Forget it? Have you lost your mind? This ranch is worth a fortune!" Ryan appeared beside him.

Tanner secured the saddle then faced his brother. "I don't see you offering to spend the rest of your life saddled to a woman you don't love."

"I'm already married, you idiot." Ryan clenched his fists. "Anyway, the will said *you* had to marry! I wasn't even mentioned. It was very clear. You'll get the ranch if you marry."

Tanner shoved his foot in the stirrup and swung up into the saddle. "Yeah, I went over that reading of the will a hundred times. You're right, Ryan. If I marry before the end of the summer, I get to keep the ranch. What the fuck is this 'keep' bullshit? The ranch never was under my name to begin with. And who gets it if I don't?"

"Huh?" Ryan peered up at him with a blank face.

"Who gets it? The will ends there, doesn't it? So who the fuck gets the ranch if I don't marry?" He took up the reins and steered Storm out of the stable.

Ryan jumped out of the way. "How the fuck do I know?"

Crouching down over Storm's neck, Tanner took off as he yelled over his shoulder. "That's what I aim to find out from

Carl. That man knows more than he told us."

Wind whipped at his face as he and Storm cleared the fence encircling the paddock. He kicked his stirrups into Storm's flank and let the horse loose.

He'd been home two weeks. Every single night he lay in bed and prayed Angel had gotten over Antonio's abuse, her father's past and his own deception. Every damn day he awoke wondering if the pain of losing Angel would finally abate.

His mother followed him around, wringing her hands, asking again and again what had happened during his trip to New York. He'd almost told her. One night after downing nearly a fifth of Jack Daniels and stumbling into the house to find his mother sitting in the dark den, he'd opened his mouth to tell her that he'd found an angel, fallen in love, then lost her.

But he'd felt his face start to crumple before the first word slipped free. Angry that he still couldn't think of Angel without wanting to bawl like a little kid, he'd held his tongue and smashed every lamp in the room before stalking back out into the night.

Two weeks. He stared up at the sky and pictured his father watching.

"Damn you," he bellowed at the top of his lungs, hoping his father heard, "damn you to hell for doing this to me."

When he arrived at the lawyer's house, he leapt off Storm's back and wrapped the reins around the post.

Bypassing the few stairs, he stomped onto the porch wrapping around the large, Victorian house and pounded on the door.

Carl's wife, Emily, opened the door. Smoothing her gray hairs back toward the braid draped over her shoulder, she peered through the screen then broke out into a wide smile. "Tanner! Come in."

"I need to ask Carl something, Emily. He home?"

She opened the screen door. "We were wondering how

long it would take for you to come by. When we heard you returned two weeks ago without a wife, we knew you'd start wondering."

Tanner followed her through the house to Carl's office. "Yeah, well, I'd better get answers before I leave."

"You know," she slowed down and wrapped her arm around his, "Carl couldn't believe you all stormed out that day without asking. He called after you all, but you wouldn't listen." She stopped and opened the door to Carl's office. "I told him that he was wrong not getting in touch with you, but he wanted to see what would happen."

He looked down at her. That day seemed like years ago, but he could still hear Carl's voice reading his father's will. Could still hear the chair crash to the oak floor behind him when he'd shot out of it and, after cursing his fool head off, charged out of the office. His mother and brother had followed. Damn if he couldn't recall Carl calling after them.

He entered the dark office and wondered, as he usually did, how the man managed to work in the dim light. The door closed behind him.

Sitting behind the massive, cherry mahogany desk, Carl grinned. "Well, it's about time!"

Standing still, unable to move and uncover just how far his father had gone, Tanner watched Carl walk around his desk and cross the room.

"Come in, Tanner."

Feeling as if his muscles had all decided to take a vacation, Tanner followed Carl to the black leather couch. Sinking into it, he considered turning tail and running. His father's will had been shocking enough. After discovering how far Angel's father had gone to keep the family business, he'd felt the wounds of his own father's transgression start to heal. He'd, after all, given Tanner some time to find his own wife.

Now, facing Carl, he wondered just how far his father had gone. Wondered if he really wanted to know.

A corporation looking to build a retirement community had contacted them shortly before his father's death. The idea of modern buildings and golf carts covering the expanse of land their ranch encompassed sickened him.

Of course, there was also the Conner family. They'd bought up so much land, the McQuades were sure the Conners would soon take the title of largest land owner from their grasp. Not that they'd ever sell to them. The Conners used up land and left it ruined faster than it took your spit to hit your face on a windy day.

And then there were the oil companies. Just picturing those rigs sickened him.

Could his father have gone that far to get his son wed?

And why? What the hell did he care if Tanner ever married or not? This was the twenty-fucking-first century.

"I gather this visit has to do with you getting married." Carl took a file from the desk and joined Tanner on the couch.

"Yeah, well, I didn't find a fucking wife."

"I've heard as much." Carl chuckled. "I told your father it wouldn't work."

"Yeah, well, it didn't! So what's the catch?" Unable to sit still, he stood up and went to the window. No breeze stirred the leaves hanging from the few trees Carl and Emily worked so hard to keep alive.

God, he missed Angel.

"No catch, Tanner."

Turning, he scowled when he found Carl smirking. "You know damn well what I mean. Who the fuck gets the ranch?"

"You know, I don't recall ever hearing you curse this much. Someone rattle you in New York?"

Tanner glared at him.

Holding up his hand, Carl laughed. "Calm down, calm down. It's not nearly as bad as you all imagined."

"Yeah? Care to tell me how losing the ranch isn't as bad

as we imagined?"

Carl's face hardened. "Sit down, Tanner."

Carl had been his father's friend and lawyer since before Tanner was born. Also Tanner's godfather, the man had spent more time at Tanner's side than any other. It took a few deep, calming breaths, but Tanner nodded and returned to the couch. He held his tongue and stemmed the desire to wring Carl's neck while the man moved around and rifled through some papers at his desk. Finally, he turned and sat on the edge of his desk.

"It all started when my granddaughter was born. Your mother made such a stink. Seems every time she came home from visiting us and finding the babe here, she fretted over you finding a wife and giving her grandchildren."

Tanner shifted. "Why me? Ryan's married."

"Ryan lives in town and made it very clear that he had no plans of living at home. And with the way he and his wife fight, your father and mother were sure they'd divorce before any grandchildren were born. You, on the other hand, let everyone know that Ryan was a fool. That you, if you were ever cursed with a wife, would build a house right next to your father's and live on the ranch." He paused.

Tanner crossed his arms over his chest. "So? What's that have to do with the will?"

"Your mamma wanted grandchildren. Grandchildren she would see every day." Again he paused.

Tanner stared back, not sure where the man wanted to take this conversation and unwilling to help him any more than he had to.

When the silence stretched on, Carl sighed. "Your father eventually came to me, one day. He'd been to the doctor. Knew he didn't have much time. You know what worried him the most? Your mamma and her keening for a grandchild. He wanted that for her more than anything. And for you. Said he couldn't bear to go thinking you'd spend so much time keeping the ranch going that you'd miss out on the best part of a man's life. His wife and children."

Tanner inwardly cursed. The telltale burn of coming tears had him blinking and looking away. Ever since he met Angel, he couldn't manage to stem these damn tears. "Yeah, well, that usually only works when you love someone."

"Oh," Carl laughed, "he knew that. And he knew that when it came down to it, you would never marry a woman you didn't love. Ryan, maybe. But not you. So he set this up. Figured he'd get you off the ranch and looking." Again Carl laughed. "I have to tell you. By the time we wrote this will up, we were sure you'd find some gal and fall in love. We even spent one drunken night naming your kids. Damn if your father didn't know you, though. He said you'd leave before ever hearing the rest of the will. Sure enough. You bolted."

"Enough of the memories! Okay?" The tears dried before falling, leaving Tanner empty, angry.

"Fine, fine. You see, when you were born, at your father's request, I put the ranch in your name."

Tanner's head snapped up. "I own the ranch?"

"Well, for two more days you do."

God, staying on the couch got harder and harder. Getting up might lead to him punching someone he cared about, though, so he stayed put.

Carl lifted a page from his desk. "Then it reverts to its original owner."

"My father is dead, Carl. Is this some sick joke?"

Laughing and shaking his head, Carl walked over to the couch and sat on the edge of the coffee table. "Your father never owned that ranch, Tanner. When he bought it, he gave it to your mamma as a late wedding gift."

All the air Tanner held in his lungs escaped. "My mother?" He laughed, a booming laugh that seemed to take all the weight off his shoulders. "So we keep the ranch! All this was for nothing."

"Afraid so. But sit, Tanner. Your father asked me to read this to you if you didn't find a wife."

Stunned, feeling as if this would sound too much like his father talking to him from the dead, he held out his hand. "I'll take it home and read it later, Carl."

Carl moved the letter out of Tanner's reach. "Sorry, son. As his lawyer, I have to follow all the rules of the will. He wanted me to read it. Wanted to make sure you heard every word."

Sitting down once again, Tanner listened as his father talked to him through Carl.

Son, I'm so sorry. Not for what I did, but because I know that if Carl is reading this, you failed to find a wife. I hoped I'd given you enough time.

Your mother and I have spent many happy years together. We started with nothing, nothing but our love for each other. If I'd never made enough to buy the ranch, we'd still have had our love and that would have been more than enough. Then we had you and we were sure that nothing could make us happier. When Ryan came along, we learned that family mattered more than anything material. And so, we both wanted that for our boys.

I saw right away that you loved our ranch more than anything. Ryan saw the wealth, but you saw it as a part of you. By the time you grew up, I knew you were in trouble. And your mamma wanted to have grandchildren. We were both worried that when we died, you be a lonely man with nothing but land to keep you company. So, I went to Carl with this plan.

There's someone out there waiting for you, Tanner. I believe God gave us all someone to love. We just have to get off our asses and find her. I only wanted you to go looking.

Like I said, I figure you're not married if Carl's reading this to you. There's another letter. One that gives you an extension if you came home with a girl but hadn't proposed yet. So I know. Then again, maybe you found your angel and let her go.

Tanner leapt off the couch. "What? Read that again."

"What?"

His heart pounded in his ears. "That last line! Read it again!"

Carl glanced down. "Oh, here it is. 'Then again, maybe you found your angel and let her go.' Shall I go on?"

"He knew. Son of a bitch, he knew!"

"Tanner, you all right?"

Tanner stared down at Carl. He couldn't believe it. Couldn't believe his father had used the word "angel". He sat down and leaned his elbows on his knees. The pain of losing Angel still gnawed at him, but something told him that his father would help him deal with it. "Go on, Carl. Please."

If you didn't find your angel, then get out there and start looking. Nothing is as sweet as holding the love of your life in your arms every night.

If you did find a lady but lost her, ask yourself this. Is your heart aching for her? Do you feel like you can't breathe without her near you? Does every day away from her seem longer than the last? God may put a lot of women we can live with on this earth, but he only sends each man one angel. One angel the man will love with all his soul. So, son, if you feel like you'll just about die if you can't have some lady, if time isn't healing your wounds, then she's your angel, and you'd better hightail it back to her before some fool snatches her away.

The ranch will be here when you get back. And son, as a wedding gift, your mamma and I will give you the ranch and all the cattle and buildings on it.

I love you and will pray you find your angel.

Dad

Tanner shook his head. "It's like he knew just what would

happen."

"So, you have no worries, Tanner." Carl held out the note. "The ranch is safe."

Taking it, Tanner reread the entire letter, but this time, he heard his father's voice. When he read the last line, he smiled. "Carl, can I use your phone?"

"Calling the family to tell them they won't lose the ranch?"

Grinning so much his cheeks hurt, Tanner shook his head. "I'll let you do that. I have to find the first plane back to New York."

Carl jumped to his feet. "Damn, I knew it! You did fall in love. Emily said your mamma told her you were moping around and spending too many nights staring up at the stars. I knew it!"

He took Tanner's arm and led him to the door. Opening it, he yelled out into the hall, "Emily, get this boy something to eat."

"But—"

"You eat, son. I'll get you that plane."

* * * * *

Picking through the rubble alongside her father, Angel wondered why they were wasting their time. Nothing survived the fire. Everything had either melted or burned beyond recognition. Her stomach churned from the odors swirling in the gentle breeze. Gasoline, burned plastic, smoke.

"Hey, look at this," her father called although she stood not two feet away. Black smudges covered his forehead and cheeks.

Stains, those made days ago, marred his yellowed tee shirt. Something had snapped the day of the fire. Her father, a man who took great pride in his appearance, now refused to shower and rarely changed his clothes. His eyes, on the few occasions he didn't avoid her gaze, frequently glazed with unshed tears. Well, as far as she knew they never fell. Before she could question him or catch one fall, he'd turn away with one excuse or another.

Now, standing where the doorway to the kitchen once was, he held up a tin box. A frail, broken man looking at garbage as if he'd found the mother lode. "Gee, Dad, that's great."

He made his way around a section of the display the workers had rebuilt the day of the fire. A horn blared from the street just as he said something.

"What?"

"It's the box your mother used to keep her coin collection in. She always hid it. Said she wanted to give it to you when you married." Brushing away soot, he shook his head and chuckled. "She didn't trust me not to touch it when business lagged. Hid it. I searched the apartment. Never thought she hid it here."

Using his soiled shirt, he continued to rub the cover. Soon, silver peeked out from the black. Spitting onto the box, her father scrubbed until not a speck of soot remained. "Never did get a good look at this. I bet this box is worth something."

Angel touched the angel engraved on the cover. "It's beautiful."

"Can't believe it didn't melt."

Surrounded by proof that the heat in the bakery had definitely reached the level to melt silver, Angel felt an eerie chill run over her skin. She met her father's eyes. Saw that he too realized the box should not have survived the fire unscathed. Goose bumps rose up on her sweat- and soot-covered arms. "Where'd you find it?"

"Right there," he pointed to doorway, "just lying on the floor."

"Open it."

He struggled with the tiny latch. "Won't budge. Guess the

fire messed it up."

"Let me try." As soon as her finger touched the latch, it popped up.

Her father rubbed the back of his neck and stared down at the latch. "Damn."

"Dad, you don't think..."

"Nah, it's just one of those strange coincidences. She must have hid it in the ceiling." He snapped his fingers. "I know. She spent a lot of time on the roof. Used to go up there to relax after a busy Sunday morning. I bet she hid it up there. By the time the roof caved in, the firemen had the temperature in here down."

Eyeing the box, she gnawed on the inside of her cheek. "I guess that would explain it."

"Open it, Angel."

With hands that wouldn't stop shaking, she lifted the cover. Music filtered out. A lullaby. After a few moments, she realized that it was her lullaby. The one her mother had made up for her when she was born and sang to her every night until Angel hit puberty and declared she was way too old to get tucked in. Even after that, she'd lie in bed and hear her mother singing it from outside her door. Tears blinded her.

"Shit! Look at that!" Her father snatched the box out of her hand.

Coins of every shape and size filled the box. Picking out one, her father whistled. "This one is over two hundred years old."

"What's that?" The corner of a piece of paper stuck out from beneath the coins. She grasped it between her thumb and index finger and tugged gently. Still, coins spilled out onto the floor.

"Watch out, Angel!" Closing the cover, he squatted and started picking up the coins and wiping them on his shirt.

"Give me the box, Dad. I want to see what that paper is.

Maybe it's a note from Mom." She reached for the box.

He jerked it away. "We'll open it at home." Moving charred slivers of wood, he cursed under his breath. "Dammit, Angel, get down here and help me find them all."

Soot covered his fingers and shirt. Clutched in his dirty hand, held against his blackened shirt, the box gleamed like a jewel in the night. Clouds of black rose up as he swept the debris back and forth. Ashes landed on his hair, shoulders and arms.

"Give me my box, Dad." Her voice shook. From fear? Anger? She wasn't sure which, but she felt them both tensing every muscle in her body. "Dad!"

Her father's head snapped up. "What?"

"Give me my box."

"This could help us rebuild the bakery."

"We have insurance for that." She held out her hand.

"The insurance won't cover it all, Angel. With this, I could buy you the finest ovens and central air instead of those useless fans." He pushed himself to his feet.

The breeze died. The stench of the burned bakery grew unbearable.

"Think about it, Angel. You'll never have to sweat through another summer day."

Dragging in one breath after another, Angel wondered why she felt as if she couldn't breathe. "Dad…"

"And you could decorate the shop any way you want. That expensive Victorian lace you saw last year for the windows. Remember? The ones they sell in Saks."

He passed her. Walked to the wall where a mural of the Italian countryside once made her feel like she hadn't spent the day trapped inside a sweltering bakery.

"And I'll hire the best painters. You pick the colors. And marble floors."

The roll she'd eaten for breakfast weighed heavy in her

stomach. "Dad, please..."

"It'll be beautiful. Better than before. I'll put up an awning outside and bistro tables imported from Milan."

The walls, what remained of them, closed in on her. Swaying, she watched her father's mouth move. Heard only a muffled moan.

"Stop!" Covering her ears, she turned and stumbled out of the bakery and onto the sidewalk. Blessed fresh air filled her lungs. The sun warmed her while a breeze cooled her damp skin. "I can't," she whispered, staring up at the sky.

"Angel?"

"You smelled of gas." No sooner had she said the words, her heart sank and she realized what had been plaguing her since the fire. Choking on a sob, she ran to the curb and vomited into the gutter.

"Angel, you're sick. I shouldn't have made you go in there. Come on, I'll take you home."

She felt his hand pat her back. Shaking her head, she jerked away. "No...I..."

Those eyes. Lonely. Empty. They swamped her with guilt for even thinking what she had. And still she had to ask.

"I smelled the gasoline that day, Dad. You reeked of it." Her stomach lurched.

"Of course I smelled of gas. When that crazy cowboy torched the bakery, I was in it!" He moved to touch her.

Backing away, Angel shook her head. The fire marshal had told her it could be the one person she least expected. She'd never, ever consider her father. Yesterday, she'd gone to his house and emptied his hamper. The smell of gasoline had overpowered her. Even then such a thought never entered her mind.

Or had it?

No. It didn't make sense. Her father loved the bakery. Nothing mattered more to him. Not her mother, not even her.

Her father shifted.

Sunlight glinted off the silver box.

"Angel, if you'd heard him that day."

"That's right," she murmured. Shuddered. "You said he blamed you."

"Crazy bastard." He stared at the ground.

"Must have made you real mad after seeing that video."

His head snapped up. His eyes focused on a spot above her head. "I don't want to talk about that."

"What'd you say he said? You sacrificed me for the bakery?"

Spinning on his heel, he yelled, "I told you, I don't want to talk about it." Shoulders slumped. Shook.

"It must have killed you to think that I went through that because of you. Because of the bakery."

"I'm going home."

As he hurried down the block, she followed. "I bet you hated the bakery at that point. Because, deep down inside, you knew he was right."

"Stop it, Angel. You don't know what you're talking about," he yelled over his shoulder.

"Mom hated her life as a baker's wife." Grabbing his arm, she tried to stop him, but he yanked free.

"I didn't know, dammit." Shoving a woman out of the way, he turned the corner.

"But you knew I did. You knew and you kept me there!" Angel sped after him. Raced around the corner and slammed into his chest.

Rage creased his face. "You don't understand. They dig their claws into you."

Sweat trickled down between her breasts. "They?"

"The founders. All the generations that followed. They dig their claws into you and hold you to that place. You think I was bad? My father told me the history of the bakery every night from the day I was born. Every night hearing that nothing mattered more than protecting the Roselli Empire. Empire!" Spittle trailed down his chin. "Do you want to know why I stayed outside? Why I only went in when I had to? Because they were there! I'd look at you, wasting away like I did, like your mother did. But if I so much as considered selling Roselli's, I'd hear them. I'd hear my father. So yes, I sacrificed you."

"Oh, Daddy."

"But they went too far. They demanded too much. That cowboy was right. I should have died in that fire for what I did to you."

She'd never seen him so enraged. Red blotches sprang up on his cheeks. His eyes glazed over. The silver box buckled under his hand.

"I should have died."

It took every bit of power she possessed but she kept herself from going to him. "Oh God, Daddy. What did you do?"

He blinked, looked at her as if he didn't recognize her. "That cowboy did it. He...he..."

"He may have wanted to, but he didn't." Brushing her knuckles down her father's soft cheek, she smiled into his eyes. "You stood up for me, didn't you, Daddy? You showed them that I mattered more."

Finally meeting her gaze head-on, he nodded.

Angel pried his fingers loose from the box.

Opening it, she shifted the coins aside until the paper slid free.

She stared at it a moment before realizing she was looking at a stock certificate for one thousand shares. "Hershey? The chocolate company?"

"She loved those candy bars. I told her she was crazy

when she bought that stock. But she insisted. Then when she hid the box, she said it had your ticket to freedom in it."

"Do you have any idea what this is worth now?" A small piece of paper stapled to the back caught her eye. Careful not to rip either, Angel separated them. She unfolded the note. Read the words aloud. "Fly free, my Angel."

Warmth spread out over Angel's chest. For the first time, she did feel free. No longer bound to the responsibility of the bakery. "Well, I have no intention of rebuilding that bakery with this." She stuffed the stock certificate into her purse and looked up with an expression she hoped would stop any arguments. But he no longer stood before her.

"Dad?" Rising up on her toes, she scanned the heads of the pedestrians. Found no sign of her father.

Chapter Eleven

The screech of the plane's tires hitting the asphalt brought a round of applause from the passengers surrounding Tanner. Gripping the arms of his seat, he continued to pray until the plane came to a halt. Only then did he release the breath filling his lungs.

Waiting while everyone gathered up their belongings took all the patience he could muster. Every minute away from Angel seemed like an eternity. He'd meant to leave Texas as soon as he left Carl's office last week. True to word, Carl had found him a flight that very day, but when Tanner had returned to the ranch to pack, his ranch hands had told him that some of the cattle had taken ill. By the time the vet left, he'd missed his flight. The next four days he'd get all set to leave, only to have to put his return to Angel off for one problem or another.

He couldn't just up and leave Ryan in the middle of a mess. After reading that letter from his father, he knew that this flight might mark the end of his days on the ranch and he wanted Ryan's transition to go smoothly.

No matter what it took, he had no intention of losing Angel.

Even if it meant putting control of the ranch in his brother's hands.

Even if it meant spending the rest of his days in New York City and having to tilt his head back for a glimpse of the sky.

Even if it meant rebuilding Roselli's Bakery and spending his days stuck behind the counter instead of riding the range.

With Angel by his side, he could face any future.

The train to Penn Station stalled. Sitting in the stuffy car, he cursed and looked at his watch.

Where was she now? He doubted they had rebuilt the bakery in the short amount of time he'd been gone, so he had no clue where she now spent her days. In Central Park, like she'd once mentioned? Shopping? Catching the last rays of summer on that Jones Beach she wistfully talked about while dozing in his arms after a long day at work?

Finally, the train jerked and took off.

An hour later, Tanner bounded up the steps of Angel's brownstone. As he pushed the button for her apartment, he noticed someone had removed her name from the panel. Telling himself that it meant nothing he continued to press the button. When no answering buzz came after a few minutes, he sat on the stoop and waited. Didn't matter how long it took for her to get home, he'd be here.

Although the sun couldn't get past the buildings to reach him, the heat was stifling. Taking off his hat, he wiped his forehead then replaced his hat and smoothed the brim.

Another hour passed. His mouth grew so parched he figured he'd start seeing mirages soon. The street sure shimmered like a pool of water.

Just when he accepted that he had to leave and find some water, the door to the brownstone opened and a petite, dumpling-shaped woman stepped onto the porch with a broom clenched in her hand.

"No loitering on my porch, sonny."

Tanner smiled and raised his hat. "I'm waiting for Angel Roselli, ma'am."

"Angel doesn't live here anymore."

His heart skipped a beat. "Angel Roselli?"

"That's right. Left just this morning." She started sweeping the porch.

"This morning?"

Dust and dirt showered down around him. Coughing, Tanner jumped up and climbed the steps to the porch.

"You wouldn't happen to know where she went, would you?"

Holding the broom between them like a weapon, she shook her head. "I don't butt into my tenants' business. All I know is she gave me the keys and said to rent the apartment, furniture and all. Said she wouldn't be back."

Tanner looked down at the people rushing by. One glance at his watch told him the lunch crowd would fill the sidewalks and intersections. So many people. He glanced up at the skyscrapers towering over the brownstones lining Angel's block. So many apartments. Running to the street, he hailed a cab.

"Brooklyn Heights." He closed the door.

The cabbie flicked on the meter and turned to stare at him.

"Brooklyn Heights," Tanner repeated.

"You wouldn't happen to have an address, pal, would ya?"

He could see Mr. Roselli's brownstone but for the life of him couldn't recall the street or number. "Just get me to the Promenade."

Again long drawn-out minutes nibbled at his nerves as the cab crawled through traffic.

Angel moved. But where? Why?

Raking his fingers through his hair, he willed the traffic to move faster.

Before the cab came to a stop at the Promenade, he'd tossed a twenty over the seat, asked the driver to wait and opened the door.

This time he knew before he even set foot on the first step that wherever Angel had gone, her father had followed. A real estate sign on the door sent his stomach right down to his toes.

Panic had him turning in circles on the sidewalk, looking for someone, anyone who might tell him where to look next.

"Yo, cowboy."

He bent over and looked into the cab.

With his arm draped across the back of the front bench, the driver chewed on an unlit cigarette a few seconds then asked, "You looking for the folks that own that bakery that burned down?"

Returning to the backseat of the cab, Tanner leaned forward. "Yeah, you know them?"

The driver scratched his head and stared at the meter. When the ping of another charge rang, he spoke. "I don't know them, but I know where that bakery was. Maybe you should hit the bakery and see if the guys working there know anything."

Tanner slammed the door. "Right, I should have thought of that."

As they drove over the bridge back into Manhattan, something told Tanner he wouldn't find Angel there. When they pulled up behind a Dumpster, the damage to the bakery appalled him. Nothing remained. If not for the pile of debris, there would be no evidence a building once stood between the blackened walls of the buildings on either side.

Guilt held him in the cab. He had left the city without ever going to see the bakery.

Two men with hardhats tossed a massive charred beam into a Dumpster. Leaving the cab, Tanner approached them.

"Excuse me. I'm looking for Angel Roselli."

The men continued working as if he hadn't said anything.

Stepping over chunks of black wood, he made his way closer. "Either of you have any idea where I might find the owners of this place?"

One, he couldn't be sure which, muttered, "Got me. I was just told to clear the place out so it could go on the market."

"On the market? They're selling the place?"

One of the men turned. Crossing his arms over a massive beer belly, he nodded toward the burned-out shell of the bakery. "I heard the owners took the money and retired. On an island."

The other man, a younger, leaner man with arms covered with tattoos, walked up to Tanner. "That's right. They found stock worth a fortune. My sister's husband's boss knows this guy who works on Wall Street. The daughter showed up with Hershey stock that was purchased at least a hundred years ago."

"You idiot, Hershey hasn't even been around that long." Beer Belly snorted.

"Well," Tattoo grumbled, "At least eighty."

"They ain't been around eighty, either."

"Fuck you, they have too." Tattoo stepped up to Beer Belly.

Tanner cleared his throat. "So they took off. Does anyone know where they went?"

"Gee, maybe asshole's sister's brother's boss knows."

Tattoo sank his fist into Beer Belly's beer belly. While Beer Belly hunched over and wheezed, Tattoo turned and grinned. "Not they. I heard her father disappeared. Then she up and left town. No one's heard from them since."

Tanner dropped his head and returned to the cab. The rest of the day passed by with Tanner and the driver going driving up and down the streets surrounding Roselli's. He stopped at every deli, dry cleaner and adult toy store in the area. Remembering a pile of books in her living room, he checked bookstores and libraries. So many knew her. No one had seen her since the fire.

Finally, as the sun began to set, he gave the driver the address of the last place he wanted to find her. They pulled up to Antonio's apartment. Tanner let out a weary sigh when he saw the "For Rent" sign in one of the dark windows.

"Where to now, cowboy? Home?"

"I'm not giving up. Take me to the Drake Hotel."

For three days, Tanner combed the city. He questioned police, the fire marshal and every stockbroker he met downtown. Tales of the Hershey stock Angel had found grew more and more exotic. They'd made a million. Two. Fifty. She'd bought a mansion, a whole state, an island.

Tales of her father's disappearance also met him everywhere he turned. But one story remained the same. Angel told everyone that she was now free to go wherever she pleased. Do whatever she wanted. Some said her eyes shone when she'd talk of the world that awaited her. Others said she spoke of finding paradise, of finding a place where she'd never smell bread baking.

On the fourth day, Tanner gave up and went home.

His mother met him at the airport. Smiling brightly, she gave him a bear hug and patted his cheek. "You look plum worn out, Tanner. Come on. Let's get you home."

He'd never told his mother why he had returned to New York, but the look in her eyes when he'd boarded the plane had him wondering if Carl or Emily had.

"Aren't you going to ask me how my trip went?"

Taking his duffle bag, she started for the exit. "Sweetie, you look like a little boy who dropped a triple-scoop ice-cream cone on the ground. I know how your trip went."

For the entire two-hour trip from the airport, his mother sang along with the blaring radio. He stared out the window and watched the desert and mountains whiz by. Feeling like a little boy, he wallowed in his grief and wondered how his mother could sing when he was so down. Almost told her to shut the damn radio and her mouth.

Clouds of dirt floated toward his brother as his mother brought the car to a skidding halt not two feet from the porch.

"Damn, Ma," Ryan yelled, brushing the dirt from his jeans, "why don't you just run me over."

Tanner's two German Shepherd Dogs raced from around the house and jumped up to greet him. Squatting down, he let them lick his face.

Coming home never felt so awful.

"Well?" Ryan came down the steps of the porch and took the duffle bag. "Did you find her?"

"Does it look like I did?"

"So then, what are you doing back here?"

Tanner looked up at the sound of Carl's voice. Standing, he shook the man's hand. "They left. All I could get was that she got her hands on a ton of money, her father disappeared and she left for some tropical island."

"Like I said, if you didn't find her, why'd you come back?"

He clamped his mouth shut and waited for the surge of anger to abate then explained slowly, curtly. "What should I have done? Spent the rest of my life searching every goddamn island in the Caribbean?"

Ryan laughed. "For a sexy angel? I would have."

Tanner scowled at Carl.

"What? I didn't say anything."

"Like hell you didn't. Ryan just up and said angel coincidentally." If the man wasn't twice his age, he would have belted him.

His mother's hand took his. "Come on, son. I have your favorite pie waiting for you inside."

Drawing in a deep breath, Tanner groaned. The scent from the jasmine flowers in his mother's garden mingled with the aroma of cinnamon coming from the house and thrust him back to that first day when Angel had walked into his arms. "I'm not up to eating pie, right now, Ma. I think I'll just take a ride on Storm."

"Nonsense! I baked that pie for you and you'll eat it while it's hot."

Following her, he muttered, "Can't be too hot, Ma. You took two hours to get to the airport and two home."

She halted so suddenly, he nearly walked right over her. "Did I just hear you sass me?"

"No, ma'am!" Tanner chuckled. Not more than five foot one, his mother always acted liked she could still put him over her knee.

Again he tumbled back in his mind. Saw Angel draped over his lap with her pink butt wriggling after each smack of his hand.

Inside, the cat rubbed against his leg. He groaned when he recalled how Angel's cat always hid whenever he entered her apartment.

"Wash your hands and remove those hats before you enter my kitchen." His mother swept past him.

"Yes, ma'am," he, Carl and Ryan said in unison.

Crowded in the bathroom, they all quickly rinsed their hands and toweled dry.

In the doorway, Ryan halted and glanced over his shoulder. "You think she's with some Hawaiian surfer doing it on the beach?"

Dealing with the cinnamon from his mother's pies and the jasmine from the garden without giving in to the unbearable sense of loss had eroded Tanner's control. The vision of his angel in the arms of another man shredded it beyond repair. He could see her, staring up at some jerk with those sultry doe eyes, moaning when he took hold of those apple-sized breasts, spreading her legs.

"You bastard." Tanner charged.

He and his brother tumbled out of the bathroom.

"Fuck, Tanner, I was only joking." Ryan, thinner and less built than Tanner, fell to the floor.

Pinning Ryan to the floor, he straddled him. But he didn't see Ryan, he saw Angel tied to her bed, Angel stretching and rubbing up against him like a cat when she awoke to find him beside her, Angel crying, Angel laughing, Angel screaming from orgasms that had shaken him to the core. "Take that back, Ryan."

"No." Ryan grinned then pursed his lips. "Oh, kiss me, cowboy. Take me away from the big bad city."

Shocked, hurt more than his brother could ever imagine, Tanner leaned over. "Take it back, little brother, or I'll beat you until you cry like a little girl."

"Tanner McQuade, don't you dare!"

He froze.

Closed his eyes.

Had he gone completely mad?

Lips brushed against his ear. "You let that boy up, or I won't let you have one bite of my pie."

The scalding burn of tears flooded his eyes. "God help me, I've gone mad."

"Open your eyes, Tanner."

Again. The voice of an angel. The only angel he would ever want.

"I can't. I'm afraid if I do, I'll find out you're just in my head."

Her laughter rippled through him. Fingers weaved through his hair. "You crazy cowboy. Of course I'm here."

"Wanna get off me?" Ryan wheezed. "I can't breathe, you big ox."

Ignoring Ryan, he peeked out of one eye. The sweetest doe eyes filled his field of vision. He opened the other eye and backed up. Lips he spent every night dreaming about kissing. Black curls he longed to bury his face in.

A lump rose in his throat. "I just spent the last few days searching all of New York City for you."

"I know, Carl told me."

"I searched for days and you were here?"

Tears made her eyes sparkle. When she nodded, her curls bounced and caressed his face. "Right here, cowboy."

"The entire time?" he asked, harsher than he'd intended.

He'd found her. So then why did he feel angry with her, with himself?

She blinked. Glanced down before once again meeting his gaze. "I-I wanted to surprise you when you got back."

"The entire time I was out searching for you, feeling like I'd die each time someone said you'd left town, you were right here."

Her hands cupped his face. "Waiting for my cowboy."

"Hanging with my mom."

"Exchanging recipes. She makes heavenly pies." She beamed. "I really like her."

He took in her dark tan. "Sunning?"

Her smile faded. "Some."

"Get to check out the pool?" He wanted nothing more than to grab hold of her and kiss her until the sun set, but it irked him that while he felt as if his heart were breaking, while he spent endless hours grieving over losing his angel, she was in his own backyard. Sunning, for Christ's sake!

"It's a beautiful pool, Tanner. I love the little waterfall."

"So, my little angel let me go on thinking I'd lost her for…how long were you here?"

She kissed his lips. A brief kiss that sent blood surging to his groin.

"How long, Angel mine?" Desire slaughtered his anger.

"That doesn't really matter, Tanner. What matters is that we're together."

"Tell him, sweetheart. We got here the day you left."

Tanner leaned over and peeked around Angel. Standing in the doorway to the kitchen, Mr. Roselli held a plate of steaming pie in his hand.

"You too?"

"Who do you think convinced her to come here?"

Angel giggled.

"Tanner, I'm dying down here."

He shot a withering look down at Ryan then faced those doe eyes again. "Your father convinced you to come here? You didn't come on your own?"

"Well...not exactly." Angel looked down.

Mr. Roselli swallowed then explained, "Well, I was coming to get you and haul your ass back to New York. She found out...God knows how...and met me at the airport. Dragged me back home. So I sold everything and convinced her to come after you. She didn't think you'd want her being that...well, I told her that if you didn't want her, we'd go live on some Caribbean island. She was all worried." He chuckled. "Thought I'd force you into a shotgun wedding. I told her you'd do the right thing."

"Shotgun wedding?" His lungs seized. Something buzzed near his ear. Swatting it away, he turned back to Angel. "The right thing?"

Angel didn't answer. Worry furrowed her forehead. "Tanner?"

His nails dug into his palms. "Everybody out!"

When Angel moved to rise, he took hold of her slender wrist. "Not you."

His mother and Carl fled to the kitchen.

Angel's father hesitated. "Now, Tanner, I'm sure you—"

"Out," Tanner bellowed.

Mr. Roselli cast a concerned glance at Angel then followed the others into the kitchen.

"Um...Tanner, I'll leave as soon as you get off me."

Tanner glanced down and realized he still sat on Ryan's

chest. Taking Angel with him, he stood up.

"Tanner, I...I..."

"Outside, Angel."

Without a word, she followed.

Striding out the door, he practically dragged her over the yard to his house. His mind felt as if it shut down. No one had to tell him what they were all hedging around. The right thing. Shotgun wedding.

As soon as they reached the porch he grabbed the saddlebags he kept next to the glider then whistled. In the paddock, Storm raised his head from the grass. Another whistle and the horse soared over the fence and galloped up to Tanner and Angel. Tanner flung the saddlebags over the horse.

"He's beautiful." Angel reached out with a trembling hand to touch Storm's flank. The horse shuddered. She snatched her hand away and giggled. "I don't think he likes me."

Grabbing hold of Storm's mane, Tanner swung up onto his bare back. He held his hand down to Angel. "Come on, we have some things to straighten out."

"I-I'm not crazy about horses." She backed away. "I don't think that's a good idea."

"Take my hand, Angel, or go back to New York."

Sunlight set her tan face aglow when she tilted it up to look at him. Her hand strayed to her stomach. "You won't let him go fast, will you?"

"What do you think?" His eyes felt as if someone had glued them open as he stared at that hand.

She hesitated a few moments longer, then slid her hand into his.

He lifted her onto the horse in front of him. Keeping Storm at a canter, he led the horse out of the front yard and toward the open range. They rode in silence. He could only imagine what was going through her mind. Knew that he should say something to allay her fears.

Words failed him.

Sliding his hand around her waist, he rested it on her stomach.

Still flat.

Gently, he drew her back until her butt pressed against his groin. Both he and Angel remained silent as they rode. Eventually, they came to the old oak tree where his father and mother had carved their initials the day after they'd bought the ranch.

His eyes strayed to the white puffy clouds scattered across the bright blue sky. Somewhere up there, his father watched. He had no doubt about that. Well, his father had better close his eyes.

Jumping down, he reached up and lifted Angel from the horse. He brought her down slow, savoring the feel of her body brushing along his with every inch. When her feet touched the ground, she raised her face up to his and closed her eyes.

Tanner grinned. Waited.

Her eyes sprang open.

"Take off your clothes, Angel mine."

Chapter Twelve

ಏ

Liquid heat seeped out of Angel's pussy. Tanner's blue eyes darkened as he ordered her to strip. The idea of making love to Tanner out here in the open left her weak with desire. Recalling how good it felt when he'd spanked her, she decided to push him a little and maybe get him to remind her just how much she liked it.

"And if I don't take off my clothes?"

He reached into one of the saddlebags and took out his single-tail whip.

"A whip? Oh now, wait a minute." She backed up. The spanking may have turned her on, but the idea of the sharp sting of a whip? Well, she had no desire to find out if he was as good as he professed.

"So, you'll take off your clothes?" He stalked her until her back hit the trunk of the tree.

"Only if you promise not to whip me with that."

He swung.

Flinching, she watched the whip uncoil and strike a branch. Leaves fluttered to the ground.

Angel shed her clothes. Quickly at first, but when he rubbed the bulge in his pants, she decided to torture him with every button, every inch of skin she bared. By the time she dropped her thong to the ground, she knew she had him on the edge of losing control.

He approached her, the whip again coiled tightly in his hand. Fingers flared. The slender leather slithered to the ground. Unable look away, she watched those fingers wrap around the handle.

Nipples hardened. Her body wept and her skin tingled from needing the feel of those fingers.

The creak of the leather snapped her out of whatever trance she'd fallen into. "You promised."

"I don't recall promising anything." He walked up to her, dragging the whip behind him.

Fear heightened her desire with each step he took. When his shirt scraped her aching nipples, tremors overtook her.

"Raise your arms," he ordered in a husky voice that told her he was just as turned-on as she.

A warm breeze caressed her skin, taunted her nipples and clit. She raised her arms and watched him walk back to the saddlebag. When he returned, he tied her wrists together then looped the rope around a low, thick branch and cinched it until she stood on her toes.

"This isn't very comfortable, Tanner."

In reply, he pinched her nipple until she squealed. As if a cord connected her nipple to her pussy, a line of pleasure streaked down her stomach and sent her juices streaming down her thigh. Feeling the warm liquid, she wondered if she'd ever been so turned-on. Her heart pounded in her ears.

Tanner turned away.

Surrounded by a vast prairie and distant mountains, Angel felt exposed to all who might be lurking in the distance. Felt as if they were the only two people in the world.

When Tanner finally returned, she gasped. He no longer held the whip.

Her vision blurred from the tears flooding her eyes. "Oh my God."

Sunlight blinked off the strand of diamonds clenched in his fist.

"Tanner, I thought you understood. I'm...maybe you should hold on to that until I know who...until we can test..." Unable to voice her doubts, she closed her eyes and silently cursed Antonio for doing this, for ruining what would have been the most romantic moment of her life.

"Oh, I understood perfectly," his soft voice caressed her, soothed her.

"I'm so sorry."

He hooked her chin. Forced her to look into his eyes. "Don't you dare ever apologize for this again."

Her heart swelled.

"But I have some questions." Frowning, he wrapped the diamond necklace around her neck and clasped it. "And..."

He stepped back. Stared. Returned to the saddlebag.

"And?"

Returning he held up what looked like a short whip with about twenty strands of purple suede hanging from the handle. Her mouth went dry.

"And, Angel mine, for each question you answer incorrectly, I'll introduce you to my friend."

The suede strands caressed up her stomach.

"Understand?"

"What do I get if I answer them all correctly?" She lost her balance. Swaying, she watched him grin. "Well?"

"Why, you get yourself a cowboy, Angel."

The handle of the whip pressed into her stomach as it made its way back down. When it bumped over her clit, she bit down on a moan. She wanted him so bad it hurt.

But she wanted him wild. "I hear cowboys are a dime a dozen here. Which one do I get?"

The handle plunged into her. Her muscles clenched around it. Quivered.

"Why, Angel, you get a bona fide, hardass, domineering, sick fuck of a cowboy who will introduce you to pleasures of the body you never knew existed. One who will tie you up anywhere he pleases so he can do whatever he pleases. One who just might show up on the night of your birthday with another domineering cowboy as a gift just so you can live out your fantasies. One who will kill anyone who ever hurts you or makes you cry. One who was all set to give up Texas and spend the rest of his days suffocating in that bakery just so he could spend them with you."

"You were?" She had realized she'd loved him the day she sent him packing, had thought her love couldn't get any stronger or hurt more. But hearing that he would have given up everything and joined her in what he'd considered a prison left her breathless from the stab of pain in her chest.

"I told you I was a sick fuck."

Angel smiled. "I don't think I've ever heard you curse so much, Tanner."

Hard eyes focused on hers. "Yeah, well, searching for an angel through the city of sin can do that to you."

The handle slid out. Returned. Slid out and returned again and again until her muscles coiled tightly and her hands clenched.

"Ask your damn questions, then. But hurry."

"Are there three of us here?" His hand smoothed over her stomach.

Her oncoming orgasm stuttered to a halt. "Yes."

"And there's a chance this baby will come out looking like a certain Italian Stallion? With chocolate eyes and dimples?" His eyes met hers. Held them captive.

"Yes," she whispered, hearing the despair in her voice.

He dropped to his knees. His cheek pressed into her stomach. "Tell me, Angel, if that happens, will you love this baby just as much as you would if it came out with blond hair and blue eyes."

She tensed. Felt her heart break.

The whip slid free. "Careful how you answer. I wouldn't want to whip a mother-to-be."

"Well, you may have to, cowboy, because the answer is yes. I don't give a damn whose sperm made this baby, it's mine and I'll love it with all my heart."

"Hm...I admit it. I was looking forward to whipping you." The smooth strands trailed down her back and over her butt. "Maybe you'll get the next one wrong."

Her heart swelled. "No, wait, I have a question."

"The answer is yes."

"I didn't ask it yet." Her blood pounded in her ears.

He stood up, stared down into her eyes. "Will I love this baby no matter what it looks like? Yes. Will I love it just as much if he is the father? I'm the father."

"I don't believe you."

The whip cracked softly as it struck her butt.

"Ow!" She swayed. Her toes skimmed over the dirt.

"Now, Angel mine, let me explain something." Dropping down to his knees again, he planted kisses all over her stomach as he spoke. "I fell in love with you way before this baby was conceived. You?"

How she wished her hands were free. She longed to touch his face. Hold him in her arms. "Way before."

"So, this baby was conceived while we loved each other. My sperm and Antonio's may have fought for the right of its genes, but I already won its mama's heart and she won mine. In my book, that makes me the father."

"Oh, Tanner. And once our baby is born, we can always test—"

The whip struck her butt.

"Ouch! What?"

"There is no need for testing. This baby is mine, DNA or not. And if it's a boy, his name will be Tanner, Junior, blond hair or not. Got it?"

Standing, he spun her around. Those heavenly strands

struck her again and again until her skin felt like it was on fire. With each strike, she lost her balance and swayed forward. With each strike, the bark of the tree scraped her nipples.

He stopped, spun her back to face him. Stared down at her nipples. She bit back the urge to beg him to suckle them. Failed to stop herself from jutting out her chest and whimpering.

Bending over, he licked each nipple one time. Dropped down to his knees and did the same to her clit.

Angel shattered. In the midst of her climax, she felt his mouth cover her pussy, heard him lap up her juices. When her body finally stopped convulsing, he sat on his heels and gazed up at her with a serious expression.

"Got it, Angel mine? No tests and that babe is Tanner Junior if it's a boy."

"Yes! Damn, that whip felt good."

"Flogger, Angel. Someday, I'll string you up in our bedroom and give you a lesson on the proper names and uses of all of *my* toys. Now a few more questions before I fuck the shit out of you."

"Hurry, I'm hurting."

He shot to his feet. "From the ropes?"

Pushing forward, she kissed him. A brief kiss. More a glancing of her lips on his before her body swayed away. Enough to make that void deep within her pussy gape and hurt with need. "No. From wanting your Long John in me. So get a move on, Tanner."

He raised a brow and the flogger.

"Please!"

He unbuttoned his shirt, yanked it off and tossed it on the ground.

"Do you ever want to work in a bakery again?"

"Oh, God, no!"

His boots, pants, socks and underwear joined his shirt.

"Do you love me?"

Sunlight caressed the ridges of his muscles. Long John, jutting out from a bed of blond curls, twitched when her gaze came to rest on it.

She drew in a deep breath. Looked into his eyes. Drowned in that endless sea of blue. Love him? The sight of him made her dizzy. His voice alone felt like a lover's caress. And when she'd believed she'd lost him?

"Well?"

"So much I can't breathe without you."

His face broke out in such a beaming, brilliant smile, she had to laugh.

"So much I'd spend the rest of my days in a bakery if I knew you'd be there with me."

Wrapping one arm around her waist he hoisted her up and untied the rope. "Tell me more, Angel mine."

She draped her arms over his shoulders and smiled down at him as he lowered her onto his cock. "So much..."

His cock rode up into her until she felt his pubic hair tickle her clit.

"Go on." Walking to a small grassy area beneath the shade of the tree, he knelt and, keeping himself lodged firmly inside her, laid her down.

"So much, I'd give up everything for just one moment like this, Tanner. One moment with you looking at me with love shining in your eyes."

"Those are tears, Angel mine. I don't know what it is, but I've cried more since I met you than I have in my entire life. Think that's love?" He wriggled his hips.

"Either that or I'm in love with a crybaby."

Laughing, Tanner cupped her face. "Call me a crybaby again and I'll show you just how good I am at handling that single tail."

His lips met hers. The grass tickled her skin, warm air

caressed her damp cheeks, but only Tanner touched her heart and soul.

He plunged into her again and again, until they both cried out from an orgasm that shattered her like no other.

Later, as they watched the clouds roll by, he told her how he'd searched the streets of Manhattan for his angel with dirty wings. Then he made love to her again. This time his every touch, every kiss told her just how much he loved her.

Gentle caresses.

Soft, lingering kisses.

Much later, as they sat on the porch of his house and listened to her father laughing at his mother's jokes, he told her that he'd build another house, a larger house and give his to her father. Then he dug into his jeans, got down onto one knee and slipped a diamond ring on her finger.

The moment that ring slid home, he tossed her over his shoulder and carried her into the house. Hanging over his back, she nearly came when he grabbed his saddlebag of toys and charged up the steps to the bedroom.

Tanner tossed her onto the bed and grinned down at her. "Like it?"

Like it? Angel took in the four-poster bed, red velvet bedspread and drapes, and the mirrored ceiling. "This room looks like it belongs—

"In a brothel?" He leaned over and yanked off her shoes.

Angel noticed metal O-rings on top of each post. She glanced around the room and gasped. Rolling away from Tanner's grasp, she scrambled off the mattress and ran over to a large sex swing hanging in a mirrored corner. Two fur-lined loops large enough for the thighs that now quivered with anticipation hung below smaller loops for her arms.

He swept a curl behind her ear. "That's—

"I know what this is." Her voice cracked. Her pussy wept at the sight of handcuffs hanging from each of the four leather straps holding up the swing. She ran her fingers over a wide cool leather strap, then glanced over her shoulder. "What is this one for?" Tanner sauntered over. Standing behind her, he reached around and started to unzip her jeans. His hot breath fanned over her ear. "That one is for your stomach. Take off your pants."

His voice, harsh and demanding, propelled Angel into action. She shoved her pants and thong over her hips and down her legs. When she bent over to take her feet out of the bunched-up jeans, Tanner grabbed her shoulders.

"No! Leave them like that. Now raise your arms."

Raising her arms, Angel stared into the blue depths of Tanner's eyes and took in the way his muscles tensed and rippled. The power and hard, unwavering determination to dominate emanating from him nearly sent her to the floor, to her knees in thankful prayer. "Why would I need a strap on my stomach when I'm on the swing? What is it, like a seat belt so I don't fall off?"

The corner of his mouth twitched as if he was trying to stop himself from smiling. He removed her shirt and bra. "It's for when I want to fuck you in the ass."

Angel's heart stuttered. "Where?"

Tanner took a step back and held her gaze for a few seconds before his eyes focused lower...and lower. As if his eyes were some telepathic aphrodisiac, they lazily meandered down her body and left a trail of fire wherever they alit.

"Turn around." An order, gruff and harsher than she expected.

Angel realized her breathing bordered on hyperventilating and took a deep calming breath. As she spun around, she stared down at her feet and blew out the breath through pursed lips. Calmer, she glanced up...at the swing just as she felt Tanner's rough palms rub the orbs of her ass. He slid his leg between hers and stepped onto her thong and jeans. "Pull out your feet...slowly."

As she slid free of her jeans, he continued to play with her ass. Kneading, sliding down to her pussy then up between her cheeks until his thumb met the entry to her anus. The sound of her erratic breathing nearly drowned out Tanner's next order.

"Bend over." He planted a hot palm between her shoulder blades then pushed when she hesitated.

Angel concentrated on his thumb as it traced a circle over her ass's puckered lips. "You said when."

"What?"

"You said it was for when you want to...you know...fuck me in the ass. Not that you were going to do it now."

"Did I say when?" He grabbed her thighs and lifted her until her back slammed against his chest.

Tanner slid Angel's legs into the loops on the swing. She closed her eyes and swallowed the sudden surge of terror gripping her. Memories, dark and humiliating, filled her mind. But a gentle kiss behind her ear reminded her that this man cared for her and would never hurt her body or pride. She'd longed for this her whole life. A relationship where she could release all her sexual fantasies into her lover's hands and feel secure that he would weed out those she would regret living out. Tanner was that man. Nothing he could do to her or make her do would ever come back to haunt her the way her own actions had. The straps cinched around her thighs.

"Now put your arms in here." More kisses along the back of her neck soothed and excited her at the same time as she followed his command. Tanner closed the handcuffs, leaving her only enough room to comfortably shift her wrists a fraction of an inch. He backed away.

Angel gasped as she swayed and dipped. She stretched her feet downward trying to touch the floor but only succeeded in making herself spin around.

"You won't fall. Relax."

Before she could answer, he left the room. As she swirled around, she tried to catch sight of the open door and prayed that no one would come in to find her harnessed to the swing with her legs spread wide. The sound of boots striking the wooden hallway floor grew louder and louder. Heat swept up her body and bathed her cheeks.

"Please let it be Tanner," she silently prayed, "please!"

Tanner stopped short in the doorway. "Damn, Angel mine. I wish you could see how beautiful you look."

She yanked on one of the straps until the swing started to move and she faced the mirror then pouted. "Well...Sir...are you talking about my beautiful face or my pouting pussy?"

Tanner strode across the room and dropped to his knees in front of the swing. His calloused hands wrapped around her knees and spread her legs wide until she felt her labia gape open. His head inched closer to her aching pussy. Damn, everything ached with need. Just when his breath caressed her wet flesh, he moved back and frowned.

"What's wrong?" She wriggled her hips and tried to swing toward his face. "Tanner?"

"I believe I had other plans. Yes, that's right. I'm on the wrong side."

Fear and desire immobilized her. "No, I don't think so."

He slid his finger along the crease of her pussy, spreading her juices down toward her quivering anus. Angel's lungs seized when she felt the tip of his finger delve into her nearly virgin ass. Gulping in a breath of air, she met his gaze and held it.

"Does it feel good?"

"Y-yes."

Tanner's brow arched. "Manners."

"Sir! Yes, Sir, it feels good." She felt his finger burrow deeper. "But I'm a little scared."

His finger stilled. "I admit, hearing you say that turns me on."

Without standing or removing his finger, he slipped

under the swing and squatted behind her. Tender kisses on her lower back sent chills up her spine. When his lips started trailing down lower, she held her breath and focused on their descent. Lower. Hesitating at the precipice of her crack. His kisses evolved into gentle nips then licks to soothe the slight sting. His hot mouth meandered lower and lower until she thought all of her nerves converged to the place she wanted, needed his touch.

He stopped. Removed his finger, dipping another into her dripping pussy and proceeded to spread more and more of her juices around and into her anus.

His clothes grazed up her back as he stood up then drew her back against his chest.

"Your ass is so open for me, Angel mine. Open for my cock." His left hand swept down her stomach until his fingertips touched her clit, took hold of it and squeezed.

Angel rested her head on his chest.

His right hand cupped her breast and rubbed those exquisite calluses over her nipple. She moaned and writhed in his arms. Tanner continued to taunt her pussy and breast, twisting her nipple and clit, pinching until she winced. She burned with need. The sway of the swing made her feel weightless, free. Through half-opened eyes, she watched in the mirror as his hands took such sweet possession of her body. The muscles deep in her vagina clenched tighter and tighter. Her anus puckered and pulsed. Nothing had ever felt this good or decadent. She only wished her hands were free so she could wrap her arms around Tanner's neck and draw his mouth down to hers. As if he had heard her thoughts, he leaned down and whispered, "Turn your head. I want your mouth."

She turned and thought she'd drown in the crystal blue depths of his eyes as his mouth closed over hers. While they kissed, while one hand left her breast and the fingers of his other thrust deep into her, the head of Tanner moistened his cock and sank into her ass. Angel groaned into his mouth as his cock stretched her tender flesh and delved deeper and deeper.

Fire. Her anus was on fire. Every gentle thrust felt like it would be the last before she ripped in two. Her safeword hovered on the tip of her tongue, but she held back from blurting it out. Tanner lifted his mouth from hers and wrapped his arms around her.

"Ready, Angel mine?" His voice purred with promise.

"Ready? I-I thought we just did it." To prove her point, she moved her hips and felt his cock deep within her ass.

"Ah, my sweet, sweet angel, this ride is just beginning."

Before she could reply, his hand rose up high above her legs. Angel watched in horror as it swept back down and landed with a stinging slap on her wet flesh. As she yelped and flung her hips back, Tanner's cock slid in to the hilt. She had no time to respond to the hot invasion. He pulled out then thrust his cock in again and again, each time slapping her pussy and pinching her nipples. Fire bathed her entire body. Suddenly her hands were free. She wrapped them around his neck and held on.

Muscles coiled tighter and tighter with each thrust then exploded free. Shudders racked her body. Her orgasm hit with too much force. Too much pleasure. Old habits told her to break free. But she held on and shoved her hips back harder. With a scream of shock, Angel tumbled over that peak she'd never had been able to reach before and fell into Tanner's waiting embrace.

Cupping her face in his hands, he tilted her head up until her gaze met his. "You all right?"

Angel smiled. "I will be when we try out the bed."

Epilogue

Standing in the doorway, Tanner watched his mother slip the last pin into the veil, securing it to the mass of black curls. His heart nearly burst looking at the fine tulle and shimmering rhinestones. Sunlight streamed through the lace curtains on the window and blinked from each rhinestone in the veil and gown, creating an ethereal glow.

The hum of the people talking outside filtered in from the open window.

Walking to the window, he gazed out. The white gazebo he'd built for today stood alongside the pool. Row upon row of white chairs filled with family and friends lined the lawn. Peacocks strolled up and down the white runner, occasionally stopping to peck at one of the dozens of red rose petals Angel had scattered on it earlier. White satin and fine china covered the tables on the patio surrounding the pool. Not a cloud marred the sky. As far as he could see, everything turned out just as he and Angel had planned.

He felt like he'd been waiting for this day his entire life.

When his mother turned and smiled, he nodded toward the hall. Without a word, she smoothed the veil and, stopping only long enough to plant a kiss on his cheek, left.

He crossed the room. Careful not to unsettle the veil, he swept it aside and slipped the diamond necklace around her neck. "Your mother would like you to wear this today."

She reached up and touched the diamonds then with a tremulous sigh, dropped her hand in her lap. "Do you think he'll show up?"

Knowing who she meant, he answered as he fumbled with the clasp. "Maybe."

"I don't know why you had to call him."

"He has a right to know, love."

She shifted. "And if he shows up today? After all these years?"

He saw her clenched hands tremble in the satin folds of her gown. Kneeling down, he took those hands and pressed his lips to them.

His love for her left him breathless. Every glance, every silken word always reminded him that she held his heart firmly in her grip. He swallowed the lump in his throat.

"Then he'll see how much I love you. How much I've always loved my little girl."

She turned and finally gifted him with one of her heart-melting smiles.

Tanner stared into bittersweet-chocolate eyes that never failed to warm his heart, trailed his fingers down her cheeks and into dimples that always gave away her every mood and thanked his father for sending him on that quest for an angel. Even thanked Antonio for producing such a special child. From the moment she'd been born, Tanner had felt her little hand wrap around his heart and squeeze. Now, seeing her in Angel's wedding gown and jewels, he felt that hand again.

"I love you too, Daddy." She turned her head and kissed his palm.

Two towheaded boys charged into the room.

"Mom said get your butts downstairs," one yelled, nearly tripping over the train spread out on the floor.

"And that dork you're marrying looks like he's going to bolt," the other said, grabbing the bouquet of roses and dropping them into his sister's lap.

Tanner held out his hand. "Ready?"

Taking the bouquet, she smiled, stood and slipped her hand in his. "I'm ready, Daddy."

Careful not to step on her gown, he led her out of the

bedroom.

At the foot of the stairs, Angel snapped a picture as he and his only daughter descended. Still beautiful, still sexy enough to make his blood boil, she tucked the camera into her purse, blew him a kiss, then took the arm of their oldest son and followed him outside.

A lot had happened since the day Tanner had bumped into his angel. Since the day he'd entered and won the greatest rodeo of his life.

Also by Doreen Orsini

ebooks:
No One But Madison
Tanner's Angel

Print Books:
No One But Madison

About the Author

೩೨

Multi-published author Doreen Orsini is highly acclaimed by reviewers and fans for suspense that captivates them from the first page until the last, for haunting descriptions that bring her books to life and for intense, in-your-face erotic scenes that make readers do the "Orsini Cross Legs & Squeeze". Between books, she entertains the members of her Yahoo fan group with her comic, kinky Breaking News posts about Orsini Fans Gone Wild.

Determined to shock, awe and bring tears to her readers' eyes, Doreen pens dark erotic contemporary and paranormal tales that break the traditional rules of romance. She writes constantly, losing herself in the worlds she creates and crying as she writes tragic scenes for the characters she sees as living, breathing people who eventually tell her where the story will lead and end.

When not writing or enjoying her time with her family, Doreen spends most of her time interacting and forming friendships with her readers.

Doreen Orsini welcomes comments from readers. You can find her website and email address on her author bio page at www.ellorascave.com.

Tell Us What You Think

We appreciate hearing reader opinions about our books. You can email us at Comments@EllorasCave.com.

Why an electronic book?

We live in the Information Age—an exciting time in the history of human civilization, in which technology rules supreme and continues to progress in leaps and bounds every minute of every day. For a multitude of reasons, more and more avid literary fans are opting to purchase e-books instead of paper books. The question from those not yet initiated into the world of electronic reading is simply: *Why?*

1. *Price.* An electronic title at Ellora's Cave Publishing and Cerridwen Press runs anywhere from 40% to 75% less than the cover price of the exact same title in paperback format. Why? Basic mathematics and cost. It is less expensive to publish an e-book (no paper and printing, no warehousing and shipping) than it is to publish a paperback, so the savings are passed along to the consumer.

2. *Space.* Running out of room in your house for your books? That is one worry you will never have with electronic books. For a low one-time cost, you can purchase a handheld device specifically designed for e-reading. Many e-readers have large, convenient screens for viewing. Better yet, hundreds of titles can be stored within your new library—on a single microchip. There are a variety of e-readers from different manufacturers. You can also read e-books on your PC or laptop computer. (Please note that Ellora's Cave does not endorse any specific brands.

You can check our websites at www.ellorascave.com or www.cerridwenpress.com for information we make available to new consumers.)

3. *Mobility.* Because your new e-library consists of only a microchip within a small, easily transportable e-reader, your entire cache of books can be taken with you wherever you go.

4. *Personal Viewing Preferences.* Are the words you are currently reading too small? Too large? Too… ANNOYING? Paperback books cannot be modified according to personal preferences, but e-books can.

5. *Instant Gratification.* Is it the middle of the night and all the bookstores near you are closed? Are you tired of waiting days, sometimes weeks, for bookstores to ship the novels you bought? Ellora's Cave Publishing sells instantaneous downloads twenty-four hours a day, seven days a week, every day of the year. Our webstore is never closed. Our e-book delivery system is 100% automated, meaning your order is filled as soon as you pay for it.

Those are a few of the top reasons why electronic books are replacing paperbacks for many avid readers.

As always, Ellora's Cave and Cerridwen Press welcome your questions and comments. We invite you to email us at Comments@ellorascave.com or write to us directly at Ellora's Cave Publishing Inc., 1056 Home Avenue, Akron, OH 44310-3502.

COMING TO A BOOKSTORE NEAR YOU!

ELLORA'S CAVE

Bestselling Authors Tour

UPDATES AVAILABLE AT
www.EllorasCave.com

Discover for yourself why readers can't get enough of the multiple award-winning publisher

Ellora's Cave.

Whether you prefer e-books or paperbacks,

be sure to visit EC on the web at
www.ellorascave.com

for an erotic reading experience that will leave you breathless.

CPSIA information can be obtained at www.ICGtesting.com
Printed in the USA
LVOW07s2044300915

456357LV00001B/73/P